NO ONE TALKS

GAVIN BECK

ISBN 979-8-9855511-0-5 (ebook)

ISBN 979-8-9855511-1-2 (paperback)

gavinbeckauthor.com

To Mom, who always encouraged me to write. You would have liked this one.

NO ONE TALKS

Chapter 1

MATT

Monday, February 13, 2017

"OK, class. Good morning," I said, trying to overcome the chatter of the students. "This course is Race and Politics. Hopefully, you're in the right place." The loud banter turned into a hush as my voice echoed off the vaulted ceilings. "Let's get started. My name is Matt Richardson. You can call me Dr. Richardson or Professor Richardson. You might even try calling me Matt. But under no circumstances are you to call me Matthew. That's reserved for my mother. Plus, hearing it makes me feel like I'm in trouble."

Some students smiled or snickered; others clearly weren't fully awake yet or didn't get my sense of humor. Honestly, it was all I could do to attempt anything close to humorous. Normally, the

1

beginning of a semester was exciting—new beginnings and a chance to open young minds. But this time was different. I was distracted. I was tired. I was scared.

I went through the normal drudgery of the first day—reviewing the syllabus and classroom policies and outlining my goals for the course. I had done this countless times over the years, experimenting with new ways of saying the same thing, semester after semester, year after year. But there are only so many different ways you can tell students that yes, they have to buy the textbook and no, attendance is not optional.

One thing I did look forward to, however, even in my present state, was meeting the students. Farrington College tended to attract smart and ambitious ones, and I loved learning about their hopes and dreams and goals. The normal way I accomplished this was to have students write a little about themselves on a note card, but today was different. It was different because of Liv. She sat on the front row, directly in front of the lectern. My attraction was immediate. She had dark brown hair and a round face. Her eyes matched her hair and lit up when she smiled. Dressed for the cold Massachusetts February, she wore a sweater that clung to her breasts, and her tight jeans revealed her long, shapely legs. I wanted to hear her voice and eye her even more, so I decided to have the students, one by one, stand and introduce themselves. That's the moment I sealed my fate.

I proceeded down the roll sheet and called each student's name. Most of those who took this course were already busy planning their next step after college—law school, medical school, graduate school. Some wanted to enter politics. Some wanted to go straight into the workforce. It gave me pride that their goals were so concrete. They were focused and determined. In some sense, I was in awe of them.

"Olivia Powell."

"Here," she answered, as she stood, smiling. "Hi, everyone. I'm Olivia, but I go by Liv. I'm from Weston, just outside of Boston if you don't know. I'm in my junior year, so another year and a half, and I'm done." She spoke with confidence and satisfaction, gesturing with her hands as she revealed her bio. She faced away from me for most of her introduction, and I couldn't help but notice her figure again. I had to be careful not to stare, as there were about thirty sets of eyes facing my direction. I wasn't the only one who noticed. Several of the male students watched her with rapt attention, their eyes fixed on her body, some of their mouths agape. "I'm majoring in political science and I plan to go to law school. I like true crime books and documentaries, so I think I want to practice criminal defense, but maybe be a prosecutor."

To get an insight into their personalities, I asked the students to name their favorite movie. Liv had evidently forgotten, as she had already sat in her desk. I reminded her.

"Oh yeah, sorry. Well, it's kind of old, but it's *The Breakfast Club*." Some students smiled while others had clearly never heard of it.

"Excellent movie," I replied. "A classic." She grinned at my affirmation of her choice. I found it difficult not to keep looking in her direction and I noticed as I moved around the room, her gaze followed me. It was distracting and alluring. It was not unusual for me to take notice of attractive women in my classes. I am a man, after all. But there was something different about Liv. She was beautiful and seemed confident, both elegant and cute. She doodled on her notebook paper as she listened to the other students. Her clear nail polish was stark a contrast with her tan skin. She had a habit--or maybe she was trying to get my attention--of tucking her hair behind her left ear after it had fallen out of place. It was seductive.

As we finished class, she lingered in her seat and I gathered my belongings to head to my office. "It was good to meet you, Liv."

"You too."

"Any idea on where you want to go to law school?"

"I'm trying to get into Yale or Columbia. I think I prefer Columbia because I love New York City. I went there last year with my family, and it's awesome. I like the idea of being able to order Chinese food at two in the morning. We don't really have that option here in Farrington."

"Indeed, although I'm not sure the availability of takeout should be part of the criteria for deciding where to go to law school."

"OK, you've clearly never had good dim sum."

"Maybe not," I grinned.

"So are you headed to another class right now or what?" she asked.

"I'm actually headed to my office."

"And where is that?"

"If you had read the syllabus, you'd know," I retorted, smiling.

"Oops."

"It's downstairs, first floor."

We walked side by side through the long, wide corridors of Edwin Hall, named after the founder of the college, James Edwin. He had wanted Farrington College to serve as the Harvard of western Massachusetts, and he placed an importance on impressive buildings and trees and ample space in the center of campus. Built in 1874,

Edwin Hall had received a few makeovers through the years, but it still retained its old charm, characterized by its granite floors, high ceilings, and prevalence of mahogany.

"So, why Farrington?" I asked her as we descended the stairs, for the first time aware of her smell. Perfume perhaps, or maybe hair products.

"I wanted to get away from home, but not too far. Plus, my grandparents live here."

"Oh, do you live with them?"

"Oh, God, no." She laughed. "I'm not sure I could take that. No, I have an apartment here in town. It's small, but close to campus, so pretty convenient."

"I see."

"OK, I have a confession," she said as she smiled. I couldn't imagine what she was about to tell me, but the thought of her confessing something to me—confiding in me—was enticing. I turned toward her, waiting for the revelation.

"You know how I said my favorite movie was *The Breakfast Club*?"

"Yeah."

"I just said that because no one has heard of my actual favorite movie."

"Try me," I said, as we both stopped outside of my office.

"It's called *The Paper Chase*. It's old, from like 1970." I furrowed my brow.

"See. I knew it. "No one has heard of it."

"So do you envision me as another Professor Kingsfield?"

"Oh my God! You know it?"

"Of course I do. It's one of my favorites, too. But I have to ask, what do you like about it? It just seems an odd choice for someone as young as you."

"Well, part of it is the whole law school thing. But there's a love story, or at least a relationship. I'm fascinated by Kingsfield. I wonder if Harvard Law School is really that way."

"I heard a former student speak on that once. He said it was pretty much like that, except the students are a lot less articulate."

"I guess that gives me hope." She smirked at her self-deprecation.

"So?"

"So what?" she asked, a look of intrigue sweeping across her face.

"Do you envision me as another Professor Kingsfield?"

"Hmmm. No. You're better looking."

And with that, she smiled, turned, and walked away. I was dumbfounded and didn't know how to respond. Finally, I was able to cough up some words. "Thanks. I'll see you in class."

She turned her head and smiled. "Bye."

I watched her walk away, appreciating her movement as she ambled toward the stairs. I became aware I was leering and, in a relief, no one witnessed it. Not that I saw, anyway.

I drove home with Liv occupying my mind but the closer I got to my house, the more my anxiety eclipsed those thoughts. I longed for more serene days, when I had fewer worries and I was optimistic about the future. Now, sometimes I felt as if I was just running out the clock.

I turned onto my street and drove under the speed limit. It was midafternoon so it was relatively quiet, a couple of hours before parents and school buses and children turned the neighborhood into a series of bustling, suburban streets. The sun was out, but the windows were cold to the touch, a quick reminder that winter wasn't releasing its grip yet.

I parked three houses away from mine across the street and reached into the glove box, retrieving the binoculars. They were a gift that went untouched for years, but I had made good use of them lately, as my paranoia and sense of doom became stronger. I pulled them to my eyes and peered into the windows of my house. I checked the two living room windows. Nothing, save for my two dogs. I scanned up to the bedroom windows. Nothing. I looked into the study, an add-on from the first year I had the house. The sun shone through the skylight, illuminating the entire room. Nothing. I tried to get a deep breath, to feel some relief, and cursed myself that this was my new life. My heart raced and I forced myself to breathe. I decided it was safe to enter.

My two German shepherds, Ann and Nancy, greeted me at the door, ecstatic at my presence, as if I had been gone for years. "Hi, girls," I said as I patted them on the head. I reached into the pantry and gave each a dog biscuit. They carried it away, escaping through the pet door and into the backyard, like two thieves fleeing a crime scene. It startled me to think this, but I envied them. They had not a care in the world. All they did was play, show and receive affection, eat, and sleep. They were void of the human, emotional complexities that form within us and drive our thoughts and feelings and actions—the very forces that motivate us to laugh and cry and love and care. But they are also the forces that motivate our selfish desires— the ones that can drive us to lie and cheat and steal and even kill.

I had taken to drinking more lately, and it was now a habit to reach into the fridge for a beer or bottle of wine after a workday. I opened a bottle of sauvignon blanc and sunk into my couch, pouring glass after glass, drinking myself numb and trying to escape, willing myself to relax and then falling asleep.

When I awoke, it was dark, and I was unsure how much time had passed. My head ached. I reached for my phone and scrolled through emails, most of which didn't warrant a reply. The ones that did I would put off until tomorrow, when I was in a much better condition to provide a coherent response. Except for one: it was from OliviaPowell@Farrington.edu. I opened it with anticipation.

Hi, Professor Richardson.

Thanks for talking with me today! I wish we had gotten to talk more. I'm really looking forward to the course. And talking about The Paper Chase *made me want to watch it again, so guess what I'm doing now lol? Have you ever spoken to students like Kingsfield does? I'd be so scared. Anyway, just thought I would say hi. And I don't know if this is allowed or whatever, but my here's my phone number: 413-555-7431. If you're not allowed to text students, I'm sorry, but I just prefer text over email. Anyway, TTYL.*

Liv

I read it twice. It was rare that a student emailed me about something other than the course, and rarer still was an email that was as friendly and open as this one. And I had never had a student give me her phone number. How should I respond?

A knock at the door with a ring of the doorbell following it disturbed my thoughts. Ann and Nancy awoke from their slumber and barked, sending a sharp pain through my already-pounding head. My heart raced and the pulse was audible in my ears. I became aware of the warming effect of the wine, struggling to stand and wavering as I walked toward the door. I snapped my fingers—the dogs' signal to hush. My loafers were new, not broken in, and they squeaked on the hardwood floor with each soft, slow step. I tried to no avail to spot the visitor through one of the front windows, and I swore under my breath for not having a front door with a window or a peephole on it. Unlocking the deadbolt, I lowered my head and closed my eyes, trying in vain to catch a deep breath. I turned the doorknob and pulled the door, terrified of what awaited me on the other side.

Chapter 2

LIV

When I was twelve, my parents got me into cheerleading. It wasn't something I wanted initially, but they said I was restless and needed an activity, so they signed me up with one of the best schools in Boston, Pyramid Spirit. I remember them talking about how expensive it was, but I know now that money was never an object for my family. When you're a kid, you don't think about how much money your family has. And why would I? All my friends had similar houses and our parents drove similar cars. We all had the best name-brand clothes. We all went to private school. So in my narrow view, I assumed all kids were pretty much like me.

Anyway, it turns out I was good at cheerleading. So good, in fact, that when I turned fourteen, the coach recommended me for a spot on the elite team at the school. That meant we entered competitions around the country. Most of them were in the Northeast and we would travel by bus, but once we got to fly to Texas.

The coach of the elite team was Eric Brandt. He was tall and muscular with dark hair and horn-rimmed glasses, and he always smelled of cologne. When I first met him, his gaze focused on my breasts and then my legs. I was wearing cheer shorts and a tee shirt with a sports bra underneath, and his stare made me uncomfortable.

"Hi, Liv. I've heard a lot of great things about you. I'm coach Brandt, but you can call me Eric."

"Hi."

"You look like you're ready to go," he said, as his eyes scanned my body. He smiled a wide, toothy grin and beads of sweat peppered his forehead. "You excited?"

"Yeah." I tried to give a convincing smile but avoided eye contact.

"Excellent. You're going to make a good addition to the team."

The other girls on the team intimidated me, at least at first. Most of them were older. They were pretty and privileged like me, and they seemed to gossip a lot. My insecurities caused me to assume I was the object of their derision, but I warmed to them over time and became friends with most of them. There were no boys on the team. Eric said he would welcome any boys on the team if they were good enough, but I know now he didn't want any boys around because that would have been competition for him, and he was too much of a coward for that.

Practice that summer was intense. It was always at least two hours a day, five days a week, and as the competitions neared, they became longer. Before practice began, we would do our stretches, starting with a basic one—bending over and touching our toes. It was then I first noticed Eric watching me. When I turned my head, he spoke because he knew I had spotted him.

"That's good, Liv, except you need to make sure you keep your legs straight. You don't want them to bend at all." He walked over and put his hand on one of my legs, just above my knee. His other hand was on my lower back. Over time, this became a routine. I was never doing my stretches differently than the other girls, but he always found a phantom flaw he needed to correct by placing his hand here or there. He would get close to my face, and the cologne smell would engulf me. His touches troubled me but when I brought it up to one of my teammates, she just said, "yeah, he's like that."

That's how my summer started, and it would become only weirder. My mom got on this kick where she decided we needed to have people over to the house on a regular basis, to connect more with our friends and neighbors. So, every couple of weeks it seemed, we were having cookouts or catered affairs. It became exhausting. My dad didn't object, but I got the feeling he didn't do so only to please my mom. Going along to get along. If it were up to him, we wouldn't have had company at all. And knowing now my mom was depressed, I can understand him not putting up a fuss in order to appease her.

Because they had the money to do it, my parents would hire a valet service for these events. Sometimes there would be hundreds of guests and cars parked on our street as far as the eye could see. When I inevitably got bored, I would venture outside and talk to the valets, mostly college-aged men who I didn't mind flirting with. It was innocent, but I liked the attention. And that's when my first theft occurred.

"Twenty bucks, baby!" one said to his co-worker, showing off a tip he had just received. He was short and stocky with a buzz cut, and a tattoo peaked out from underneath his shirt sleeve.

"Put that away, you dick," the co-worker responded. "Have a little class." This one was tall with red hair and wore glasses with round frames.

"You guys must make good money," I said.

"It depends," replied Red Hair. "At stuff like this, we do pretty well."

"Like how much?" I asked.

"Something like this? Probably a hundred fifty bucks. Two hundred maybe.

"Are you kidding?" I replied. "I'm going to drop out of school." They both laughed.

"You don't want this job," Buzz Cut replied. "There's too much running, you get sweaty, and your feet kill will you. It's exhausting."

"That's just because you're fat," replied Red Hair.

"Fuck off."

"It's only you two here tonight?" I asked Red Hair.

"Yup. Just us." An older couple came out and handed Buzz Cut a ticket. He opened the door to the podium containing all of the keys to the parked cars, found the match, and ran off into the night to retrieve the couple's car. I made small talk with Red Hair and the couple and soon, Buzz Cut arrived in their car—a Mercedes as I recall. They thanked him as the man handed him a tip. Buzz Cut walked over, opened the podium door, and placed the tip on a tall stack of dollar bills. I watched this process repeat itself a few times. There was a key in the door of the podium but because they were lazy or careless, or maybe because they trusted me, neither Red Hair nor Buzz Cut bothered to lock it.

Not too long after, I saw my chance. Both valets were off retrieving cars. The three people waiting were all talking, paying me no attention. I opened the podium door, eyeing the trio the whole time. My heart raced, yet I felt a strange calm in the moment. I reached for the money, skimmed some bills off the top, and stuffed them in my bra.

I told Red Hair and Buzz Cut goodnight when they returned and headed to my room. Pulling the wad of cash out was exhilarating. I counted it quickly, noticing the twenty-dollar bill that Buzz Cut was so proud of. Seventy-three dollars. I half expected someone to come barging in my room, accusing me of stealing. I didn't know how I would react. Would I cave and admit it, or would I become defiant? But no one ever came. I placed the money behind a drawer in my dresser.

I can't say what compelled me to take that money. All I know is that it was exciting—planning it, carrying it out, and counting my reward afterward. It made me want to do it again and again. And I did. Throughout that summer, I took a little over five-hundred dollars. The last time I did it, though, I got caught.

It was my mistake. I was careless, and I vowed afterward I would never repeat such an error. Red Hair had gone to retrieve a car and I thought Buzz Cut had as well. It turns out, though, he had stepped inside the house. I opened the podium door, felt the money and as I was pulling it out, a strong hand grasped my arm. It startled me and hurt, and my face turned hot. Buzz Cut pulled me over to the side of the house.

"Give it to me," he demanded, as he ripped it out of my hand.

"I'm sorry," I said. He turned to look toward the couple waiting for their car. Engrossed in their conversation, they hadn't witnessed the theft. Buzz Cut glanced at the money and then stared at me.

"Why would you do this? Jesus Christ, look at your house. You're loaded."

"I don't know," I said, a pathetic response. He glanced around again before glaring at me.

"You want the money?" he asked.

"No, you can have it."

"Of course I can have it. It's mine. I'm asking if you want it."

"What do you mean?"

"Do you want it?" he asked, raising his voice.

"Yes."

"Show me your tits."

"What?"

"You heard me. If you want the money, show me your tits."

I was still reeling from being caught and terrified my parents would find out. But now, here was my escape.

"Are you serious?"

"As a heart attack."

I lifted my shirt and then my bra. Buzz Cut smiled as he stared at my breasts before looking me in the eye.

"Nice. Here you go."

He handed me the money and I ran toward the back yard, pulling my bra down and stuffing the money inside. I felt ashamed and violated, but I was excited too. I entered the back yard through our gate. The night was warm and loud with crickets. I sat on the wooden tree swing attached to our giant oak tree. I used to swing on it for hours when I was young, the breeze whipping through my long hair. If I got high enough, I could see into the neighbor's back yard, their shaggy dog objecting to my presence.

And now, as I gripped the tattered ropes that held me, I couldn't help but contrast the innocence of my younger years with what I had just done. I reached into my bra. Seventeen dollars. I smiled. Not exactly the crime of the century. Buzz Cut got a good deal. I noticed my dad out of the corner of my eye, walking toward me.

"Hey, I could use some of that," he said, eyeing the money. I grinned.

"Has everyone gone home?"

"Yeah, thank God. The caterers are cleaning up and the valets are about to leave. What are you doing out here?"

"Nothing. Just relaxing I guess." I slipped off my sandals and ran my feet through the cool, summer grass.

"I brought you a gift." He reached into his pocket and pulled out a napkin. He unfolded it slowly, prolonging my anticipation. "Ta-da." He revealed the prize, a frosted sugar cookie, with white icing. Green icing in the shape of a dollar sign adorned the top.

"Aww, thanks, Dad. Who brought these?"

"That would be one Ryan McCormick.

"Moneybags McCormick?"

"You got it."

Moneybags was a co-worker of my dad's who had earned that nickname for inheriting a fortune from his deceased parents. Instead of shying away from such a name, he embraced it.

"A dollar sign, huh? Makes sense I guess." I took a bite.

"Any good?"

"Very," I replied, my mouth full of cookie.

"Well, I guess you can afford the highest quality ingredients when you're worth hundreds of millions of dollars."

"So if he's worth that much, why does he still work?"

"Good question. Honestly, I think some people just don't know when to stop. He could do nothing for the rest of his life and make a fortune off the interest alone."

"Didn't he get married again?"

"He did. Last year. She was here tonight. I think she's already miserable."

"Why's that?"

"Because Moneybags is an asshole. Pardon the language."

"I want to start working so I can earn some money."

"Earning it is one thing," he replied. "Moneybags fell into his."

"Well, whatever. I want money. I want a job."

"Yeah, I think they have child labor laws that would prevent that," he replied, kissing my forehead.

"Not fair," I said.

"Oh, you don't want to work yet. The world is full of corrupt people, and that's especially true when money is involved. You're still innocent. Embrace it."

If he only knew.

Chapter 3

MATT

Monday, February 13, 2017

After opening the door, I realized I had nothing to fear except mindless banter.

"Hey, Ms. Sorkelson."

"Honey, you really need to turn the porch light on. For a minute there, I thought you might already be in bed. You weren't, were you? I guess not, judging from your clothes. You don't look so good. Are you sick?"

"No, I'm OK. Just relaxing."

Evenette Sorkelson was my elderly next-door neighbor. A good neighbor in that she kept her place tidy, gathered my mail when I was away on trips, and occasionally brought me food; a bad neighbor in that she was retired and had a lot of free time, jumping at the chance to make small talk, day or night, as this encounter proved. She was plump and wore glasses, and gravity had long-since betrayed her. Her neck sagged and shook as she talked, and her red-dyed hair convinced no one that she wasn't hiding her natural gray.

"Oh, good. Well, I didn't want to disturb you, but I got concerned because your porch light isn't on but your car is in the driveway. It just seemed strange." I reached to the side and flipped on the porch light. She returned a smile, her old eyes squinting behind her glasses.

"I appreciate it Ms. Sorkelson. You know, nobody else checks on me."

"Well, that's a shame. You know, they should. That's what neighbors are for. When I was growing up, we knew every person on our street. And now, no one seems to talk to their neighbors at all. It's just a shame."

"It really is," I replied, feigning interest.

"And you know what else is a problem?"

"I'm sorry, Ms. Sorkelson, but I've got to make a phone call, and I really can't wait any longer." I crushed her spirit.

"Oh." A long pause followed. "Well, that's OK. We can talk later."

"That sounds good. You have a good night."

"You too, honey."

I closed and locked the door and climbed the stairs to my bedroom. My feet felt heavy, each step a struggle. Undressing and still frazzled by the late-night knock on the door, I peered into the mirror at the revulsion that was my current appearance. My brown eyes were bloodshot, and the constant worry and paranoia had taken their toll. My hair was a mess, and the lack of sleep and repetitive boozing had advanced my middle-aged appearance. I took three ibuprofen, lay on the bed, and as so many other nights of late, the self-loathing began.

After letting my mind drift, I reread Liv's email and texted her.

> Hi, Liv. This is Professor Richardson. Thanks for the email. How was the movie this time around?
> Hi prof. The movie was great as always! And how are you tonight?

In her email, she had mentioned the propriety of students and professors texting each other. There was no explicit rule against it, although every professional bone in my body told me it wasn't a good idea. My fatalistic attitude and reduced inhibitions from the wine, however, dictated my actions.

> A little bored at the moment, but that's really nothing new.
> I know the feeling.

Are you hungry?

Frequently.

:) Do you know Maxwell's Diner?

I don't.

I can send you the address. You want to meet there?

Sounds good.

Great. See you in about thirty minutes.

Maxwell's was a small, 24-hour diner on Route 116 on the north side of town, away from the bustle of bars and restaurants that surrounded the college. I chose it because there was much less of a chance of someone seeing us together.

I leapt from the bed and splashed some cold water on my face, rationalizing that not having shaved for five days was a rustic look, as opposed to shabby. The consequence of downing an entire bottle of wine was still with me and I knew I shouldn't drive, but the anticipation of the meeting obscured my judgment. So, I drove on, sitting in silence, increasingly nervous as the miles accumulated on the odometer.

Maxwell's was an unexceptional brown-brick building, colored only by the purple neon sign that read DINER out front. There were three steps leading to the entrance, and I had to steady myself with the handrail as I opened the door. A quick scan revealed Liv had arrived before me, sitting in a booth near the back. I smiled and waved as I made my way there, appreciating the strong smell of bacon and coffee.

"Hey, there," I said as I slid into the booth, scanning the restaurant to assure myself no one was there who might recognize me.

"Expecting someone else?"

"It might be hard to explain why I'm at a diner at ten o'clock at night with one of my students."

"So why did you come?"

"I was hungry." I smiled and she returned it. She was as captivating now as she was earlier. She wore jeans and a sweatshirt, and atop her head was a pink, knit beanie that accentuated her eyes.

"So, Liv, tell me about yourself," I asked, unsure of what to say and afraid of an awkward silence setting the tone for the rest of our meal.

"Didn't I do that already in your class?"

"Good point. But what else should I know?"

"Well, for starters, I ordered you a cup of coffee. I figured professors and coffee go hand in hand." An old waitress with a scowl and a sharp chin set a cup in front of me.

"You'd be right. So what else goes hand in hand with professors?"

"Well, you're smart. That's a given, I suppose. But not necessarily wise, you know, being out with a student this late at night." Our eyes met for a second before she turned her gaze downward.

"We're on the same page with that. It's definitely not wise. No argument there. But that wouldn't be the first unwise decision I've made in my life."

"Do tell," she lifted her head and beamed, like a schoolgirl about to receive a juicy piece of gossip.

"Well, let's see. I could be serious and tell you how I screwed up my marriage of thirteen years, or we could go with something more amusing, and I could talk about the time I taught a class while drunk."

"OK, that's no contest. Drunk teacher it is."

"It was a night class my first year at Farrington. I went to dinner with some colleagues and, three Long Island iced teas later, I was standing in front of a class, most likely babbling incoherently."

"Did anyone say anything?"

"Only one. An older student came up to me afterward and said she'd like to have whatever I was drinking."

"Wow. I didn't know alcohol and professors went hand in hand."

"You have a lot to learn, young one."

"Do I, now?" A deceptive grin creeped across her flawless face.

"Actually, you seem a lot more with it than I was at your age."

"Maybe, but I feel a lot of pressure to be *with it*."

"Why's that?"

"My family. My dad is OK, but my mom is screwed up, and there's always this expectation I have to succeed at this or that, always have to be involved in something. Always have to get good grades."

"Are you happy you chose Farrington?" I asked.

"Yeah, I like it here. Some of the students can be pretentious, but I guess that's true almost anywhere. And some of the professors are arrogant assholes."

I laughed. "Like who?"

"Whom," she replied, smirking.

"Who's the arrogant one now?"

"Do you know Ms. Carlisle who teaches English?"

"I don't," I lied.

"Well, she's an asshole. Did you ever have to read Paradise Lost in one night? It's torture. And then we had to write a critique of Beowulf."

"Sounds exciting," I deadpanned.

"But I'm looking forward to your course."

"And why's that?"

"Are you kidding? This stuff is right up my alley. Race and politics. I can't wait. Plus, you're cute," she said, biting her lower lip. "Sounds like you're the one who's been drinking the Long Islands."

Over the next two hours, we ordered food and several cups of coffee, and I laughed as I hadn't laughed in months. It was a release, a cathartic jolt from the doldrums and dread of my current life. I was enamored with this girl across the table—my student. Her beauty, her smile, her mannerisms—it was all intoxicating. She spoke in a gentrified way that suggested an age older than her twenty years, but her laugh and pop-culture references that eluded me were reminiscent of an exuberant teenager. Jesus Christ, what would people think? I was old enough to be her dad. But I didn't care. The moment had captured me, and in that moment, nothing else mattered. And I needed nothing else to matter for a change. For far too long, I resigned myself to apathy in the resignation that I couldn't find any happiness or value in much of anything. But here she was, so full of life and optimism.

"Hello, are you there?"

"I'm sorry," I replied, aware I was daydreaming and hopeful I hadn't revealed the far-off gaze of a love-struck schoolboy.

"No worries. I didn't know if you were deep in thought or if I was boring you."

"You're definitely not boring me. Quite the opposite."

"OK, good." With that, I felt the slightest presence of her shoe against mine. *Was that on purpose?* She wasn't moving it, and neither would I. I let the feeling travel throughout my body, surrendering to the fantasies that danced in my mind. She continued to talk and I continued to listen, but my attention was elsewhere, the excitement of an illicit relationship outweighing the sobering thought of that same relationship ruining my career.

"OK, your turn."

"Turn for what?" she replied with a quizzical look.

"Have you ever made an unwise decision in your life?" She bit her lower lip again in the midst of a smile, a most sensual gesture I would have no problem recalling later. "Let me rephrase. Everyone has made an unwise decision. What's one of yours?"

"Oh, wow. Let me think." She stared at the ceiling for a few seconds before fixing her eyes on mine. "All right, one time I caught our neighbor looking into my window from behind our backyard fence. Yeah, I should've had my blinds closed, but he was being a total creeper. The very next night, the same thing happened. I caught him again. The third night, I decided to give him a show. I thought it would be funny. This guy is like sixty. It's not like I was trying to entice him or anything. So when I saw him looking in, I undressed to my underwear and bra." She lowered her head, as if ashamed.

"So that's it? That's the bad decision?"

"No. That's coming. Later that night, my mom called me downstairs and my parents were waiting there looking pissed. It turns out the guy called and told my parents I was undressing with my blinds open and there could be a sexual predator out there. Who does that? Who hangs around for a peep show and then rats out the person giving the show? It was so stupid. Plus, he was the one walking through the woods behind our house at night like a psycho. So, later that night, when I knew everyone was asleep, I got my keys and keyed the shit out of the guy's car. There were marks all up and down the side. He called the police but nothing ever came of it. I always wonder if he suspected me."

"Wow. Keying a car. And you think that was unwise?"

"Don't you? I mean, I don't like what he did and I probably shouldn't have given him the show, but I think keying his car was a little disproportionate, right?"

"That's a fair assessment," I said, sympathizing with the sentiment.

"It's interesting, isn't it?"

"What's that?" I asked.

"The choices we make."

"How so?"

"Well, my parents always told me I, and I alone, am responsible for the decisions I make."

"Yeah. And you don't think that's correct?"

"Only up to a certain point. I think our life is determined as much by the choice of others as it is our own decisions. Like tonight. I took you up on your invitation and if I hadn't, we might not have gotten to know each other and then who knows? Maybe our lives might have taken different paths if I hadn't joined you."

"So you're saying this meeting has forever altered the course of history." She gave me a wide grin.

"Maybe."

The old, scowling waitress had stopped refilling our coffee, a sign we had worn out our welcome. Upon paying the bill, we made our way to the parking lot. Our cars were in opposite directions from the exit, and we shared an awkward goodbye. I wanted to hug her and kiss her, to hold her close in the cold, nighttime winter air, but I had missed my chance. I knew, however, there would be others.

She had shown too much interest in me for this to be a one-time occurrence. It was nearly one in the morning and I drove home wide awake. The intoxication from the wine was gone. Now, my only intoxication was from the anticipation of thinking about the next encounter with my new favorite student.

Chapter 4

LIV

When I realized no one knew or even suspected I took the money from the valets, I began to wonder what else I could get away with. I can't explain that compulsion, but it was palpable, a desire to be daring. I began snooping around the house. I was particularly curious about my parents. What were they hiding? Everyone hides something and everyone has secrets; they were no different. I waited until they left one afternoon and entered their bedroom.

It was spacious, and I was jealous of it. The blinds on the French doors were open, revealing the balcony. I remember thinking as a young girl if I had this bedroom, I would never leave. Everything was nicer than what I had—their bed, their dresser, their TV, the open bathroom with its vaulted ceiling. They even had a sitting area next to a seldom-used fireplace. I had been in this bedroom many times, but I had never paused to reflect on the opulence of it. The plush carpet soothed my feet with every step and my mom's perfume infused the air. I stretched across their soft bed and enjoyed the thickness of their pillows.

Afterward, I rummaged through their dresser drawers and my mom's jewelry box, taking a bracelet in the process. She didn't wear it much and likely wouldn't miss it. Dad spoiled her with all sorts of gifts and this was one of dozens of pieces of jewelry he had given her through the years. I moved to their closets which, with their enormity, resembled changing rooms in a fancy clothing store. Dad filled his mostly with suits for work, and all his other clothing he arranged in a haphazard manner, much to the disapproval of my mom and her penchant for order. A safe sat on one of the shelves. I recall them buying it, but I had never bothered to ask what they planned to put in it. Dad kept his acoustic guitar propped up in a corner. I lifted it and strummed it, trying to remember the last time I had seen him play it. In another corner, I discovered a stack of old *Playboys* tucked behind some tee shirts. I found and donned his old red sweatshirt emblazoned with CORNELL on the front. I borrowed it occasionally with his permission, always appreciating the softness of it and that his smell permeated it.

I moved to mom's closet next. She had more dresses than one person would ever need, all hung with velvet hangers and spaced evenly. From floor to ceiling, there were shirts and blouses and pants and shoes, and her wedding dress occupied a large space near the back. The bottom of the dress almost touched the floor and below it was a small, wooden box. I knelt and saw the keyhole on the front. I picked the box up and studied it, trying to lift the lid, but it was of no use. It was locked. I shook it and the contents rattled from side to side. Something was inside, and I had to find out what it was.

I had a lot of time on my hands that summer, and I devoted much of it to looking for the key to unlock that box. I searched everywhere I could think of—in my mom's closet, in her dresser drawers, in my parents' bathroom, in the basement, and in the attic. I tried every key on my mom's key ring, and none of them worked.

I had resigned myself to the idea I would never find it, until one night when my mom asked me to help her prepare dinner. In doing so, I reached into a drawer with cooking utensils—a drawer only she ever accessed. And there, beneath a spatula, was a key, and I knew immediately it was the one I was searching for. It was silver, with three holes on the bow and one bit toward the end. I left it in the drawer on the chance she would use it that night, with plans to retrieve it when I was alone again.

The opportunity presented itself the next day. Dad was gone to work and my mom was running errands. My younger sister, Sarah, was in the house but glued to her phone, and there was no chance she would catch me. I grabbed the key and climbed the stairs toward my parents' bedroom. The box was still there and my anticipation grew. The key was a perfect fit. Turning it, the lock snapped back, and I lifted the lid.

Inside was a phone wrapped in a cocktail napkin. On the napkin was a phone number in handwriting I didn't recognize. I pressed the home button on the phone and, to my surprise, there was no passcode for it. I went to the contacts and only one existed—someone named Andrew. I scrolled through the texts, all of which were conversations between this mysterious Andrew and my mom. Some were explicit and others mundane, and many were sprinkled here and there with an "I love you." I went to the photos next. There were many, a lot of them selfies of my mom and the man who I presumed to be Andrew. There were some explicit ones, too, both of them nude and grinning for the camera. A video, which I quickly shut off, showed my mom fellating Andrew, his moaning a dissonant cliché of male pleasure.

I found it hard to believe what I was seeing. I never thought about my parents cheating, and I doubt many fourteen-year-olds do, but here it was, as plain as day. I had so many questions. Who was Andrew? When did this affair begin? Did she really love him? What would happen if my dad discovered this?

I put the phone and napkin back in the box as I had found them. I closed the lid, locked it, and placed the key back in the utensil drawer. The rest of the day and well into the night, I had to process my discovery.

I wondered if my mom was happy with Andrew. She seemed happy in those photos, but how much can really be gleaned from a photo at all? They're snapshots—a brief moment captured in time and in no way a reflection of an ongoing reality. Even at such a young age, I knew cheating spouses were seeking something they weren't receiving at home. Attention, affection, love, sex—there was some shortcoming. But what did Andrew offer? Did he give my mom something my dad couldn't give or wouldn't give? Was my dad inadequate in some way?

My parents seemed happy with each other, or at least that's the impression I got. They doted on each other and occasionally kissed. They sat close together when watching TV. They still seemed to be two people in love. But as a mother, my mom was a different story. I often wondered whether she loved me or saw me as an inconvenience. Her hugs were infrequent and even then, they were short, shallow interactions that offered precious little in the way of affection. She was obsessed with cleanliness and order that I jokingly said bordered on psychosis. She inspected my room and my sister's room daily and anything that fell outside of her expectations for what a clean room should be, became the target of her wrath. Her punishments were always severe. She would spank me in my younger years or lock me in my closet. She once grounded me for three days for tracking mud in the house. My friend Grace kidded me that one day my mom would crack. Maybe the affair with Andrew was her cracking. I knew she felt pressure to meet the expectations of what she thought she should be—a pretty wife and mother in a big, glamorous house with two perfect kids. Maybe Andrew was her release.

But analyzing her motives didn't satisfy me, nor did it make me feel any better. So I wondered what to do. Should I pretend I didn't see any of it and go about my business as usual? Should I confront her? Should I tell my dad about it? As I lay awake in bed that night, jumbled thoughts running through my head, my feelings became clear. I was angry. How could she do this to my dad? How was that fair to him? And how was it fair to me to discover this and to see those disgusting images? I already had to tolerate her oppressiveness and emotional distance, but now this? No, it wasn't fair to me at all. But wait. Did she want to be caught? Why leave that key in a conspicuous place when she knew I would be retrieving items from that drawer? Why leave the phone unlocked? Maybe it was a cry for help. Maybe she wanted this out in the light. If she did, my plan wouldn't work. If she intended this to be a secret, however, I suspected my idea was nothing short of splendid.

Chapter 5

MATT

Whenever someone does something for the first time, there is no indication the act will become an addiction. The first time someone has sex or takes a particular drug or takes their first drink, he or she isn't thinking about how doing so could alter their behavior in the coming days, weeks, or years—how it could adversely affect their health and relationships. Such was the case with gambling and me. What started as an innocent bet on a football game turned into a nightmare of deceit, divorce, and out-of-control debt. My life spun so far out of control I couldn't see a way to recovery.

It was my junior year in college at the University of Texas in Austin. And it's odd—I can't remember what the game was; the fog of addiction has clouded my memory. But I won, and I knew I liked the feeling. My friends and I would sit around the TV on Saturdays and Sundays, making bets on individual plays—"I'll bet you ten bucks they throw it," or "I'll bet you twenty bucks they get a first down here." It became addicting, so much so I was betting on dozens of games over a weekend and hundreds of individual plays.

After a few months, I learned I could make even bigger bets with a bookie. I don't remember how I learned of his existence, but I found myself one night in a small, nondescript apartment. I figured a bookie would be akin to what I had seen in the movies—a shady character with dark glasses, plumes of smoke engulfing him. This wasn't the case at all. This man, Kyle, was short and frail and probably about 40-years old. Every time I saw him, he wore a visor, as if he were heading out to play a round of golf. He mumbled when he spoke and had the annoying habit of saying "what?" when I would ask him a question and then answering the question before I could repeat it.

I made a lot of money my junior and senior years. Of course I lost some, but I had found a knack for making good picks, or maybe I was just lucky. Or maybe I was doing my homework and making smart bets. Whatever the case, fifty dollars here, a hundred dollars there, I was doing fine. Kyle kidded that I was going to put him out of business.

The addiction was consuming me. I would often lay awake in bed, unable to sleep, statistics and trends occupying my brain. There were many nights where I wouldn't drift off until three or four o'clock in the morning, offering myself only a few hours of sleep. Emily, my wife, knew I was betting, but she didn't know the extent of it, nor did she know I was addicted. Any stress I showed I passed off as work related. Then I got the job at Farrington, and that's when things took a turn for the worse.

We packed and moved in less than a week, excited for our new life in Massachusetts. Being a teacher, Emily had no problem finding work, and I was nervous but eager to start my professorship. Through Kyle's connections, I contacted a man in Springfield with whom I could place bets. The problem, however, was that he wouldn't take bets over a hundred dollars. I, acting like a big shot, felt that smalltime betting was beneath me. I needed a bigger score, so he arranged a meeting for me with a man named Rex in Boston.

Rex lived in an apartment building above a small convenience store on the South Side. It was my first time visiting Boston and all the images I had in my head of Southie made me nervous— dilapidated houses, street toughs, Whitey Bulger. As I approached, however, the neighborhood wasn't what I imagined. New buildings or refurbished ones with late-model cars parked out front gave the area a gentrified look. I parked on the street under a dimly lit streetlight and entered Rex's building through a side door. He lived on the fourth floor, and I ascended the creaking, wooden stairs, passing a family speaking what sounded like an Eastern-European language. They looked at me too long, as if they knew I didn't belong there.

The first time I knocked on Rex's door, no one answered. A neighbor stuck her head out of her door and looked at me before shutting it and slamming the dead bolt into place. I knocked a second time, and a large man opened it. Dark, scraggly hair adorned his head and he seemed to have razor burn on his face from a fresh shave. I guessed he was in his late 20s. I smiled and said hi, but he said nothing in return and motioned with his head as if to say, "follow me."

A small entryway opened into a living room, and the only light came from the TV. A young man and woman sat on the couch close together, paying me no attention. The large man led me into a bedroom and closed the door behind me.

"You got any weapons on you?" he asked.

"No," I replied, raising my arms a few inches.

"I have to check." He gave me a cursory pat down, his plump hands maneuvering their way across my shirt and pants. He stepped back and eyeballed me, and his breathing sounded labored. "OK, look, if you're wearing a wire, you need to turn around right now and walk out. I'm about to search

45

you, and if you have a wire on you, I can't guarantee you'll make it out of here safely. You understand?"

All I could think about at that moment is what would be the reason for anyone wearing a wire or carrying a weapon? I should have known I was in over my head and left the apartment, but the questions unnerved me and I froze.

"I'm not wearing a wire."

"Lift your shirt and turn around."

I did as he instructed and, once satisfied, he told me to lower my pants.

"Is that really necessary?"

"It is if you want to see Rex." I unfastened my belt, unbuttoned my pants, and lowered my zipper, letting my pants fall and losing a little dignity as one tends to do when his pants are pooled around the ankles.

When the man confirmed I had no wire on me, he led me down another short hallway and knocked on a door that was slightly open. "Yo, Rex. That guy's here."

"What guy?" replied a voice from the room.

"The guy from Farrington."

"Oh, yeah. OK, send him in."

I entered the room. It was small, and a king-size bed filled most of it. The room's walls were powder blue, covered in posters of rock bands and women wearing not much more than a smile.

"What's up, man? I'm Rex." He ripped earbuds out of his ears and fumbled with the wires. He didn't put his hand out for a greeting, and I didn't offer mine. I could hear my large escort breathing behind me, and Rex stared at me for several seconds before speaking again. I didn't know if this was meant to intimidate me or if he was socially awkward. He looked to be in his early 30s, had dark, unkempt hair, and several days' growth on his face. He wore jeans, a faded red tee shirt with a giant crosshair on it, and sat in a rolling desk chair that squeaked at the slightest movement. "A little birdie told me you like to gamble a little, huh?"

"You could say that."

"Ha! I like it. What do you like to bet on?"

"Football mostly."

"All right. So what do you want? What are looking to lay down?"

"I'm just looking for somebody to take my bets."

"I know, man. I'm asking like how much are you looking to bet?"

"It depends."

"Well, we have to agree on it, you know?

"Of course."

"But here's the deal. Straight-up bets. Nothing less than a thousand, all right?"

"OK."

"I'm not a bookie. I just do this for fun, and I got too much shit riding on my other business, so I don't want to mess with that small stuff. High risk, high reward. You know what I'm saying?"

"Yeah." I didn't ask what his other business was but judging from the search earlier, I suspected it was drugs.

"Now, I'm always good for my money. It might not look like it from this little shithole, but I'm pretty well off, man. This is what I call my flophouse. I don't have a problem paying. But there's something you need know." He stood and got close to my face. His breath stank and his dark eyes frightened me. "I don't play around with people who don't pay. You lose, you pay, we're good. I lose, I pay, we're good. You lose and don't pay, it will go badly for you. You got it?"

"Yeah, I got it. I'll pay. No problem."

"You met Mike, right?

"Who?"

"Mike. This fat fuck who led you back here," he said, pointing behind me.

"Oh, yeah."

"Well, he's very loyal to me and he has, on occasion, had to force people to pay. And it's not pretty. Me, I'm just a businessman. But Mike? He's rough. Right, Mikey?"

"You could say that."

"Mike's not one to brag," Rex said, "but he knocked a guy's teeth out last year. Every single one. Dude was crying, bleeding all over the pavement. That was for not paying on ten grand. Hell, his dentist bill will be more than that."

I didn't know how to react to that. If Rex was trying to intimidate me, mission accomplished. I smiled uneasily and thought I might leave, drive back home, and never see him again. But my addiction wouldn't allow that. It was as if some unrelenting monster had me in its jaws, ready to eat me alive.

"So, speaking of that, I need to take a picture of your driver's license."

"What? Why?"

"I have to know where all my contacts live. You know, in case you don't pay, Mikey can pay you a visit." I hesitated before reaching back and pulling out my wallet, slipping the license out of the plastic sleeve and handing it to Rex. He snapped a pic after snickering, presumably looking at my awful picture.

Over the next two years, I made more and bigger bets, and I started to lose. My first big loss was a thousand dollars. I tried to erase the deficit but kept digging a deeper hole. I went behind Emily's back, maxing out my credit cards with cash advances and taking out a loan from a bank. After I had exhausted those funds, I decimated our savings account. After that, I cashed out my 401K. I couldn't stop.

I made so many trips to Boston I lost count. My stomach knotted every time I ascended the stairs to Rex's apartment, and the feel and smell of the place nauseated me, yet I always returned. In all, I paid Rex about fifty-thousand dollars, all of which he placed in a suitcase under the bed. It seemed an odd choice to reveal the location of the money, yet I figured Rex knew I was intimidated and not a threat to him. I was sure in his drug business—if that's indeed what it was—he was used to dealing with tougher characters.

When Emily found all of this out, she was livid, an understandable reaction. She tried to stop me and begged me to get therapy, but I would have none of it. I didn't need therapy, I told her and myself. I needed to start winning again. Once she saw I was hopeless, she packed her stuff and left. I don't blame her—I was ruining her life, too. But I cried and pleaded with her to stay, to no avail. Two weeks later, she served me with divorce papers. The force of my addiction caused me to worry, not about the dissolution of my marriage, but about my next bet. I had to get out of the hole. I was desperate. Then came the Super Bowl.

It was the Patriots against the Falcons. In the weeks leading to the game, I studied all of the trends and statistics I could find. I pored over injury reports and dissected each team's offense and defense. I felt confident, because gambling junkies can talk themselves into any bet and convince themselves that it's a wise one. I called Rex and told him I wanted fifty-thousand dollars on the over-under. I took the under, Rex took the over, and in a matter of seconds, I had the most money on the line I had ever had.

I was antsy that entire weekend. I couldn't eat or sleep. I paced around the house on the day of the game. The over-under was 57 points, the highest ever for a Super Bowl, and things looked good early. There were only 24 points at halftime, well below the pace needed to get over 57. Then, in my most agonizing moment to that point, I watched my chance crumble. Fucking Tom Brady. The Patriots orchestrated the biggest comeback in Super Bowl history. The game went into overtime, but the score at the end of the fourth quarter was 28-28. Regardless of how the game ended, I had lost.

I threw a glass against the wall and shattered it. I cursed and screamed in anguish. Panic set in. How could I pay this? I couldn't. There was no way. Mike would break my legs or maybe kill me. My phone rang.

"You're not on a ledge are you?" Rex asked, the sound of a smile in his voice. I didn't respond. "Bring me the money by the end of the week."

"Yeah." That was all I could muster. I ended the call, but I might as well have ended my life. I was doomed.

Chapter 6

LIV

The next morning after I found my mom's secret phone, my dad left for work at his usual time, around eight A.M. I typically slept in on summer mornings until I had to get ready for cheer practice, but on this day, I was restless and nervous for what I was about to do. My mom performed her usual routine—30 minutes on the treadmill followed by her low-calorie breakfast of sugarless oatmeal and a cup of black coffee. She forbade us to eat anywhere but at the table, so I would wait until she was in the shower to eat my breakfast on the couch or from the comfort of my bed.

This particular morning, she gave me a cursory greeting and reminded me of my chores before taking a shower. I waited until I was sure she was in there and made my move. I opened the utensil drawer, got the key, and carried it to her closet. She was humming a tune I didn't know and I could smell her body wash. I opened her closet door, and the box was just as it had been when I found it. I unlocked it, verified the phone was still in there, and shut the lid, keeping it unlocked. I put the key back in the kitchen drawer and closed it, hearing a noise behind me.

"What are you doing?"

I whipped around to see Sarah. "Oh, nothing. You want some breakfast?"

"Sure. But none of that shit mom eats."

"You shouldn't talk like that."

"What's the difference? It's not like Mom and Dad can hear me. Besides, I hear you curse all the time."

Sarah was only two years younger than I was, but she had more than her fair share of precociousness. She was feisty and I liked that about her, but her personality and my mom's personality meshed like oil and water. They fought frequently, which often ended with Sarah being grounded and my mom shutting herself off in the bedroom for the rest of the day.

"Well, don't let them hear you or you'll get into more trouble than you usually do."

"Whatever," she retorted.

"Hey, do you know anyone named Andrew?" She stared at the ceiling and cocked her mouth.

"There's a guy in my homeroom class named Andrew."

"No, I mean like an older guy, like Mom and Dad's age."

"Nope. Why?"

"Don't worry about it. It's nothing."

She didn't press me further, thankfully. I made her some waffles, which she promptly drowned in syrup. She downed some chocolate milk and headed to her room, and my stomach jumped with butterflies because the moment had arrived.

I watched my mom descend the stairs in her pink robe, her hair damp from the shower. My throat was dry and I took a deep breath.

"Hey, mom?"

"Yeah."

"Can I talk to you for a second?"

"Sure," she said. "What's up?" She leaned on the kitchen counter with her elbows, her dark eyes peering at me above her high cheekbones. She had a way of looking mean, as if she were waiting to punish me for the latest atrocity of not eating at the table or not performing a chore to her standards. Then, however, she could radically transform her thin face by beaming—a beautiful smile that lights up a room—and make me forget why I resented her. She gave me such a smile on this occasion and I almost nixed my plan, but I reminded myself why I felt motivated to carry this out in the first place.

"Yesterday," I started out, my voice quivering, "I went up to your closet. I was curious and wanted to see your wedding dress, and that's when I noticed the box." Her eyes widened, and her look became one of fear. That's when I knew she didn't intend for her secret to get out. "I opened it and saw the phone."

"Liv, why are you searching through my things?" Her voice was loud. "You have no business doing that. Would you like it if I went searching through your stuff?"

"It was an innocent mistake, Mom. The box was unlocked, so I opened it."

"Unlocked?"

"Yeah."

"Oh my God," she said, and buried her head in her hands.

"Mom, who is that guy?" I asked, referring to Andrew.

"He's a friend from college."

"How long have you been seeing him?"

"Liv, I really don't want to talk about this." She was clearly uncomfortable, as I had hoped.

"Why not? I mean, this affects me. It affects Sarah. It definitely affects Dad. He has a right to know."

"Liv, you can't tell your dad. Please. It will crush him." Her eyes welled with tears and one tumbled down her cheek. "Please, I'm begging you. What do you want?"

And with that statement, so clear it cut the air, we were on a level playing field, two negotiators ready to talk terms, like a prospective car owner and a salesman. It was time for me to name my price. "What do I want?"

"Yes. Tell me," she said, wiping her eyes with her sleeve. "What do you want to keep quiet?"

I pretended as if I hadn't thought it over, but I had played this scene out in my mind many times the previous night.

"A hundred dollars a week." She began sobbing, a quiet but full cry. I knew this wasn't a cry of guilt, though. This was a cry of regret that I'd caught her. She was sorry only that her big secret was out.

"That's kind of steep, Liv."

"What's it worth to you, Mom? What's it worth to you not to have Dad find out?"

"OK," she replied, knowing I had backed her into a corner. "A hundred dollars." She was broken. Her eyes were red and strands of hair fell about her face. She was a pitiful sight, but I felt no empathy. I smiled inside. I got what I wanted and for the first time in my life, I felt empowered.

That night, as my mom moped around the house and played it off to my dad as her not feeling well, I reflected on what I had done. I felt no remorse. It was not on me to feel guilty for my mom's sin. I simply took advantage of the situation and parlayed it into cash, which is what any prudent person should do given the circumstances.

The thing that surprised me the most, however—the thing that kept coming back to me repeatedly—was how easy it was. It was like stealing the money from the valets. I had a goal, devised my plan, and followed through with it. I had a teacher in middle school who loved the phrase, "By failing to prepare you are preparing to fail." That stuck with me—I had done most of my work before executing my plan. And the next year I employed the same tactic, but with far more serious consequences.

Chapter 7

MATT

Farrington College has the odd practice of starting the spring semester in February, as opposed to most other schools that begin a new semester in January. Supposedly, the inception of this was one of personal desire. The former president of the college had a mistress who liked to ski and, late January being prime ski season, he whisked her away to Aspen every year until mid-February. Even more peculiar than that was the president's wife was aware of the mistress. Evidently, she wasn't fond of her husband, but she had quite the affection for his money, and that was enough to tolerate his dalliances.

The result of his carnal desires was Farrington had some courses where class meetings were five days a week in order to accommodate the school's quarterly term system. And such was the case with my Race and Politics course that included Liv.

Normally, I dreaded these five-days-a-week courses, but not this one for obvious reasons.

Tuesday, February 14, 2017

Liv was sitting in the same spot the second day of class. I arrived right on time, determined not to pay too much attention to her. I hadn't yet crossed a line with her, but I had already decided I would, and I resolved myself to maintain my professionalism in the classroom. She had other ideas, however. As I stood at the front of the class, she gave me a knowing, seductive smile that suggested only she and I were in on a joke.

I didn't tell Liv about my gambling problem. I thought she might think less of me, and I wanted to project the image she likely had of me—a successful, smart, and charming college professor. Was I kidding myself? Possibly, but she seemed attracted to me, and I didn't want to jeopardize that by revealing a major shortcoming.

So, on that day in the classroom, my mind drifted far away from my teaching duties. Even as I talked, my gambling debt occupied my mind. I expected to hear from Rex at any moment. It had been three days since I was supposed to pay him. But my mind oscillated between worry and elation.

Here was this beautiful woman right in front of me, using her big, brown eyes to flirt with me, catching every glance I made toward her. I was teaching, but I was on autopilot. In fact, I wasn't sure what I said during much of the lecture.

A student raised his hand. It was Zack, a student whom I had taught in a few previous classes. Among the sea of liberalism that is Farrington College, Zack was the resident conservative, and never afraid to speak his mind. He was also smart as a whip and, if being conservative wasn't enough to stand out, he played the part by wearing a blue blazer and a bow tie.

"Yeah, Zack?"

"Professor, you said the First Amendment means we're free to speak our minds, but I disagree. There's no doubt many people are being silenced."

"How so?"

"With cancel culture."

"And what do you mean by cancel culture?"

"It seems whenever a conservative wants to voice his opinion, they are shouted down or outright banned from, for example, giving a speech."

"Well, forgive me if I'm wrong, Zack, but you're conservative, right?

"Yes."

"And you're being allowed to speak your mind here, right?"

"Well, yeah."

"And no one is shouting you down."

"Can I say something?" Liv raised her hand as she spoke.

"Sure," I replied.

"I think you might be confused between being canceled and being held accountable." She turned to face Zack. Noticing her body, I found myself fighting not to drift from the conversation. "Conservatives get angry because they get kicked off Twitter or Facebook. But those are private platforms, right? So the First Amendment doesn't apply to them. Twitter and Facebook are simply cracking down on people spreading lies and misinformation, not to mention racists and misogynists. So sure, people are free to be racists, but private companies aren't forced to accommodate their views."

Zach replied with a statement I didn't hear because I was transfixed. Not only was Liv beautiful, but she impressed me with her eloquence and intellect, which attracted me even more. The previous night we mostly joked around and laughed a lot, and I saw her as a funny, mostly carefree young woman. Here in the classroom, however, she took on the air of a scholar, someone who had more college courses under her belt than she currently did.

We made small talk after class, and she whispered she would text me later. I responded with a bland acknowledgment as she turned into the hall and out of sight. Driving home, reality hit me with a thud. I again scouted the inside of my house with the binoculars. I saw no one.

Upon opening the back door, I noticed something was amiss. The usual jingle of Ann and Nancy's collars was absent. I walked through the kitchen toward the living room and there, in the center of the room, I saw them lying still. My knees buckled and I buried my head in my hands. I yelled, anger and sadness combining to produce a mournful wail. Then, a massive force against my back toppled me over. It knocked the wind out of me, resulting in a terrifying few seconds of an inability to receive any oxygen—an instantaneous suffocation.

I turned to look up and braced myself for another blow and there, holding a baseball bat inches from my face, was a massive man. His large hands swallowed the bat's grip and his enormous belly made it difficult to see his face, but I knew then it was Mike.

"You knew I was coming, right? You're not stupid." He kicked me in the ribs. "You should really be more prepared."

I struggled to speak and placed my hands in front of my face. "Please. I'm going to pay. I just don't have it yet."

"That's not very creative. Every person I've ever had to collect from says the exact same thing: 'I'm going to pay.' If every person were going to pay, I wouldn't have to do this shit. Now, listen to me. Are you listening?"

"Yes," I replied, sheepishly.

"What?" he said, kicking me again.

"Yes!"

"You're kind of a nice guy. Nice home. You seem pretty put together. I don't want to have to kill you. But you see, it's my job. Rex calls the shots, not me. You were supposed to pay three days ago. So what happened?"

"I'm going to pay. It's just going to take me a few more days, I swear."

"Consider this your final warning. You've got one week from today to pay him all the money. Understand?"

"Yes."

"And don't even think about trying to run. I've tracked guys all the way across the country with no problem. And don't think for a second about calling the cops either. You try any of that shit and you're signing your death warrant."

"OK."

"Did you see how this time I hit you with the bat and made my presence known? Next week, that won't happen. You won't even see me, and boom, just like that, it's all over. You got it?"

"Yeah." He turned to walk away but stopped and kicked me hard, this time in the back where he had hit me with the bat.

"And don't worry about your pooches there. I just gave them something to keep quiet. They'll be up in a few hours. I like dogs. You, however, are a piece of shit."

He left through the back door. I struggled to breathe and wondered if my ribs were broken. My torso ached and I felt lightheaded as I stood. I stared at Ann and Nancy, their midsections moving in a rhythmic up-and-down pattern, reflective a deep slumber. In all this time, I knew it was coming. I knew I had no way to pay Rex and I knew Mike or some other goon would be after me, but I was in shock from the whole experience.

After a few minutes, I managed to get a deep breath and wanted nothing more than to crawl into bed and try to forget everything. I took some Vicodin left over from a dental procedure, gathered two ice packs, and inched my way toward the bedroom. I lay in the bed, my body became heavy from the medicine, and I felt shame for what I had done and what I had become. This was how my life would end. I had no out. There was no way I could produce fifty-thousand dollars, certainly not in a week. I couldn't run. The only people who can successfully disappear are those with money, and I had none. Going to the police was not an option, as Mike made clear. It was hopeless, and it was all my fault. A pathetic ending to a promising life, all for selfish gain. I thought of Emily. I still loved her and I wondered if that was mutual. I wrecked her life and there was nothing I could do to repair it. The day she walked out, she had tears in her eyes. That alone should have caused me to see the light, to get the help I needed. It pained me now to think about that, but in that moment, my brain told me she was the irrational one, not me. She was the one who was abandoning the marriage, not me

So there, on the bed with an aching body, with the sun setting outside and on my life, I reached the depths of my despair. I thought of killing Rex and Mike. But how? It would take planning, but my medicinal haze prevented any rational thoughts, and I drifted off, a temporary reprieve from the immeasurable weight upon my shoulders.

Chapter 8

LIV

Over the next year, my mom and I didn't talk much. She continued to pay me the money she owed, and I suppose she continued to see Andrew, but I didn't know for sure. She sank into what I know now was a deep depression. There were some days when she didn't get out of bed. On some others, she would sit in a darkened room and only once in a while venture outside the house. I suspect she started medicating herself after that because there were some days where she seemed happy, like the mom I remembered in my younger years. But I knew she was fragile, and the claws of depression scratched at the door, haunting her, waiting for the right moment to enter and seize control once again.

During the school year, I was on the cheerleading team for school, but in the summer, as in the previous year, I joined the elite team at Pyramid Spirit, coached by the perverted Eric Brandt. I saw a lot of opportunity with my cheering and figured I could go on to cheer at the college level, so I tolerated his behavior. He continued to correct my stretching that didn't need correcting and interjected his perverted comments. In isolation, the comments might have seemed innocuous but taken together, they established a pattern exemplifying his depravity.

The summer I was fifteen, we got new cheer uniforms in preparation for a tournament in Florida. We had gotten new uniforms in the past and, to assure proper fitting, the assistant coach, Jane, would have us try them on and she would inspect them. On this particular day, however, I arrived to find that Jane wasn't there.

"Hi, girls," Eric said, greeting us with his big, toothy smile. "Jane had something she needed to take care of so she can't be here. But we have to make sure these uniforms are ready to go for Florida, so I'll be the one inspecting them. They have to be a perfect fit. It's part of our presentation score, and I don't want to lose the tournament because someone's uniform is too baggy or too tight or too short or too long."

The other girls and I exchanged uneasy looks when we heard this. We were used to Eric leering at us, but the thought of modeling a cheer uniform in front of him was even more uncomfortable. We filed into the dressing room to change while he waited in a lounge area immediately outside. One by one, he called us to stand before him so he could approve of the fit. I was nervous. I didn't like the thought of being alone with him. It didn't scare me, as the other girls were in the next room, but it was distressing nonetheless.

When the girl in front of me returned from the lounge area, I made my way there, returning his smile because that's what he expected me to do. He gave me several directions. Stand with your feet together. Stand with them apart. Turn around. I complied with all of them, ready for it to be over. When I turned back around, his brow was furrowed. He stood and walked toward me, staring at my skirt. He touched the hem of it and grazed my thigh. "Does that feel OK? It seems tight."

"Yeah, it feels fine."

"It looks a little uneven. Can you adjust it a bit?"

It wasn't uneven at all, but this was his chance to keep staring and to solidify his power over me. I shifted the waist of my skirt, and his eyes locked on mine. I averted my gaze.

"Can you turn around again?" he asked. "I need to make sure this fits properly in the back." With my back to him, he creeped closer. He put his hands on my hips and he pulled me into him. I felt his erection. I think this episode lasted for a second or two, but it seemed much longer.

"You look great, Liv. All right, send in someone else." I walked back into the dressing room, motioned for the next girl in line and went to the bathroom. I hid myself in a stall and cried, humiliated and scared. I knew Eric had planned for Jane to be gone so he could ogle us and, at least in my case, touch us. I exited after a few minutes and tried to compose myself around the other girls, but they could tell something was wrong. I dismissed it, unconvincingly, as not feeling well. I was too ashamed to ask any of the other girls if Eric did the same thing to them. Ultimately, it didn't matter. It mattered only what he did to me and it was at that moment I realized Eric didn't only make me uncomfortable, but I hated him. It was a deep-seated hatred where I envisioned hurting him or even killing him. I wanted him gone. I couldn't tolerate him any longer. I thought about quitting the team, but why should I quit? That's punishing me. He was the one who should be punished. He should have to pay.

For the first time in my teen years, I wanted to confide in my mom and to feel the comfort only a mother can provide. But she was never one to console, the chasm between us was wider than ever, and her depression wouldn't allow it. I couldn't go to my dad either. If I had told him, he likely would've taken matters into his own hands, and I'd be off the team for sure. I decided to say nothing, the traditional anthem of girls and women subject to sexual assault and harassment. That is, until the swim party.

In keeping with the idea of the previous year, my mom wanted to host a lot of parties. It seemed odd, given that she was more withdrawn than ever, but my dad, being the good soldier he was, went along with it. The last party of the summer was a Saturday, two days after the latest incident with Eric, and my mom decided to have this one outdoors. She invited neighbors, friends, and family, and she allowed me to invite some friends from school and the cheer team. My dad, fulfilling his proper role, cooked on the grill.

As the smell of burning charcoal and cooked meat filled the air, my friends and I frolicked in the water and the older attendees mostly sunned themselves, away from the unmatched chaos that is a group of kids in a pool. It was the last vestige of summer and I consciously tried to appreciate the moment, knowing the short nights and long days of the school year were approaching. Out of the corner of my eye, I saw him. Eric had arrived. He had a bathing suit on and a tight, yellow tee shirt, his glasses fastened to his face with a piece of string. He flashed his repulsive smirk as he talked to others, making his way toward the pool.

I turned away from him and made a beeline for my mom. She was reclining in a lounge chair, her face hidden under a big floppy hat. "Mom."

She peeked out from the hat and shielded the glare of the sun with her hand. "Hi, Liv."

"Did you invite him?"

"Who?"

"Eric."

"Yeah, why?"

"Why did you invite him?"

"I figured it was the nice thing to do. The rest of the cheer team is here. I invited Jane, too, but she had plans. What's the big deal?"

I chose not to elaborate. I figured if I said any more, she might pry further, and I didn't want to have that conversation at the party. "It's nothing," I said. "I just didn't know he'd be here."

I walked back toward the pool and hopped in. I pretended not to notice him and started interacting with my friends, but Eric greeting me was inevitable as he came closer.

"Hey, Liv," he said, removing his tee shirt and slithering into the pool.

"Hey."

"Two weeks from today we'll be in sunny Florida. You excited?"

"Yeah." Another cursory response.

"I really think we have a good shot at winning. There's tough competition, but I feel like we're ready. The only thing is that last routine where you're the flyer. I think we need to work on that. I looked at some video of it from practice and we're a little sloppy, especially with your toe touch at the end. Don't get me wrong, you're great, it's just a hard routine and finishing it with a good toe touch is incredibly difficult. If we can nail that, the judges will be impressed."

"OK." That was all I cared to say. He was disgusting. He videoed every practice, which was reasonable, but I have no doubt that while watching them, his perverted pleasures overtook his coaching concerns. Knowing I was on display on his computer screen, him fantasizing about me and pausing me and the other girls in vulnerable positions made me sick.

I emerged from the pool and felt his eyes upon me as I walked toward the grill. My dad was there, sweating and looking like he had just exercised. "Hey, sweetheart," he said, as he saw me approaching. "I'd give you a hug, but . . . ", he added, pointing to his sweat-drenched shirt.

"I appreciate the offer. It's the thought that counts."

"Indeed. You having a good time?"

"I guess. Hey, did you know mom invited Eric?"

"No. You know me. I more or less do what I'm told and go along for the ride." He said all this without looking up, focusing on his task, checking the beef and the chicken and applying the right amount of sauce on each piece. His Red Sox cap protected his head and face, but the fair skin of his arms and legs were pink from the sun.

"Why did you want to know?" he asked.

"No reason, really. I just didn't know he was coming, and it feels kind of awkward having a coach here."

"Especially him."

"What do you mean?" I asked.

"Just between you and me, he's always creeped me out a little. He reminds me of a teacher I had in high school."

"Who was the teacher?"

"Mr. Selatori. He taught chemistry. He wore glasses just like Eric's. A weird guy all around. He was always flirty with the girls, definitely inappropriate with them sometimes. And one day, we found out he was no longer at the school—that he had been arrested for statutory rape. We never found out who the victim was, but he got twenty years in prison. We called him Mr. 'Statutori' after that." I snickered.

"Wow. twenty years."

"Yeah, so I guess he's out now."

"So statutory rape gets you twenty years?"

"Well, I imagine it depends on the circumstances but yeah, it's a serious thing." He sipped on his bottle of beer, placed a meat patty on a plate, and handed it to me. "There you go. Well done for you, as always." He smiled and gave me a wink.

"Thanks, Dad." I turned and walked toward a patio table, careful to avoid Eric. It was amazing to me how much more comfortable I was around my dad than my mom. How he could instinctively make me feel loved and secure and how she was so cold and detached. I wondered what they saw in each other, but they still at least seemed in love. Even then, I knew having an affair didn't automatically mean she had lost her love for my dad. It was complicated, but I felt bad he didn't know—that he was in the dark. Even if I hadn't blackmailed my mom, though, I wouldn't have told him. It would have broken his spirit and I couldn't bear to see him like that. Ignorance is bliss.

I sat to eat my burger alone at a table and, as if he had been tracking my movements, Eric sat opposite me, holding an unopened bottle of Coke. On all our cheerleading trips—on the bus rides and plane trip to Texas and the hotel rooms—I had avoided being alone with him and now, in the span of two days, he had cornered me so he left me with no choice but to interact with him. He droned on about something I can't remember. I tried to disengage, but he kept at it, with his annoying habit of trying to make jokes and laughing to himself afterward. Still shirtless, he stretched, arms extended over his head, eyeing me the whole time. After several minutes of me giving brief responses to his comments and questions, I could tell he was about to leave.

"Well, I think I'll head home." He lifted his bottle and stood, pushing his chair away from the table. "By the way," he said, "I really like your bathing suit."

"Oh, thanks." He gazed at me with a predatory stare, fully aware I saw his erection beneath his bathing suit.

"I'll see you Monday at practice," he said.

I didn't say anything in reply. I was too disgusted and I vowed then I was through tolerating his behavior. I would make him pay, and I knew just how to do it.

Chapter 9

MATT

Tuesday, February 14, 2017

The buzzing stirred me, but then it stopped. It happened again. Periodically, like a song on repeat, it kept coming. Its occurrence was now predictable—an annoying hum followed by the still of the night. My body felt heavy but I reached for the source, shuffling my hands around on the sheets. I forced my eyelids open and saw the light from my phone. Forcing myself to wake, I reached for it. The texts were from Liv.

I scrolled through them to find a simple "Hey" followed by more small talk, a few emojis and, finally, an apology for "blowing up my phone." I checked my watch. It was almost 8:00 P.M.

I responded immediately, afraid an opportunity might have passed.

Hey, sorry. I took a nap. Three dots danced below my message signifying she was typing.

Who takes naps at eight o'clock at night?

Me, evidently.

You want some apple cider?

The alcoholic kind or the hot kind?

:) The hot kind.

That sounds nice, although I would've said yes to either.

710 Fairmont Ln. Apt. 4.

See you in a few.

My anticipation grew at the thought of being with her in her apartment, but my pain soon overcame it. The Vicodin had helped, but I struggled to remove my shirt. My ribs were sore but I was breathing fine, so I figured they were intact. Turning toward the mirror, I eyed the source of my biggest ache—the mark of Mike's bat—a misshapen mix of purple and red cascading down my back. It pained me to see it and I turned away, reaching for the ibuprofen.

I changed into some casual clothes—a sweatshirt and jeans—and put on my coat. Blessed by tolerable temperatures in recent days, the cold, dark hand of winter had returned to the state, and it began to snow. Before leaving, I hugged Ann and Nancy, who were groggy but alert, and gave them a rawhide bone, partly as an "I'm sorry" for having to ingest whatever the hell Mike had given them.

Driving toward Liv's apartment, I turned the heat on and fumbled with the radio but was unable to concentrate on any song. I was nervous, like a schoolboy approaching his crush to ask for a date. I popped a couple of mints in my mouth and checked for any lingering bits of spinach left over from lunch. On one hand, it felt ridiculous to be nervous; on the other, I seemed out of my element. I was going to see a woman a quarter of a century younger than I was, a situation no rational person would put himself in. But given all that had transpired over the past week, I made a conscious decision to abandon rationality. There was no point. I might be dead in a matter of days. Why not have a fling? Why not fulfill the ultimate cliché and play the classic fool of a professor falling for his student?

I made my way toward the main road in front of the campus and its tree-lined streets. Massive oak trees towered above the road and met in the middle, their limbs free of the leaves that usually provided a natural canopy. Eventually, though, the trees thinned out and gave way to restaurants and pubs catering to the college crowd, and students presumably doing schoolwork filled the trendy coffee shops that dotted the area.

Fairmont Lane was a two-way road a few blocks from the campus, filled mostly with old modest homes maintained well for decades. Liv's dwelling was an old Victorian-style house, which stood out from the rest. It had been converted into apartments—a massive structure of three floors and three, looming turrets covered by fish-scale shingles. I had passed this house many times, always finding it mysterious and foreboding.

I parked out front, trying to be as conspicuous as possible, and walked through the wrought-iron gate on the stone path toward the porch. The wind was biting and the trees on the front lawn blew freely, giving the setting a haunted feel. Ten steps led me to the double front doors beneath an imposing archway. I reached for the doorknob but someone beat me to it.

"Excuse me," I said with my eyes downward.

"Professor Richardson?"

Startled, I raised my gaze to see Zack, my student. "Hey, Zack."

He wrinkled his forehead and pursed his lips as if trying to solve a riddle. "What are you doing here?"

"I might ask you the same thing," I said, smiling.

"My girlfriend lives here."

"I see. And I noticed you've ditched the blazer." I pointed to his unbuttoned parka and sweatshirt underneath.

"She hates it."

"Is that right? And you're still with her? It must be true love."

"Slow down, professor. I don't know that I'm ready to be tied down just yet."

"I never figured you for a ladies' man, Zack."

"We're all full of surprises, I guess."

"I suppose that's right. Good night, Zack."

"Good night. See you in class."

I entered the house and the door behind me closed with a thud. Finding Liv's door, I knocked, trying to calm my nerves by breathing but I felt the sharp, stabbing pain running through my back and ribs.

"Hey," she said, opening the door and leaving it, walking back toward the kitchen as if she were tending to something. Her apartment occupied two rooms. The living area was long and narrow with dark, hardwood floors. A small couch occupied one wall and a large TV the other. The kitchen was in the far back corner next to a small window. I shut the door behind me and, while walking toward the kitchen, noticed the other room was her bedroom.

"OK," she said from the kitchen. "This is a recipe from my mom. I've made it only a few times."

81

She came toward me carrying a mug that was white with a green four-leaf clover on it. She was beautiful. Her hair was in a bun, and she wore a red sweatshirt and black yoga pants.

"Here you go," she said, handing me the mug. "And be honest. It's ok if you don't like it."

I sipped the cider. Its spices hit my tongue and it warmed me as it coated my throat. "It's really good."

"You swear?"

"I swear. It's delicious."

"Oh, good. I was afraid you'd hate it. I think it's the cinnamon sticks that do the trick."

I took another sip and began to feel awkward. The previous night in the diner, there were no expectations for what would happen between us. Our interaction hinged on the food and the coffee, nothing more. Now, however, there was a void, a series of awkward pauses infused with small talk and cider sips.

"OK, let me give you the grand tour," she said. "It's not much but as I said, it's convenient. I walk to class on most days. I really like it, although the landlord is a bit of a dick."

"And why's that?"

"He lives down the hall and complains about my TV being too loud. He also blamed me for smoking weed once. I wasn't smoking at all, but he wasn't convinced."

I turned toward a sprawling painting hanging above her TV. It was an abstract of a young woman or girl, her hair obscuring one eye, the other a forest green. Her hair, accentuated by four white flowers with yellow pistils, was an array of reds and yellows, and her lips were shaded scarlet.

"Believe it or not, that's me. My aunt is an artist and she painted that for me. What do you think?"

"It's beautiful. I could never paint something like that in a million years."

"You and me both. OK, follow me." I set my cup on her coffee table and followed her into the bedroom. She flipped on the light. "Yeah, I know, it's pretty small."

And it was. A four-post bed overwhelmed much of the space and a cedar chest lay in front of it. The walls were wallpapered—no doubt a holdover from years past—a sunflower yellow with white, circular designs interspersed throughout. The smell was pleasant, comprised of a mix of candles and lotions and body washes, the kind that rarely emanated from a man's room. The bathroom was mere feet from one side of the bed and on the other side was a closet with sliding, louvered doors, slightly open.

"I like it." I said. "It's cozy."

As I said it and before I could react, she was kissing me. I returned it, with all of the pent-up passion I had felt since I first saw her, a passion that had been slowly building each time I talked to or even thought of her. Our tongues touched and I let my hands wander over her body. We undressed and fell onto the bed, an awkward moment that caused us both to smile. My ribs and back hurt, but I put the pain out of my mind and concentrated on her. A bruise to my male ego, I hadn't been with a woman since Emily, and our sex life dwindled to almost extinction before the divorce, so I was nervous.

We continued to kiss and her legs slowly spread, inviting me. My thrusts and the bouncing of our bodies made the bed squeak, and I wondered if her landlord would complain. With her legs wrapped around me, she bit her lip in that sexiest of ways and closed her eyes, emitting a soft, rhythmic moan that became louder and louder, stopping just short of a scream. The headboard banged against the wall and I didn't care, continuing to push until I climaxed. I gazed into her eyes and we joined our mouths, a soft, sloppy kiss that ended too soon. The episode was over in minutes. It was quick, it was passionate, and the forbidden nature of it made it even more so.

I was dizzy, my heart pounded, and I rolled over onto my back, letting out a moan, not one of ecstasy, but of pain.

"Are you ok?" she asked.

"Yeah, I'm fine," I replied, in a strained whisper.

"Is your back hurt?"

"Yeah, but it's not a big deal."

She nudged me a bit to have a look. "Oh my God. How did that happen?"

Maybe it was the Vicodin or maybe the hope of sex clouded my mind, but I hadn't prepared a story to explain the wound on my back. I had to think quickly.

"I hurt it playing basketball."

"Basketball? Is this some kind of full-contact basketball I don't know about?"

I smiled. "I happened to run into the wall on a fast break. Stupid, I know."

"You want some ice?"

"No, thanks. I just want to lie here with you."

"I can do that." She pulled back the covers and we slid underneath. She rested her head on my chest and her breasts fell against me. As much as worry and fatalism consumed me the previous week, at that moment, they were gone, and there was no place I had rather be than holding her. The smell of her hair was glorious, a hint of coconut-scented shampoo that filled the air around it. I smoothed her hair and ran my hands along her back.

"Wow," I said, breaking the silence.

"What is it?"

"That was nice. I have to say, when you said you would give me a tour, well, I can't say I was expecting *that*."

"Well, I did say it was the *grand* tour."

"Grand indeed. I hope you don't mind that the bed might have scuffed up your wall a bit."

"I don't care. My landlord might, but fuck him."

"Yeah, fuck him."

"It was worth it anyway," she replied. "Hey, I have a question."

"Uh oh."

"No, it's not a big deal, but what happens if the college finds out about students and professors who are in a relationship?"

"Well, it ultimately means I'd get fired. If you weren't my student it might be different, but that's a moot point."

"Well, I won't say anything. There's no way they could find out anyway unless we start acting weird around each other."

"Not a problem. I have to say, though, I do find you distracting in the classroom."

She smiled and looked at me. "Really?"

"Yeah. From the moment I saw you I found it hard to concentrate on teaching."

"I'm flattered."

"I'm sure I'm not the first professor who's felt that way about you."

"I wouldn't know. I've never had a professor tell me that, and you're the first one I've fucked." She ran her hands below my stomach and gripped me, causing a slow arousal. "Not yet, prof. To be continued," she said, disappointing me. "Remember Ms. Carlisle?"

"The English professor."

"Yeah. I'm in her American Lit course and if I don't finish *The Great Gatsby* tonight, she'll embarrass me tomorrow in front of the entire class."

"Plus you have to read chapter two in the book for my course," I said with a smirk.

"Oh, yeah. That too." She grinned.

"You didn't read *Gatsby* in high school?"

"The only thing I read in high school was *Twilight* and *Cosmo*."

She climbed out of bed and shut the closet door completely, reaching for her clothes. I stared at and admired her body, lithe and taut, untainted by age. We both dressed and she led me to her door before giving me a final smooch. We said our goodbyes and I kept my head down, avoiding eye contact with anyone who might recognize me. I was on a high as I drove home. The snow was getting thick on the roads and I took my time, happy for what I experienced and craving more.

Few things can bring contemplation and clarity like a quiet drive. I sat in silence, and it astounded me to think what I had done. I met a beautiful student whom I liked. She was engaging, outgoing, and energetic, and seemed to possess so many qualities I either didn't have or had lost some time ago. On top of that, we had now had sex which, as it was inclined to do, could present a problem. However, I was too far gone to care. I was like someone running up a credit card bill with no intention of ever paying it. Yes, I had crossed a line. But where, exactly, was that line? Did I cross it when I texted her? Or was it when we met at the diner? Or maybe it was when I crossed the threshold of her apartment. Regardless, I was now well beyond that line. I was playing with fire, and I rather liked the heat.

Chapter 10

LIV

Sunday afternoon, the day after Eric invaded our pool party, I told my parents I was going for a walk. My sister asked to come along but, to her dismay, I said I wanted to be alone. I slipped out of the front door and made the long walk down our driveway toward the road. It was a beautiful day. There wasn't a cloud in the sky and only a slight breeze. The sun was warm on my face and I smiled at the passers-by out for a jog or a stroll. I exited our neighborhood and walked along the sidewalk on Sourek Street until I arrived at Cowler's Drug Store. Before entering, I put my hood over my head, enough to obscure my face. It was odd to wear a hoodie during the summer, but no one would be able to identify me if they ever viewed the surveillance footage.

I scanned the aisles for a bit to locate what I needed. Finding and then standing in front of them, though, I felt self-conscious. Condoms are as common as any other drugstore item, but there is a stigma about them, as if the person buying them is doing something illicit. I searched for the type I needed. It had to be the ones with spermicide in them. Finding the correct box, I grabbed it and headed to the counter, praying no one I knew would see me.

I placed the box in front of the clerk, a middle-aged woman who leered at me when she saw my purchase. Upon exiting the store, I ditched the bag, receipt, and the box, and placed the roll of condoms in my bra. My plan was coming to fruition.

The next day, I performed my usual routine. I waited until my mom was clear of the kitchen so I could eat my breakfast in my room. My sister was watching TV and oblivious to everything else. Cheer practice started at 10:00 A.M., so I still had time.

After eating, I put my dishes away, avoiding my mom's wrath. I gathered a sandwich bag and took it into the bathroom. I took a shower, shaved my legs, and dried off. Fetching the tweezers, I reached between my legs, plucked several hairs, and placed them in the bag.

I went into my bedroom and decided on my outfit for practice. First, I put on a black sports bra followed by white cotton underwear with a rainbow design on the front—distinctive and not easily forgotten. Normally, I didn't wear underwear beneath my cheer briefs, but today was different. Today was special. I completed my outfit by donning a white tee shirt I acquired at a cheer camp the previous year.

It was about time to leave. My mom was already in the car ready to drive me, so I placed the bag of hairs in my gym bag along with an extra change of clothes, a towel, my purse, my water bottle, and the roll of condoms. I tore one condom package off and placed it between my mattresses. As usual, when I exited the vehicle at the gym, my mom said nothing except "pick you up right after noon."

Eric always started practice on time and only a few seconds after ten, we were performing our stretches. We performed our routines for the Florida competition the entire time. The whole team was exhausted. Practice ended a few minutes before noon and those of us who weren't old enough to drive waited around outside for our rides.

"Oh, I forgot something," I said to the five others who were still lingering. Eric was also outside, chatting with Jane and the parents who didn't mind small talk. "I'll be right back."

Moving quickly, I headed to Eric's office. His desk was metal with a wooden top and in front of that was a file cabinet. The flooring was gray vinyl tile carpet and it smelled of sweat. I glanced at the picture that hung on the wall of him, his wife, and his son. Then, I went to work.

I opened my gym bag and retrieved the sandwich bag with my pubic hairs. One by one, I placed them on the floor and one on top of his desk. Next, I plucked a few hairs from my head and scattered them on the floor. Afterward, I removed my gym shorts, cheer briefs, and underwear. I heard a sound outside and people talking. There was no way to explain my presence in Eric's office, so I had to move faster. My heart raced. I opened the bottom right-hand drawer of the desk and placed my underwear and the roll of condoms in it. Closing the drawer without a sound, I put on my shorts, stuffed my briefs in my bag, and zipped it. I walked to the locker room so if anyone saw me, explaining my presence there would be a piece of cake. Sure enough, not five seconds after entering, Eric came in.

"Hey, what are you still doing here?"

"Stupid me. I thought I left my water bottle in here but I just checked and it's in my bag."

"Ah, I see. Well, Jane is already gone, so I need to lock up."

"Yeah, I'm going."

"You looked really good today, as always."

"Thanks," I said, looking over my shoulder and giving him a smile. Then, and I don't know what possessed me to do it, I turned around and reached for him, giving him a hug. Maybe it was the fact that this was his last day as my coach. It definitely wasn't remorse for what I was doing. He didn't expect the hug, but of course it lasted longer than I wanted.

I walked outside. My mom was waiting in the car and the other girls had already left. I had to play the part, so I got in, said nothing, and donned a pair of sunglasses. I leaned back in my seat and, to my relief, my mom didn't try to engage me in conversation. As we pulled out of the parking lot, I saw Eric locking the gym doors and I smiled to myself.

Once home, I closed myself in my bedroom. As tense as it was removing my underwear in Eric's office, what was next was the most difficult part of my preparation. I removed my shorts, grabbed my hairbrush, and lay on my bed. Then, slowly at first, I put the handle inside me. This was not for pleasure; it was for revenge. I pushed harder and deeper and faster to the point of tears. The pain was sharp and made me squirm. When satisfied I had done enough, I removed the brush. Streaks of blood were smeared on the white handle. I cleaned it and reached between my mattresses for the condom package. Opening it, I rolled it onto two fingers, and inserted it into me for a few seconds. Then, putting

on my cheer briefs and shorts, I rehearsed my lines
and prepared for my biggest lie yet.

Chapter 11

MATT

Wednesday, February 15, 2017

Want to see where your professor lives?

I texted the words to Liv, uneasy at the response I might receive.

> Ms. Carlisle? No thanks.
> Lol. That makes two of us. I was talking about me.
> :) Sure. When?
> Around six? I can order in some food.
> You don't cook?
> Not unless you're in the mood for mac and cheese.
> OK, OK, we'll order in.
> You like Italian?
> Definitely.
> Great. I'll see you in class.

I'll try not to be a distraction.

No, please distract me all you want.

Be careful what you wish for.

That's probably good advice. 23 Greenwich St. You can park in the driveway.

See you later.

It was a date. I felt butterflies, reminiscent of my first date with Emily many moons ago. I dressed and headed to work but concentrating on anything besides Liv was a lost cause. The dizzying intoxication of sexual energy controlled me, and I found myself checking my watch too often, counting down the hours until Liv and I could meet. I went through the motions in my classes. Perfunctory statements and hurried responses to students' questions carried the day, and I left earlier than I was supposed to, neglecting my office hours. I descended the steps from Edwin Hall and walked across campus toward my car, appreciating the beauty of the college and its impressive, gothic structures, many of them covered in ivy, which provided a stark contrast to the white of the fresh snow. For the first time in a long time, there was a spring in my step.

As six o'clock approached, I began peering outside my front window, waiting for her arrival. The butterflies were still there and I felt like a kid waiting to open presents on his birthday. Right on time, she arrived. She drove a recent model BMW, a glaring difference parked behind my six-year-old Honda Civic with a dent in the rear bumper. She walked the short brick path toward the porch and stopped briefly, and I backed away from the window to avoid looking desperate. Eventually, the doorbell rang and I greeted her, quieting Ann and Nancy's barks with a snap of my fingers.

"Hey," she said, smiling. "So I just met your neighbor."

"Shit. Mrs. Sorkelson."

"She's sweet. She asked me who I was."

"And?"

"I said I was your fuck buddy. What else?"

My heart skipped a beat, but then I realized she was joking. She let out a large chuckle and tilted her head   back.

"You should see the look on your face. No, I told her I was your niece."

"Thank God." I introduced Ann and Nancy to Liv, and they sniffed their way toward accepting this stranger into their house.

"They're adorable." She extended her hands to greet them. "Interesting names for dogs, though."

"They're named after the Wilson sisters."

"Who?"

I grabbed my chest and exhaled, feigning disappointment. "You don't know the group, Heart?"

"Sorry, I don't."

"No worries. We'll correct that in due time. OK, so now it's my turn to give you a tour."

"Is it a *grand* tour?" she asked, referring to the previous night at her apartment when we ended up in her bed. I smiled sheepishly at the question.

"It can be grand," I responded, "but we have to eat first."

"I understand. You old guys need your strength."

I made the chest-grabbing motion again. "Ouch," I replied. She gave me a "just kidding" and the welcomed gesture of touching my arm. I took her coat and placed it on the couch and smelled the now-familiar scent of her shampoo. As always, she was stunning. She wore a black turtleneck and a black-and-white checkered skirt with black leggings. Her ankle-length boots gave a discerning thud as she traversed across the hardwood floor. Despite her jest regarding the "old man" comment earlier, I was now self-conscious about my beige chinos and blue pullover sweater. My threads were so plain compared the modernity of hers.

I led her around the house as we made small talk. Emily and I had found this two-story, early

20th-century colonial available when we moved here three years prior, and we jumped on it. We both fell in love with its white paint and red shutters and doors, and its towering trees surrounding it only added to its beauty. It provided more space than we needed but we couldn't resist, and we both envisioned a bright future growing old here—a future that, thanks to me, would never be.

The food arrived and I placed it on the small, square dining table adjacent to the kitchen. Liv sat and I noticed her pearl drop earrings as she pushed back her hair. "OK, delicate question," I announced as I opened the refrigerator. "I'm a big believer that wine is a necessity with Italian food. I have a bottle, but I also know you're not twenty one yet. Would you like a glass? Or we could stick to something else."

"Start pouring," she replied.

"OK then." I opened a bottle of pinot grigio and poured us both a glass. This untoward decision fit right in with my ill-advised interaction with this young woman, but I pressed on.

"OK, Professor Richardson. Matt." She smiled and sipped her wine. "Rumor has it you went to law school."

"That's the rumor, huh?"

"Is it true?"

"It is."

"So why did you stop practicing?" she inquired, leaning forward.

"It was no single reason. I was tired of it. I didn't find it fulfilling at all. It was a lot of hours and not a lot of happiness."

"Where did you go to school?"

"University of Texas. In Austin."

"Is that where you're from? Texas?"

"Yep," I said with a Texan drawl.

"Oh my God. I never would've guessed that. You don't have an accent at all."

"Thanks."

"So how did you make it all the way up to Farrington?" She sipped her wine and maintained eye contact.

"I drove."

She placed her hand in front of her mouth and I thought for a second she might spew her drink in reaction to my silly remark. "Oh my God. I didn't know you were a comedian."

I smiled. "After leaving the practice of law, I decided to get my master's and doctorate in political science. I taught at the University in Austin for a few years and, voila, here I am."

"I don't want to pry, but I noticed you don't have a ring on and, well, I never would've pursued you if you did. So—"

I cut her off. "You're not prying. I'm divorced. Six months."

"I'm sorry."

"Thank you. Sometimes things don't work out. I think we're both better off now," I lied. "So what about your parents?" I asked, changing the subject. "Are they still together?"

"Yeah."

"You don't sound too happy about it."

"It's complicated. I guess they love each other, but my mom's been cheating on my dad for years. He has no idea. At least I don't think he does. I would've never known unless I saw pictures of her and her lover together."

"Wow. So I guess that was pretty jolting—to see that."

"It was. I was only 14 at the time. But in a weird way, I think it helped me. It made me realize people can't necessarily be taken at face value. And everyone has secrets. Honestly, before I saw those pics, I would've said my mom was one of the most boring people in the world. She's definitely not, although she's still a bitch."

"For cheating?"

"Yeah, and for other shit I don't want to get into."

"Fair enough," I replied, happy not to pry.

"You know, secrets, they can be empowering," she continued. "Don't you think? Like you and I have this secret between us and no one else in the world knows. It's just us. I find that invigorating."

"I know what you mean. And that secret has an element of danger, at least for me."

"Right? Which makes it more exciting. I used to do that as a kid. I would put myself in situations where I had a secret, where there was a danger to someone finding out. It made me feel . . . alive in a weird way. I don't know, maybe I should be telling a therapist this instead of you."

"I don't mind listening, but I'm definitely not a therapist. And you can tell me anything, Liv. There's nothing about this relationship that's not secret. I have no reason to tell anyone about any of it."

"You have everything to lose and," she thought for a second, "what do you have to gain?"

"Are you kidding? I like you. You're beautiful, smart, funny. The sex was amazing." She smiled and moved her eyes downward as her fingers traced the rim of her wine glass.

"Thank you. I'm not used to receiving comments like that. But it's like what you said in class today—how political decisions don't always involve rational choices. People vote against their self-interest all the time, right? So you can persuade people to make impassioned decisions based on short-term gain or a gut feeling."

"Very true," I replied. "And yeah, you're probably right. My decision to be with you is not the most rational decision. But all I can say is I'm living in the moment. I haven't done enough of that in my life. It's been too structured."

"So, you're sowing your wild oats."

"Well, I don't know. Maybe I'm the one who needs to be in a therapist's office." She took another sip of wine and brushed her hair back, revealing her earrings again. I complimented them.

"Oh, thanks," she replied. "My grandparents own a jewelry store here. My mom's parents. That's where I got these."

"Really?"

"Yeah, it's Holland Jewelers. It's in that shopping center near downtown, on Sycamore Street."

"I'm guessing you get a discount."

"Yeah, well, I wish they owned a clothing store instead."

We continued talking. My plate was empty and our bottle of wine was half-full. I was enjoying the night as I had enjoyed no night in recent memory. I was falling for Liv. There was no other way to say it. It's ridiculous—I had known her for less than seventy-two hours—but I couldn't ignore that fact.

I was smitten. But what did she see in me? That question remained in the back of my mind from the moment we met at the diner. I was forty-five years old. Were there not other guys nearer her age who offered just as much? She did seem, however, physically attracted to me and genuinely interested in me as a person. The problem was my self-doubt. I was inclined toward it lately and as I sat across from this beautiful woman, I determined I would not let that doubt ruin my night.

I took out my phone and connected it to the speakers in the living room. I selected a Heart playlist and turned it on.

"What is this?" she asked, as "Barracuda" began, the guitar's rumble and the thundering drums filling the room.

"I told you I would correct your lack of knowledge regarding Heart."

"Oh, I know this! My parents listen to this."

"And now, I feel old again."

"Awww." She gave a pouty face, stood, and walked toward me. "You're not old. Age is just a number, right?" She sat on my lap and began to kiss me.

"Or," I replied, "you're only as old as you feel. And right now, I feel like a spry eighteen-year-old." I returned the kiss. Our tongues danced as my hand crawled beneath her skirt, caressing her bare thighs above her leggings. She arched her back and placed her feet on the table. I pulled her panties to the side, inserting a finger. The moans from the previous night returned, and we continued to kiss as "Barracuda" blared.

She turned around and eyed me with a devilish grin as she took her feet off the table. She lowered herself in front of me and her hair fell about my torso. Unzipping my pants and feeling her way with her hands, she took me into her mouth. I held my head back and closed my eyes and the moment engulfed me. The tricks of her tongue complemented the warmness and wetness of her mouth, and I exhaled a deep and long, satisfying release of tension and worry. I opened my eyes to watch her performance and she returned the gaze with her dark brown eyes.

"Hi, professor," she said as she paused, and then resumed as quickly as she had stopped. I held back, eager to prolong the moment, and pulled out of her mouth. I stood and helped her to her feet, prepared to escort her upstairs to the bedroom. She turned, however, and leaned over the kitchen counter. I got behind her and pulled her panties down, awkwardly, over her boots, and began exploring her legs and butt and with my hands. I entered her, starting slowly and gaining speed, regular pushes culminating in the loud slapping of our bodies. She yelled, uninhibited without her neighbors or a cranky landlord, and her animalistic screams of pleasure fueled my desire. I continued until resistance was futile, and I exploded.

She turned back around and we embraced, kissing once again. I don't know how long all of that lasted, but we had blown through several Heart songs. My legs were weak and I told her as much. "Old man," she said with a smirk.

"I'll show you who's old." With that, I lifted her over my shoulder and she squealed as I began to climb the stairs toward my bedroom.

"Impressed?" I asked as I tossed her on the bed.

"I was already impressed."

"You mean I did that for nothing?"

"Well, now I know you can rescue me from a burning building."

"I'm a man of many talents."

"I'm finding that out."

We finished off the bottle of wine in bed while we watched TV and at some point, we fell asleep as I cradled her. We awoke early in the morning and made love again, the sun just beginning to peek through the blinds, illuminating her exquisite, nude figure as she straddled me.

"Shit," she said, as she rolled off of me. "Look at the time. We have class."

"I could cancel it."

"Really?"

"Of course. I'm quite powerful," I replied, causing her to grin.

"With great power comes great responsibility," she replied.

"I like the power part. The responsibility part, not so much. I'm not going to cancel it. There's no doubt those with more power than I have would ask me why I didn't hold class. Plus, politics in the civil rights era is not going to teach itself."

"I have to hurry," she said. I don't think I even have time to go home and change."

"Also, your panties are still downstairs."

"Keep them. Consider it a souvenir."

"So you're going to class with a skirt on and no panties?"

"I'll give you a show in the middle of the lecture."

"Now I'm definitely not cancelling class."

She dressed, kissed me, and bounded down the stairs and out of the door. I watched through the window as her car sped out of sight, faster than was prudent for the snowy conditions. I checked my watch. Class started in exactly twenty minutes, not enough time to shower. But I didn't care. I wanted her smell on me, a tattoo of pleasure from the previous night. I hurried down the stairs and fed the dogs. Spotting Liv's panties, I took them from the floor and smelled them, the intoxicating aroma enveloping my senses, a smell I would not and could not soon forget. As I drove away, I blasted "Barracuda" again and smiled, looking forward to Liv's mid-lecture show.

Chapter 12

LIV

When I told my mom the story of how Eric raped me in his office, she was indignant. She asked me a ton of questions, which made her seem skeptical, but then she called my dad at work and he came home immediately. I knew he would be sympathetic, but I must also give my mom credit. Both parents were supportive and when my dad arrived, he called the police. Seeing that police vehicle parked in front of the house made me nervous because that made it real. It was too late to turn back. I was entrenched in the lie and if I caved, I would be the one to get into trouble—not Eric, and I couldn't bear that thought.

To my surprise—and I was thankful—the detective was a woman. She exited her vehicle, a jet-black Tahoe with police lights under the grille. My dad opened the door before she could ring the doorbell and welcomed her in. She greeted my parents with what seemed a firm handshake, the strength of which can set the tone of an entire meeting.

"Hi, Olivia. I'm Detective Larsen." She didn't offer her hand to me, which I found odd. She was tall with broad shoulders and brown eyes. The top of her hair was brunette but as it flowed away from her scalp, it transitioned into a dark blonde. She wore jeans and a button-up white shirt, and her badge was fastened to her belt. I caught a glimpse of her gun beneath her black coat. "I'd like to ask you some questions if that's OK. And Mom and Dad, I need to be alone with her," she said, turning toward my parents. "Is there somewhere we can go or if you two want to leave the room, that would work too."

My parents walked upstairs, both in tears. The detective sat beside me on the couch, but I didn't make eye contact. At that point, I was scared she would see right through me—that this was all a farce.

"Olivia, I want you to go slowly and tell me exactly what happened. The important thing is to take your time. We're not in a rush, and you're perfectly safe here, OK? I'm going to take notes on my phone so I can refer back to the information later. Does that sound good?"

"Yes." I stammered at first, not sure how to begin and still not looking her in the eye. I took a deep breath and steeled myself, remembering why I was doing this in the first place. After that, it was easy. "So, it was after practice."

"Cheer practice, right? At the gym on Rosemont?"

"Right. And I was standing outside with the other girls waiting for my mom to pick me up. But I thought I forgot my water bottle, so I went back inside. Eric was in his office and called me in there."

"Eric is your coach?"

"Yeah. Eric Brandt."

"And then what happened?"

"He's always been, I guess you could say, creepy."

"Like how?"

"He's always touching me during stretches and once he came up behind me and I could . . . feel him."

"He stood behind you?"

"Yes."

"And you said 'feel him.' Do you mean he had an erection?"

"Yes."

"And you said he would touch you. Where would he touch you?"

"On my legs usually, sometimes my back."

"Does he do this to the other girls?"

"Yeah."

"OK, so let's go back to today. He called you into his office, and then what did he do?"

"He told me I looked really good and did a good job at practice. Then he told me to come over to his desk. When I did that, he shut his door. And I didn't know what he was doing. I thought it was weird he shut the door, but I thought he just wanted to talk, like I might be in trouble or something."

"Did anyone see you go into his office?"

"I don't think so. We were the only ones in the gym at that point."

"OK, and then what happened?"

"He grabbed me and kissed me and put his hands all over me. Then he put his hand over my mouth and said we had to be quiet."

"Then what?"

The detective kept alternating her gaze between her phone and me. It was repetitive. She asked a question looking into my eyes, an intent stare of sympathy and scrutiny, and when I answered, she immediately turned to her phone to type. On this question, then, I forced myself to cry. I had to be believable, and real tears were the way to do it.

"He put me on his desk, and then he pulled my cheer briefs and underwear down."

"Did you say anything to him?"

"I told him I didn't want to do it, but he wouldn't stop." Tears were now sliding down my cheeks.

"Did he penetrate you then?"

"He put on a condom first."

"Where did he get the condom?"

"It was in one of the drawers."

"Do you remember what it looked like?"

"It was orange."

"All right, now it's ok if you can't remember, but do you know about how long it lasted? Was it more like seconds, or was it over a minute? Or maybe several minutes?"

"I'd say seconds. Less than a minute."

"After he did that, what did he do?"

"He took the condom off—I don't know what he did with it—and he kissed me on the stomach and . . . went down on me."

"Do you know for how long?"

"It wasn't long. Like maybe ten seconds."

"Did he say anything during or after?"

"After it was over, he told me to get my bag and go, like he was in a hurry. He handed me my cheer briefs and I put them on and—"

"What is it?" the detective asked.

"I don't think I put my underwear back on."

"You think you left them at the gym?"

"Maybe. But I don't have them on now."

113

"So you had on your shorts, your briefs, and your underwear before you went into his office? And now you have just your shorts and briefs on?"

"Right."

"Do you remember what your underwear looked like?"

"Um . . . white with a rainbow design on the front."

She asked a few more questions after that and summoned my parents downstairs. I was crying—an Oscar-worthy performance—which made my parents cry even more. The detective arranged for me to go to the hospital for an examination, and she was adamant it had to be sooner rather than later. So, off I went with my parents.

When I concocted my plan, I knew this examination was coming. As unpleasant as it was, I had to do it. If Eric wasn't held accountable for his despicable behavior, he would eventually rape someone for real. I was doing this to save others. If I had to have a head-to-toe examination, have my mouth and vagina swabbed, and have tons of pictures taken of my naked body, so be it. It was for a greater cause.

I was there for a few hours. They handed the report to my parents and I saw phrases and words on it that made me cringe, such as "penetrate" and "vaginal bruising." We drove home in silence. The sun was low in the sky and I put my head against the window, relaxing myself with the hum of the tires on the road.

Things seemed to happen in a rush after that. The detective called our house and talked to my dad. They arrested Eric that night after they found condoms and my underwear in his desk drawer. He was released on bail but he had to wear an ankle monitor and stay in his house. The police searched the rest of his office and found pubic hairs and long hairs that appeared to be from a head. They sent those to the lab for analysis, but I knew the results already: those hairs were from me, and they would serve to tighten the screws on Eric.

We didn't get to go to Florida for the competition, which upset me, and I didn't see any of the other girls on the team. Several texted me and called me to offer their sympathies and we shared stories about Eric and his nasty ways. My appearances at practice became sporadic and I eventually stopped going completely. Over Christmas break, the prosecutor in the case called us and asked for a meeting.

The courthouse in Farrington is a mid-century, unsightly building comprised of brown brick and very few windows. The inside is as drab as the outside, long hallways with low ceilings and brown, church-like pews along the walls. The prosecutor in my case was Haley Olman, and this was the first we had met her in person. She was young and likely fresh out of law school, which concerned my parents. She had caramel skin and long, black, straight hair that tended to obscure one side of her face. Her high heels made her seem taller than she was. She introduced herself with a big smile and directed us to the chairs in front of her desk.

"I guess they're hiring kids these days," my mom remarked to Haley. My mom could be such an asshole sometimes.

"I'm not exactly a kid, Mrs. Powell," Haley replied, still smiling.

"You're just younger than I expected."

"Well, I'm likely older than I look."

"Where did you go law school?"

"You can read all my qualifications on the wall," she replied, pointing to the area behind her, which contained her framed credentials. Columbia Law School, Magna cum Laude. My mom shut up when she saw that.

"OK," Haley started as she took her seat at the desk. "It looked like for a while this thing would go to trial, but the defense has hinted they're open to a deal. And honestly, I think our chances are pretty good at trial, but it's certainly not a slam dunk. It never is. There are some things, though, the defense would have a hard time explaining: the vaginal bruising, the presence of spermicide in Olivia, the underwear in Mr. Brandt's drawer, and Olivia's hair in his office. Given all of that, it looks like he's ready to accept a plea deal. Plus, all of the girls on the team have given statements about Eric's lewd comments and occasional inappropriate touching."

"What kind of deal?" my dad asked.

"We're prepared to offer twenty years. If he got convicted at trial, his sentence would likely be at least twenty, maybe as long as thirty."

"What about parole? Could he be out sooner than twenty years?" my dad asked again.

"Technically, yes. But the parole board doesn't take kindly to people convicted of child rape. If I had to bet, I would guess he would serve the full twenty. Definitely at least three-fourths of that."

"So he could be out in fifteen years?" my mom inquired.

"Conceivably, but I wouldn't count on it."

My mom placed her elbow on the arm of her chair and rested her forehead in her hand. My dad exhaled and stared at the bright lights on the ceiling. I knew they would ask me what I thought. For me, I wanted Eric put away as soon as possible. I didn't want a trial. I didn't want to testify. And there was a chance the jury would find him not guilty, which would mean my plan was all for naught.

"Liv?" My dad turned toward me. "What do you think?"

"I'm fine with twenty years."

"Another selling point with offering the plea is that Olivia won't have to testify," Haley noted. "That can be a difficult experience, mentally and emotionally. Keep in mind, though, you don't have to decide now. You can have some time to sleep on it."

My parents looked at each other, and I knew their answer before they said it. They were tired of thinking about this every waking hour, as was I. Everyone wanted it behind us, and the plea deal was the way to make that happen.

"I think that's what we want," my dad said.

Haley turned her head in my direction, observed me for a few seconds, and spoke. "Olivia?"

"Yeah, that's what I want."

"Mrs. Powell, are you in agreement?"

"Yeah."

"OK. Here's our next step. As soon as we're done here, I'll call the defense attorney and make the offer. Assuming Mr. Brandt accepts it, we'll draw up the paperwork, file it with the court, and have a hearing scheduled."

"And if he doesn't accept it?" my mom asked.

"Then we haven't really lost anything. We can go back and make another offer, but we definitely have the upper hand here," Haley replied.

As we had done after my examination, we drove home in quiet, hardly a word spoken among us. My family had lost the camaraderie we had when I was much younger and this situation with Eric exacerbated the proclivity for silence, as I'm sure my mom's affair and depression did as well. We used to laugh and joke as a family, and it seemed those days were gone. My parents were both hurt emotionally, and I was not in a good emotional state either. That, however, was a small price to pay for putting Eric where he belonged.

Not too long after we arrived home, Haley called and notified my parents that Eric's attorney had counteroffered with a ten-year sentence. After a few phone calls among my family and Haley, she notified us Eric was open to splitting the difference—a fifteen-year sentence. Although reluctant at first, I agreed to it along with my mom and dad.

The sentencing hearing was scheduled three weeks out and I, along with the rest of my family, decided we didn't want to be there. There was no point in attending, as Haley told us it would be a short procedure. I, however, knew deep down I would be there. I would be in my Sunday best to see

Eric hauled away in handcuffs, that perpetual smirk gone from his face.

The sentencing day fell on the Friday before I had to return to school from Christmas break. I didn't tell my parents I was going because I knew they would accompany me, so I lied and told them I was going to a friend's house. That was technically true; I just had to stop at the courthouse first. My friend had recently turned 16 and had her license, so she waited in the parking lot while I went to the hearing.

The courtroom was smaller than I expected. There were only a few benches available for spectators, and I sat on the back row in the corner. I saw Eric as soon as I walked through the door. His back was to me, and he conversed with his attorney. He had regular clothes on because he was out on bail, but I knew he would be in a prison jumpsuit soon enough. The judge was old and gray with a large face. His neck sagged over the collar of his black robe and he had a raspy voice. Glasses sat far down on his nose and he peeked over the lenses when he spoke.

Asking Eric to stand, the judge spoke for several minutes. After both attorneys spoke, the judge asked Eric if he wanted to say anything. To my surprise, he said no and shook his head. Then, also to my surprise, he started crying. He wept hard and loud like a little boy separated from his mother. How pathetic. I put my hand over my mouth and smiled. Eric's wife and son were also there and they were crying as well. I felt bad for them, but it's not my fault they have a scumbag for a husband and a father.

When the judge announced the sentence and banged his gavel, Eric continued to cry. He turned around to try to hug his wife and son but the bailiff wouldn't let him. When he turned around, though, he spotted me. We glared into each other's eyes, an unspoken secret communicated between us that no one else knew. The corners of my mouth began to travel outward, the genesis of a grin. But I stopped it. He knew I had him, and there was nothing he could do. Smiling at him was pointless. We continued the stare-down until the bailiff turned him around and placed handcuffs on him. And, in matter of seconds, Eric was hauled out of the courtroom and out of my life.

Chapter 13

MATT

Thursday, February 16, 2017

Liv did indeed give me a show in class, spreading her legs surreptitiously while I lectured. A devious grin adorned her face and I had to resist becoming the butt of all student jokes as the professor who sprang an erection in the middle of class. She texted me later in the day to tell me she had to write a paper for another class and probably wouldn't get to see me that night. Disappointed, I locked myself in my office and for the entire afternoon, completed the work I had neglected because of my preoccupation with Liv and my anxiety over my Rex-and-Mike problem. I set off for home under the gray sky, morbid thoughts and questions drowning out the music on the radio as I drove along the wet, freshly plowed streets. Would Rex and Mike kill me? If they didn't kill me, what would they do? Pull my teeth out? Break my legs? It was a gruesome curiosity I couldn't shake from my brain.

I pulled into the driveway and Ms. Sorkelson spotted me from her front porch, flagging me down like a stranded motorist. I greeted her as I exited the car. I was never one for small talk and, given my current situation, had little tolerance for it. But I knew she was lonely and I felt badly for her.

"Hi, honey. How about this weather? It's nice and sunny one day and it snows five inches the next."

"Well, you know what they say. If you don't like the weather, just stick around and it'll change." She smiled at my obligatory statement.

"If it's not too much trouble, would you mind shoveling my walk?" Not too long after I moved into the neighborhood, an implicit agreement was formed between the two of us that I would clear her front walk and sidewalk of snow. She knew she didn't have to ask me, but I think she felt guilty if she didn't. I don't know how that practice started, but once you start shoveling snow for an old woman, you can't really stop and tell her to find someone else.

"Of course. Just give me a few minutes."

"Oh, I almost forgot," she said.

"What's that?"

"I met your niece last night." She gave me air quotes as she said the word "niece." I gave her a half-smile and she returned it with a knowing grin.

"She wasn't convincing, huh?"

"Not at all. Hope she's not trying to become an actor." She crinkled her nose and giggled. The belt of her beige robe flapped in a gust of wind and she folded her arms, trying to prevent the inevitable chill.

"Not that I know of."

"Oh, don't worry about it, honey. We all have our needs. But let me tell you something. She's a looker. You should hang on to her."

"I'll remember that," I said, waving as I entered my front door. It concerned me she had seen Liv, and it concerned me even more she could probably deduce Liv was one of my students. I had to trust she wouldn't say anything if given the opportunity.

I changed clothes and performed my neighborly duty, but I knew I would be doing the same thing tomorrow. The thick, gray snow clouds gathered in the waning daylight, and it was only a matter of time before a fresh blanket shrouded my progress.

I knew I had only one play left to avoid whatever irreparable harm Mike and Rex would bestow upon me, so I got in my car and headed to Emily's apartment. She moved into it before we divorced, and the thought of her alone in there always saddened me. Or maybe she wasn't alone. It was conceivable she could have found a romantic interest by that point. After all, I had. Or at least something resembling a romance.

I parked, ready to exit my car when I saw her leaving her apartment. She didn't see me as she walked across the parking lot to her BMW X5, a splurge we had made a few years ago before moving to Farrington. At the risk of seeming like a stalker, I followed her. I needed to talk to her, but curiosity consumed me. I wondered if she was going on a date. Who was she seeing? I was like a jealous boyfriend, although I had no right to be jealous or even to know where she was going. We neared downtown and she parked along the street next to the ever-growing snow piles. I found a spot several feet back and watched.

She exited her vehicle and entered Confessions, a restaurant and bar—mostly bar—that had been in existence for decades. It was converted from a Catholic church, and stained-glass windows still adorned the sides. Small tables now sat where pews once did, and the bar was located below where the organist would have played. Its wooden floors and high ceilings made for a noisy environment.

I entered a few minutes after Emily and spotted her alone at a table, unsure if she was waiting on someone. Uneasy at the reception I might get, I walked toward the bar on the chance she would spot me first. She did.

"Matt?"

"Oh, hey," I replied, failing to sound surprised enough.

"What are you doing here?"

"Nothing, just grabbing a drink. You?"

"I'm hungry and too tired to cook."

"No obligation to say yes, but do you care if I join you, or are you waiting on someone?"

She hesitated. "No, that's fine. I'm here alone."

I sat across from her. God, I missed her. She had aged gracefully. Her dirty-blonde hair with large curls flowed to just below her shoulders, and her green eyes were as lovely as I remembered in my dreams. I cursed myself for the millionth time for ruining it all—for letting my one, true love slip out of my life.

"It's been a while since I've been here," I said.

"Funny we should get here at about the same time." She stared at me as she brought her glass of water to her lips.

"What, you think I followed you here?"

"Didn't you? I doubt you would just come here because you wanted to. You always said you hated this place. You said anything related to church gave you bad vibes and you couldn't stand the fact all they have on the menu is hot dogs and hamburgers."

I sighed. "Busted."

"So why are you here, Matt?"

"Can we just slow down? Let me buy you a drink."

"Fine. Red wine." I strolled to the bar, our tense interaction on my mind. I ordered her wine and myself a beer, and it wouldn't have surprised me if she had left when I wasn't looking. Thankfully, she was still at the table when I returned.

"House wine. I see you're splurging," she remarked after taking a sip.

"Sorry."

"I'm kidding." A waiter approached the table and asked if we were ready to order. He was Exhibit A if anyone accused this establishment of hiring underage workers. He was short and frail and his face screamed prepubescence.

"I'll have the burger with cheese, no onions or tomatoes, mayo, medium. And she'll have the burger, no cheese or lettuce, mustard, well done."

"You remembered," she said, exhibiting her first smile since my arrival.

"Lots of practice."

"Remember the Boxcar Bar in Austin? How many burgers did we eat there?"

"A thousand? Give or take a few." She was still smiling and revealed that soft, effeminate giggle I fell in love with many years ago. It was so familiar yet now so distant. "I have to ask, Emily. How are you?"

She sighed and took a few seconds to answer, as if she were really considering the question instead of making small talk. "I'm doing fine. Work is fine, although this is the time of year when the students are driving me crazy. I'm getting used to living on my own. I can't say I enjoy it, but it comes with the territory, I suppose. How about you?"

"Under the circumstances, I'm OK," I lied. "I'm actually thinking of selling the house."

"Why?"

"It's too much room for one. It doesn't make any sense."

"I always thought it was too much room for two."

"Yeah, same here. And then we went and added on a study." We both chuckled.

"You hate yardwork, too, and that house has quite the back yard. Is all that belladonna still back there?"

"Yeah. I've given up on trying to get rid of it. It comes back like herpes."

"That's a lovely image. Just make sure Ann and Nancy don't get in it."

"Oh my God, Emily," I replied, exasperated. "That's like the thousandth time you've warned me about the belladonna. Yes, I know it's dangerous. Yes, I'll get rid of it. In the meantime, I fenced it off. The dogs are safe."

"You know, I thought we were on our way to having a decent conversation," she said, annoyed, "but it doesn't look like that's going to happen."

"I'm sorry. My mistake."

After a long pause, she resumed our conversation. "So, I asked how you're doing and I think you avoided the question."

"Did I?"

"Mostly."

"I think I said I was doing OK, but that's not really true."

"Have you gotten help yet?"

"No," I said, ashamed. "But I plan to. Soon."

She shook her head. "You know, a year ago I would have given you a big speech about how your gambling is ruining your life and everything you care about. But now? I'm saving my words. It won't do any good and truthfully, I don't owe you anything at this point."

Her words hurt, mostly because they were true. "I know, and I hesitate to even say this, but I'm done with gambling."

"Oh please, Matt. You know how many times I've heard that?"

"I know, but this time is different."

"And how many times have I heard that, too? So tell me, why? Why is this time any different than the other thousands of times you said you were done?"

"Because . . . I've done something foolish." She stared straight at me. Her stunning green eyes were no longer inviting; they were piercing. It was a look I had seen too many times during my downward spiral.

"I made a big bet on the Super Bowl."

"And let me guess, you lost."

"Yeah."

"Matt, why did you come here? Why did you follow me? I never took you for a stalker."

"Emily, I'm in trouble."

"What kind of trouble?"

"The guy I was making bets with in Boston is a bit of a dangerous guy, and I can't pay him."

"Dangerous how?"

"I'm pretty sure he's into drugs and one of his goons paid me a visit."

"What does that mean?"

"He roughed me up a bit." I was embarrassed to say it. Why, I didn't know, but it was like it bruised my ego.

"So, what happens if you can't pay?"

"That's the thing. He'll come after me, and I really don't know what he'll do. He scared me with stories about knocking a guy's teeth out."

"Jesus Christ, Matt."

"Yeah. I'm worried."

"At the risk of being upset and knowing more than I want to, how much did you lose?"

"Fifty thousand." Her mouth fell open and she lowered her head. She took a deep breath and sighed, amazed at my stupidity and further bestowing the shame on me I didn't need.

"I don't even know what to say."

"There's nothing to say, and believe me, I've beat myself up over it countless times."

"That still doesn't explain why you're here."

"Please, Emily. Is there any chance your parents could lend me the money? I would pay them back."

"I can't believe you just asked that. You want me to ask my parents to lend my ex-husband fifty-thousand dollars? The same guy who decimated our savings and ruined our marriage? Are you serious?"

"Please, I didn't know where else to turn and I know they have the money."

"That's not the point. Of course they have the money. But you know as well as I do if they bail you out, you'll be gambling again next week. It'll never end. Sometimes you have to learn things the hard way, Matt. And I figured losing me and our marriage might be enough to set you straight. It obviously wasn't. I can't help you, and I'm damned sure not going to get my parents involved. I'm leaving."

She stood and kicked her chair out with one motion and made a beeline for the door. I didn't try to stop her. It was pointless. I could feel the eyes of the other patrons upon me but I was too embarrassed to make eye contact with anyone.

"Two burgers, well done for the lady and here's yours," the waiter said as he set the food on the table. I couldn't muster a "thank you." I was too upset, and I knew deep within I was wrong to follow Emily, I was wrong to invade her space, and I was wrong to ask her to get her parents involved. I was at the end of my rope, and I had nowhere else to turn. Desperate times.

I ordered two more beers and finished off Emily's wine, placing a fifty-dollar bill on the table before walking out. I felt the buzz of the alcohol as I sat in my car. I stared into the cold night, unsure of what to do at that point. I couldn't plan anything beyond the next hour, much less figure any way out of the mess I was in. Since I met Liv, I had been living only in the moment. Instant gratification was the order of the day, and I was unable to envision another sunrise. I had six days until the money was due and I had no plan.

I texted Liv and she responded immediately.

> How's your paper?
> Shitty.
> At least you're honest. Need a break?
> I'm sorry. I can't.
> Disappointed, but I understand.
> I can't see you, but you remember that story I told you where the guy was looking into my window and I gave him a show?
> Yeah.
> Come to my building, go around back, and look in my window. I think you'll like what you see.
> On my way.

The roads were slick and, still buzzed from the alcohol, I shouldn't have driven. But my desire to see Liv overtook any sensible thought.

I arrived and walked toward the large house. It was deathly quiet and I felt like a prowler as I made my way toward the back, the snow crunching beneath my feet. Someone exited the front door and I ducked behind a large tree trunk. I proceeded farther and eyed the series of windows that adorned the back of the house. There was only one room lit, so I assumed it was Liv's. I didn't see her, however, so I waited. Despite the warmth of my coat pockets, my hands were uncomfortable in the frigid temperature. I started to text her when I saw her appear. She wore a white bra and her hair was in a ponytail. She looked in my direction, but I was unaware if she spotted me. She turned her back toward me and then, as if right on cue, she unsnapped her bra and slid it off her body. She turned to face the window, exposing her breasts.

As I gawked like a teenager, a bright light illuminated the area around me. "Hey," a voice said. I turned to face the light and, unable to see the shadowy figure behind it, I ran.

"Police!" a man's voice shouted. I should have stopped but my flight instinct took over. I ran through the snowy yard and jumped a chain-link fence, hearing his footsteps behind me. I heard the jangle of the fence as he scaled it, and I kept running from yard to yard. The idiocy of what I was doing wasn't lost on me. I wasn't a peeping Tom—Liv had given me permission to look in her window. It was consensual. But here I was, failing to cede to this officer who clearly had the authority to stop and question me. I turned to the right down a narrow alley and slipped on some ice, falling on my shoulder. Rising to my feet as fast as I could and wincing from the pain, I heard more shouts to stop.

My lungs were cold, my breathing heavy, and my chest ached.

I was breaking some law by not stopping but I couldn't risk anyone at the college learning of this nonsense, so I pressed on. I could see the campus, the buildings getting bigger as I approached. I ran as fast as I could, not looking back, and found the gym. I opened the heavy, metal door and slipped inside, noticing the stark contrast of the chill outside and the heat within. Trying to look as inconspicuous as possible, I ventured toward the men's room. I found an open stall and locked it.

I didn't know if the officer had seen me enter the gym. If he had, my capture was inevitable. So, I waited, listening to the sounds of pick-up basketball games. Yelling and shouting and squeaking shoes filled the air as my heart rate slowed. Liv texted me and promptly returned an "LOL" when I told her what happened. I can't say I wouldn't have done the same, but I was in no mood to laugh. Fearing walking back to the scene of my "crime," I asked her to rescue me. She arrived moments later. I lowered my head as I exited the gym and walked to her car, but I never saw the officer.

"That was too close," I said, breathing a sigh of relief.

"I can't believe that!"

"That makes two of us."

"No, I can't believe you ran."

"Wait, you can't believe I ran because you think I'm old or because it was a stupid thing to do?"

She laughed. "The stupidity. Well, was it worth it?"

I sat in silence, considering the question. "Well, it was a good show, but I wanted more, preferably without the long arm of the law breathing down my neck."

"Fair enough."

"Shit," I said, as she began driving me to my car.

"What's wrong?"

"Besides almost everything, you mean?" She seemed surprised at the answer.

"What do you mean?"

"Nothing. Just feeling a bit stressed." An understatement, yet one that reeked of existential dread and despondency, but I wasn't ready to reveal anything of that nature to her. I wanted to go home. She didn't say anything in response, and she took me to my car in silence. We kissed, a soft but short peck. Her eyes drifted downward and I could see them welling with tears.

"What's wrong?"

"It's nothing. Just . . . school stuff."

I suspected it was more than that, but I didn't have the energy to pry. I wasn't in the mood for dealing with any more emotional baggage than I was already carrying.

"I'm sorry. Let me know if I can help." She mustered a smile and wiped a tear away from her cheek.

"Thanks. I'll talk to you tomorrow."

I drove home and contemplated a night that could be described only as a failure. My shoulder smarted from my fall on the ice and, as I was inclined to do, numbed the pain with alcohol in the form of wine. I opened a bottle and drank it too fast, leaving no time to appreciate the flavor. After finishing, I fell onto my bed and surrendered to my stupor, having no idea of the trouble that awaited me the next day.

Chapter 14

LIV

I met Darin Duclair my senior year of high school at a birthday party of a mutual friend. He was two years older than I was and attended Boston College. I was impressed he showed an interest in me—a college man talking to a lowly high school junior. He had an air about him that reflected his privilege. A native of Beacon Hill, his parents had even more money than mine and he talked like a Kennedy. He was thin with pale, smooth skin, and the short, brown hair on the sides of his head provided a glaring contrast with the long hair on top, which he periodically swept away from his deep, blue eyes.

I was instantly attracted to him. He was confident and I admired his blasé attitude. He regaled me with stories about college life and how great it was to have the freedom of being away from the strictures of parents. He invited me to his apartment in Chestnut Hill and before long, I was spending nearly every waking hour with him. He would take me to fancy restaurants, and we'd go to movies and make love late into the night. I told my parents I was staying with a friend and they always bought it, or at least pretended they did.

Darin also introduced me to weed. I was nervous to try it at first, but eventually I gave in and we used it almost every time we were together. I loved the way it made me feel and for the first time in my life, I felt I could be myself around another person. Darin never pressured me into being something I wasn't. In his world, there was no pressure from school, no overbearing, distant mother. Only him and me. It was bliss.

After a few months together, I began to see another side of him. That side might have turned a lot of girls off, but I became more attracted to him. He started carrying a gun. I asked him why he needed it, and he always said for protection. I couldn't imagine what he needed protection from, but I would soon find out. Anyway, he liked carrying it. It made him feel more powerful. He tucked it away neatly in the waistband of his designer pants or the breast pocket of his coat. Twice I saw him flash it to another person to deescalate a situation. Once was over a parking space. The other is when a man gave me a "Hey, baby" outside a restaurant. Darin opened his coat and told the guy to keep walking. A peacemaker. Isn't that what they call guns? It was true in Darin's case anyway.

Attending Farrington wasn't my first choice. I considered other schools in or around Boston, but my parents encouraged me to move away. In truth, I think they wanted me out of the house, especially my mom. And Farrington offered me a full scholarship, which meant I wouldn't have to get a job and could concentrate on my studies. I wanted to be near Darin, but we decided a two-hour drive wasn't a big deal. We could meet in the middle and visit each other on the weekends. My friends said a long-distance relationship would never work, but I proved them wrong. We stayed together, and our periodic separation increased my desire for him.

When he graduated BC, he decided to move to Farrington. I was ecstatic. I expected him to move to Boston, but he wanted to be near me. He said he couldn't bear the thought of being so far away from me any longer. He rented a house on the outskirts of town and by the beginning of my junior year of high school, I was going there every weekend. The house was ugly—a two-bedroom frame job with an unkempt yard surrounded by a chain-link fence. But it was our ugly, and I loved being there. Only us, no one around to bother us or tell us what to do. The ultimate freedom.

I entered his house one cold, January day and did a double take when I saw his kitchen table. On it sat a gym bag that appeared to have cocaine in it. I was taken aback and, judging from the look on my face, he knew he needed to explain.

"We have a delivery to make."

"A delivery? What do you mean?"

"I have to deliver that to a guy in Boston.

"Who?"

"Just come along and I'll explain it."

"That's got to be like thousands of dollars' worth of . . . what is it, cocaine?"

"Yeah, and that's kind of the point—the money." He zipped the bag, lifted it, and looked me in the eye, as if he were expecting me to say more. "Well? Are you coming?"

I didn't want to, but I was worried about rebuffing him, and there was still that part of me that found his dangerous side exciting. So I said yes. He put the cocaine in the trunk of his Mercedes and we sped off, headed toward Boston. As he often did, he stared straight ahead, not saying a word. Sometimes getting him to speak, much less open up, was an exercise in futility.

"So where are we going?" I asked.

"It's a place on Eighth Street."

"Eighth Street? Isn't that Southie?"

"You got it."

"Who do you know there?"

"So here's the thing," he began to explain. "I got hooked up with a guy at BC who knows this guy in Springfield who can get a lot of drugs, but he doesn't have the contacts to sell it all. He asked me if I would drive it to Boston and meet a guy named Rex and give it to him. So that's what I did. At first, it was weed, but now I deliver coke for him."

"Why doesn't the guy in Springfield deliver it himself?"

"I asked the same thing. He said he's scared of getting caught. He knew someone who got busted on I-90 with a trunk full of weed and now he's doing ten years in prison."

"And you're not concerned?"

"No. As long I go the speed limit, headlights are working and all that, I'll be fine."

"Where does the guy in Springfield get the cocaine?"

"I don't really know. I think he has contacts out west."

"And now you've graduated to cocaine?" He looked over at me for the first time on the drive.

"Is that what it's called? Graduating?"

"It seems a little more serious than weed. More jail time too. Shit, Darin. Why do you do this?"

"Does it bother you?"

"Not really. Well, maybe a little. I just think it's odd. You have all the money you could want. Why risk it?"

"That's the thing. I really *don't* have all the money I want. My parents are loaded, but they never give me money, not since I graduated. I have a trust fund I have access to now. They paid for my college, but that's it. So whatever money I have comes from that trust fund.

"How much?"

"It's enough. For now."

"Why don't they ever give you money?"

He sighed and began to spout off lines as if he had heard them a hundred times before. "Because learning how to make it in the world builds character. If you always have a safety net or someone to give you money, you'll never amount to anything."

I smiled at the admonishment from his parents and their hypocrisy that spurred their son to make it on his own using trust-fund money. "You believe all that?" I asked.

"Fuck no. Look at all the rich people in this country. Did they all make it on their own? Do they all have character? Of course they don't. They have money. And when you have enough money, you don't need to have character. Hell, you don't even have to be a good person. You can be an asshole, but you'll still make it for no other reason than you have money."

"OK, so why drugs? Why deliver drugs?"

"It's exciting. You know how boring life can be growing up in Beacon Hill?"

"You should try Weston," I retorted.

"It's the same thing. Never wanting for anything, living in a gigantic house, all to get good grades, go to college, and do the same thing your parents did—work, work, work, and for what?"

"You sound like a hippie."

He snickered. "Maybe I am. We should ditch everything and go live off the land."

"OK, let's not get crazy."

"I've got tens of thousands of dollars of cocaine in the trunk. We're already there, baby."

I loved when he called me that. And there, sitting in his car speeding along the freeway, eyeing his profile against the fading sunlight, I would have gone anywhere with him or done anything for him. I loved him with every fiber of my being.

We approached South Boston, Darin obeying every traffic law under the sun. My parents always warned me this neighborhood was dangerous, but it didn't seem so. A lot of the buildings appeared new and people milled about in bars and restaurants and, even in the chilly evening air, spilled onto the sidewalk, holding their drink of choice. Darin found a small parking lot and pulled into a narrow space between two jalopies, which made his car stick out like a sore thumb. He opened the trunk and looked all around him before retrieving the bag.

"So who is this guy anyway? This Rex?"

"I don't know him that well. I've been here only a few times. He has a fat guy who works for him though who scares the shit out of me. Just don't say anything and it'll be ok."

"What do you mean don't say anything?" I had a lump in my throat and butterflies in my stomach. I almost asked to wait in the car but I didn't want Darin to think less of me.

"Just stay close to me. Look like you belong. He'll take the bag of coke and give me some money. That's it."

We ascended a dark flight of stairs and down a narrow hall until we reached Rex's place. Before Darin could knock, a big guy opened the door and stepped back so we could enter. Without saying a word, he led us down a hallway to a bedroom. A man I assumed to be Rex was sitting at a computer. He didn't resemble my vision of a drug dealer. He was short and clean cut with a nice smile.

"Wow," Rex said, turning toward us. You didn't tell me you were bringing company. "What's your name?" he asked, looking into my eyes before his gaze drifted to my body. His walls were plastered with posters of half-nude women and even though I was clad in a big coat and jeans, he undressed me with his eyes, matching his mind with the images all around us.

"I'm Liv."

"Liv. It's good to meet you. That big guy behind you is Mike, and I'm Rex. You're beautiful. How did you get mixed up with this guy?" He gestured toward Darin. I didn't know how to respond to that and Darin seemed too nervous to say anything, which added to my trepidation. Darin always seemed so confident but here he was, evidently out of his element. "Not really one for words, huh? No worries. I like the pretty, silent type. All right, show me your ID," he said to me. I cut my eyes at Darin.

"He just needs to see it. He checks everyone's," Darin explained. I reached into the back pocket of my jeans and pulled out my driver's license. Rex snapped a photo of it. I still had my parent's address on it, which made me concerned but also relieved that it wasn't my Farrington address.

"Yeah. I have to check who everyone is and where they live because, well, sometimes we have to pay people a visit. All right. Put the bag on the bed," Rex commanded. He reached under the bed and pulled out a scale, placing it on the desk. The red, digital numbers were all zeros, and fear overcame me. It didn't occur to me that Rex would weigh the cocaine. It made sense but in my naiveté, I thought it was as simple as trading drugs for money. I wanted to escape but I knew I couldn't. *What if there wasn't enough cocaine? What would Rex do? God, why had I even come here? A drug deal? It was ludicrous.*

Rex took the cocaine out, placed it on the scale, and the numbers began to move. He cut his eyes at Darin before turning his attention toward the numbers. I didn't look at Darin because I knew his fear fed mine, and I couldn't bear it at that point. My heart raced and my cheeks felt warm. The numbers stopped moving. *Fuck.*

"You're short," Rex said.

"That's all the guy gave me."

"Well that's not what I ordered. There's supposed to be a pound and a half here. Do you see one point five anywhere on that scale? You're short three quarters of a pound." Mike stepped in front of me holding a gun. Before I could react, he hit Darin in the face with it, spinning him around. His face was bloody, and Mike continued to pummel him as Darin fell to the floor. I turned away in shock. Mercifully, Rex said "stop." He kneeled close to Darin's blood-covered ear. "When I order a specific amount, I expect it. You got it?"

"Yes," Darin responded, a soft whisper that reflected his pain.

"I got people counting on me and now I'm short, so it's going to be my ass. That means that three quarters of a pound is coming out of your pocket, you piece of shit. And if you come here again and pull this, you won't walk out of here alive. You might want to invest in a scale. Just a thought." Rex reached into a briefcase under the bed and pulled out a stack of bills. He peeled some off, counting them one by one, and threw them down at Darin. "Now get the fuck out of here. Although you can stay, baby," he said to me. "You want to stick around or are you late for dinner?" He snickered at his dull joke and for a second, I was worried he might actually keep me there.

Darin struggled to his feet, gathering the money and staggering out of the door. Blood poured from his eye and would soon be swollen shut. He grabbed a towel from the trunk of his car and held it to his face, transforming the floral patterns on it into a disgusting discoloration of crimson. He handed me the keys and said nothing. As Southie disappeared in the rearview mirror, I imagined his drug-dealing days were over, that nothing was worth the pain and suffering that accompanied such a dangerous game. But then he took the stack of bills from his pocket and fanned them out, displaying his ill-gotten gain. He turned to me with his bloody face and smiled like a prizefighter holding his championship belt. I

knew then he would never quit. The reward was too
great and the risk be damned.

CHAPTER 15

THE GRAVESITE

Friday, February 17, 2017

A small crowd gathered under the gray sky that threatened another snowfall. Dressed mostly in black, a few fought back tears, some stared in the distance, and the young kids fidgeted. The casket was teal, Muriel Norman's favorite color, but it was cheap—the least expensive option. Atop lay a giant bouquet of red and white roses whose scent wafted through the chilly morning breeze.

The Reverend, Chris McCaley, performed dozens of these a year, especially as his flock at the Hilltop Presbyterian Church in Farrington advanced in years. The process was always the same: speak with the family about the deceased, learn more about their likes and dislikes and favorite hymns, note several relevant passages from the Good Book, and prepare a eulogy the family would remember fondly. Muriel's ultimate demise was trickier, however. Hardly anyone liked her. For various reasons no one quite knew, her family alienated her, and she died alone in her small house that began to crumble around her after her husband died.

The reverend began to speak and, because of the deceased's estrangement from her family, today's talk was generic. He spoke of the temporary nature of life and Muriel's new home. He read a few scriptures and eyed the crowd, asking if anyone had any parting words. No one spoke, and he finished with a short prayer, afterwards encouraging the supposed mourners to go in peace. It was a sad ending of a sad life on a sad day.

Later that day, in this remote part of the New Life Cemetery, the workers lowered Muriel's casket into the ground. Using their shovels, they filled in the grave with dirt. Upon finishing, one of them retrieved a plastic marker standing against a tree. He carried it over to the grave to mark the final resting place of Muriel and to guide the proper placement of a headstone, in the unlikely event her family decided to shell out the money for one. The marker read "Muriel Beatrice Norman, July 28, 1933-February 14, 2017." The worker placed it on the soft, cold dirt, which no one would ever disturb again. Or so he thought.

Chapter 16

LIV

Friday, February 10, 2017

I don't believe in fate. Saying things are left to fate is a cop-out, a way of saying we don't exhibit some control in our lives. Sometimes, however, something happens that causes me to waver in that belief; moments occur that seem gripped by fate, and no force great or small can change that destiny. Such was the case on that night.

As his face had begun to heal from Mike's pummeling and retake its perfect form, a series of events unfolded I could have never foreseen. Darin picked up a shipment of cocaine in Springfield and readied to deliver it to Rex in Boston the next day. Someone, however, was watching him. As he approached his car, someone hit him and pointed a gun in his face. The person pulled the trigger, but the gun jammed. The next thing Darin remembers is waking in an alley, bloody with a throbbing headache.

When that happened, however, I didn't know it. I expected him to come home or text me or call me as he always did. But the minutes turned into hours and I became worried. I texted him and called him countless times. I feared the worst. He always responded to my texts and calls immediately, but that night they were met with a foreboding silence. Finally, minutes after midnight, he called. His voice was weak and he sounded disoriented. I wanted to help him, to hold him close and protect him, but I could do nothing. There was a reason he no longer let me go on these drug runs. It was he who was protecting me.

He mustered the strength to make the short drive from Springfield. I met him at his house, horrified at the grotesque shape of his face. His lips were swollen and the bridge of his nose was misshapen. The front of his shirt was ripped, revealing a large welt on his chest. He walked with a limp and when he saw me crying, he began to cry as well.

I took him to the emergency room. They performed all sorts of tests on him—X-rays, CAT scans, and the like. His nose was broken but, according to the doctor, it would heal on its own.

He also had a concussion. The doctor prescribed some pain meds and sent him on his way.

As we sat in his living room with the lights off, tending to his wounds and parsing out his medicine, it occurred to us how much trouble he was in. The mugging he had endured was the least of his problems. He told me that cocaine shipment was worth at least $60,000, and Rex and Mike had already threatened him for being short. Now, not only was Darin short on the money he owed, he had lost an entire shipment of drugs.

He called Rex early the next morning and told him about the mugging, but he lied and said he still had the cocaine stashed away, that he was in the hospital and would be out in a few days. That must have satisfied Rex because he told Darin to bring it to him in a week. That meant we had time to devise a plan, to figure out how to keep Darin alive by satisfying Rex.

Replacing the cocaine wasn't an option. There was no hope of getting the batch back that was stolen, and there was no way to obtain a new batch. I asked Darin about his trust fund, but he was defiant—he didn't want to use that money and he exaggerated the amount he had in it anyway. It was also a nonstarter to ask his parents for the money. We thought of running, but to where? And that would mean leaving our lives behind—our family and friends, and we had seen enough movies to know that people rarely disappear. They're usually found, and the results aren't pretty.

With each passing idea guaranteed to fail, we were running out of options, and the dread of the situation loomed larger. Darin fell asleep, but I was wide awake, scrolling through my phone when I saw it. It was one of those moments that fate had me in her grasp, and I was powerless to resist.

I ran the plan through my head repeatedly. I covered all the scenarios—the what-ifs and potential backfires. I also weighed the consequences. It was risky for sure, but it could save Darin's life, and that's what I cared about more than anything. I didn't care to go on without him. He was my world.

I stared at his bruised and battered body on the couch, unable to contain my excitement that I had a solution to his problem. I spoke in a whisper to wake him. His eyes opened halfway as his concussed brain tried to comprehend my plan. I went over the details and, as any good man will do, he supported my idea. Knowing we had a solution to our problem, I watched him fall back asleep and sauntered into his bedroom, my mind at peace. I removed my clothes and lay naked in his bed, savoring his smell from the pillows and relishing in the softness of the sheets against my skin. I couldn't get enough of that smell and now, because of my brilliant scheme, it would be with me forever.

Chapter 17

MATT

Friday, February 17, 2017

I woke in a fog, my brain fuzzy from the previous night's events. It came back to me, though, all too quickly. The meeting with Emily. The invitation from Liv to be a peeping Tom, and running from the police officer. It was all so stupid, and I wanted to block it out of my mind. And I did, for a while at least.

I went through the motions of teaching—Liv was absent and hadn't texted me—and I anticipated the respite that I hoped the weekend would provide. I wanted rest, but I wanted to be with Liv even more. Like a drug, she was my fix, and I didn't get enough of my fill the previous night. I texted her after my final class of the day.

You OK? Missed you today.
Yeah, I'm fine. Didn't sleep well.

Sorry to hear that.

Before I could type something else, she responded.

Can you come over?
Sure. When?
Now is good.
I'll be there soon.

Upon arriving and exiting my car, I saw a police officer driving his car in the opposite direction. I had no way of knowing if he was my pursuer from the peeping-Tom incident, but I dared not make eye contact. I kept my head down as I approached the giant house, skipping every other step as I approached the front door.

I knocked on Liv's apartment door and it opened immediately. Stepping in, I noticed Liv behind the door and an unknown figure on the couch. His face appeared bruised and he stared into my eyes, refusing to avert his gaze. "Hey," Liv said, slamming the door. "You look confused. Let me help. This is Darin."

"Hey," I said, nodding my head in his direction.
"He's my boyfriend."
"What?" I asked, the claim perplexing me.

"Yeah. I didn't mention him before because that would've caused problems, so I figured it was best to keep him out of it. Well, in a manner of speaking, anyway."

"What's going on, Liv? I asked, turning to face her.

"You should go ahead and sit down, Matt. Everything's fine." I approached the couch and sat at the opposite end from Darin. As much as his swollen face would allow, he exhibited a wry smile. "So, these past few days have been fun," Liv said. "I'm not going to lie. I actually enjoyed it. You're fun to talk to and hang out with. But there's another reason this all happened. Did you actually think I would fall for someone like you? Someone old enough to be my dad?" She laughed at the absurdity of the idea—an idea I had been too reckless to see through. My blood ran cold. "What is this?" I inquired, turning toward Darin and his disgusting face.

"Remember I said my grandparents owned a jewelry store here?"

"Yeah."

"We need to you to do something."

"Do what, exactly?"

"We need you to rob it," Darin chimed in.

"You're out of your fucking minds," I retorted.

"It will be an easy job. Trust me," Liv said.

"Trust you? That's rich. Why would I ever trust you again?"

"Fair point. But this is in your best interest."

"How so?"

"Well, if you want to keep your job. I don't think the college would take too kindly to a professor fucking one of his students."

I scoffed. "It's your word against mine."

"Only partly."

"What does that mean?"

"Show him, Darin." At that prompt, he took out his phone and leaned closer, showing a video of Liv and me in her apartment, our naked bodies intertwined. I remembered—her closet, next to her bed, the door was slightly open. Darin was standing in there the whole time.

"You bitch," I said averting my eyes from the phone and turning toward Liv.

"You can call me what you want, but I had to do it, Matt. I really didn't have a choice. It's to save Darin's life."

"How does robbing a jewelry store save his life?"

"He owes some money to some very bad people."

"Who?"

"It doesn't matter. The point is, this will get him out of the jam, and you don't lose your job."

"And then we just go about our lives like everything   is   normal?"

"Exactly."

"What about your grandparents? Jesus Christ, Liv. You want me to rob your grandparents? What kind of a person are you?"

"They'll be ok. And they have everything insured. They'll get all the money they're owed."

"I can't believe you. You had sex with me for money. You know what that makes you, right?"

"Again, call me what you want. I don't care. Remember that night in the diner?"

"You mean the first night you pretended to care about me?"

"Easy, Matt. We had a good conversation. Remember what I said, how our lives are just as much determined by the choices of others as they are our own choices? Well, this is a good example."

"Fuck you."

"So hostile. Just calm down. You're not losing anything here. Well, except for me. But deep down you knew that wouldn't last anyway."

I was seething. An unadulterated rage replaced the anticipation I had walking toward Liv's apartment. I hated her and I hated her stupid boyfriend. The stunning young woman I knew was no longer there. Standing before me now was a devil with a cold heart that obscured her delicate beauty.

I wanted to hit her. I wanted to bash Darin's face in more than it already was. I rose from the couch. "This is blackmail."

"Yeah, so?" Darin responded.

"It's illegal."

"Whatever, man. There's no way you go to the cops with this. They'll find out what the blackmail is for and then you're fucked." I approached the door and reached for the knob.

"Be here tomorrow morning at 8:00," Liv said. "The store opens at nine. We need time to plan. And Matt?" I turned to look at her. "Bring your gun."

"I don't have a gun."

"Bullshit. You have a permit to carry one. If you have a permit to carry a gun but don't actually own one, you'd be the first in history."

I said nothing and stormed toward my car, my blood now boiling with contempt. How could I have been so careless? How could I have been so naïve? Even without knowing what exactly Rex and Mike had planned for me, I made the ultimate mistake, all for a girl—a girl who was now my enemy.

I sped on the way home, not giving a damn if a cop saw me. I raced around slower cars and gave a driver the finger who honked at me. I found it hard to breathe and my chest was tight. I slammed into my driveway, the front end scraping the pavement for all the neighbors to hear.

Giving a cursory greeting to Ann and Nancy, I reached for the fridge. *Shit.* No more wine. No booze at all. I slammed the door shut and yelled at the top of my lungs. I sat and tried to calm myself, contemplating my situation.

I had a professor in graduate school who was fond of telling us to learn from our silence. He had an affinity for meditation and his point was, I think, that we can all take a few moments to calm ourselves and relax, which, supposedly, will give us clarity of thought. So I did. I sat in my recliner in silence and dwelled upon how fucked my life had become. I thought of my parents back in Texas and our home. The countless hours I spent outside with friends playing tag or hide and seek or riding my bike for hours on end. I thought of Emily, how she was the best thing to ever happen to me. A true, undeserved gift. I thought of the accolades I received through school and my professional career and how, now, sitting alone in the stillness, they seemed so pointless.

If clarity of thought was the goal, perhaps it worked. I didn't know how much money Darin needed, but I was short fifty thousand. This was my chance, my opportunity to lift the heavy burden off of my shoulders. I could take the proceeds from the jewelry, get the cash I needed, and pay Rex. Liv was right. As evil as she was, her point that insurance would pay for everything rang true. And her grandparents wouldn't be hurt. Even if I brandished my gun, I wouldn't use it. The whole thing would be over in a matter of minutes. It wasn't lost on me how sick this was. How sick I was. But this was a gift. Liv was the ultimate manipulator, but she had given me an out.

As I sat and further rationalized my impending crime, my heart began to slow and I was breathing again. I felt a strange calm, a peace I hadn't felt in months, maybe years. The still, dark of the night surrounded me and I relished in the tranquil state I was in and didn't want to leave.

I stood to grab a glass of water, flipping on the kitchen light. As I passed the fridge, I noticed a magnet that one of Emily's friends had given her years ago. It contained a quote from the famous photographer, Yousuf Karsh: "Character, like a photograph, develops in darkness."

Chapter 18

JOHN AND

LINDA

HOLLAND

Saturday, February 18, 2017

For the past forty-five years, on every day except Sunday, John and Linda had the same routine. Wake, shower, get dressed, eat breakfast while reading the newspaper, and travel the five miles to Holland Jewelers, located the past 30 years in a shopping center filled with small shops and a large grocery store. They always traveled together except on the rare occasion when one was sick and had to stay home.

Such was the case on a dreary Saturday in February. John woke his wife early to tell her he couldn't go in that morning. He felt terrible. It was his stomach. He'd been diagnosed with an ulcer previously and, although he had medication for it, he hated the way the medicine made him feel—lethargic with an occasional bout of dizziness.

"That's fine," Linda reassured him. "I'll handle things. You stay in bed."

"Thank you, Dear." John often thought through their fifty-one years of marriage he didn't deserve her. She was kind and considerate and not in any sense self-serving. When he went off to Vietnam, she wrote him every day. Most were short notes—three or four lines—but she never missed a day. And upon putting pen to paper, she couldn't fend off the macabre thoughts that this note might be the last one he ever read. She would stare out of the front window of their small house watching, almost with anticipation, of some army official exiting a black car, removing his hat as he ascended the steps to the porch, ready to deliver the horrific news. But that news never came and, despite John's war trauma that still affected him, they made a happy life together.

Besides John not getting out of bed, this morning was no different than any other so, as was her inclination, she scrambled some eggs, put some biscuits in the oven, and brewed some coffee. Before leaving the house, she took John his breakfast and a cup of coffee—straight black, as he liked it. He was snoring when she walked in and, although she was hesitant to disturb him, he needed to know she was leaving. She set his food and drink on the nightstand and kissed him on the forehead. He roused and thanked her for the breakfast, the strong smell of coffee obscuring Linda's perfume.

"I love you," he whispered.

"I love you, too. Call me if you need me."

"Thank you."

In a matter of seconds, she was out the door and on her way to open the store, as she done countless times. She had no idea this day would be different from all the rest.

Chapter 19

MATT

Saturday, February 18, 2017

I arrived at Liv's early, my small, black .22 revolver tucked inside my coat pocket. How Liv knew I had a gun, I have no idea. We had never talked about it, and the gun wasn't important to me. I got it several years ago. Emily and I took a class together to obtain our permits to be able to carry them. She scored better on the written test and on the proficiency exam, which didn't surprise either of us. That was the last time I fired a gun, and having it on me made me nervous.

Darin came to the door, his wretched face greeting me. Without acknowledging his presence, I walked past him, too nervous to sit. Liv strolled in from her bedroom, giving me a faint smile that wasn't returned. He hair was ruffled, as if she had recently rolled out of bed. Plopping on the couch, she started our business.

"You know where this is, right?" she asked, referring to the jewelry store. "It's the shopping center on Sycamore. It's right in the middle."

"Yeah."

"OK. My grandparents get there around 8:30. They prepare for the day—whatever that entails. Here's the layout of the place." She began to draw on white printer paper. "There are three display cases. One along the right wall, one along the left wall, and one in the middle at the back of the store, which is where the register is. Behind that is a little hallway, and at the end of it is their office. It's small, basically only a desk and a phone. You have to make sure no one is in there. They both have to be out of there when you rob it because of the phone."

"What about cameras?"

"There's one in the corner, up and to the right as you walk in. Darin has a mask you can use." *How thoughtful.*

"Is there any kind of a switch like banks have that allow them to notify the police?"

"No. At least I've never seen one. And I've been behind that register a lot.

"So what's the plan?" I asked, increasingly concerned none of this would work.

"The key to the display cases is in the register," Liv continued. "The same key works for all of them. You have to get them to open the register. That's the first thing you have to do. Grab everything you can from the cases and stuff it in the bag. Walk out and that's it."

Use this," Darin said as he pitched me a black gym bag.

"A simple plan," I said, my statement dripping with sarcasm.

"Don't complicate it, Matt," Liv retorted.

"Don't complicate the armed robbery. Got it."

"You put yourself in this position," she shot back.

"The hell I did. This is your hair-brained scheme, along with your idiot boyfriend." Darin reached behind him and pulled a gun out of his waistband, aiming it at my face, inches from my forehead.

"Shut the fuck up!"

"OK, please," I responded, raising my hands and turning away from the barrel.

"Can you put it away, baby?" Liv asked him, calmly, as if she was asking how his day went. He placed it back in his waistband and gave me a smug smile. "Now, we need to talk about where to park your car. As you're facing the store, there's a covered walkway just to the right, and there's a small parking lot behind the store. Park there—don't park in front. Hardly anyone uses that back lot. It should be close to empty or there might not be any cars at all since it's Saturday morning."

I wanted to say so much to Liv, but I couldn't form the words. Thoughts ricocheted in my mind, prohibiting anything coherent, much less anything worth saying. She was no longer the person I knew, or at least the person I *thought* I knew. She betrayed me. Was it all an act? Was this all planned from the beginning? Was it a coincidence she took my course, or had she sought me out? In that moment, I struggled to make sense of it all. I made an ill-advised choice for sure, but I was her prey—a wounded animal to be used and feasted upon.

"Anything else you want to know?" Liv asked.

"Where will we meet?"

"Back here. We'll be waiting."

"And listen, both of you" I said, exerting some authority in this fucked-up situation for the first time. "Don't call or text. If you have to, make your statements generic. Everything you say over texts can be tracked, and every outgoing and incoming call is logged."

Darin tossed me a black ski mask. I put it on as a cap and headed to my car, driving at a snail's pace toward the strip mall. The sun was out, low in the sky but bright, and vehicles on the road were sparse. I entered the parking lot and spotted the jewelry store, sandwiched between a Sheridan's grocery store and a dry cleaner. Its sign read, in fancy gold script, "Holland Jewelers, Since 1971." The store was still dark inside—I was early. Locating the parking lot in back, I found a space close to the front, turned the engine off, and waited. A fellow motorist drove in the lot a few minutes later. An old, beat-up Ford, it creeped toward me, coming closer by the second. Afraid of the driver parking close to me, I lowered my head and turned away, obscuring my face. Seconds later, after catching the nerve to look for the car, I saw the back of it, exiting the lot and onto the street. I tried in vain to catch a deep breath. I was fidgety. I checked my watch too many times and the hands seemed to stand still. I forced myself to look away from it.

I was well aware of what I was doing. No, I had not committed the robbery yet, but I knew enough law to know that I, along with Liv and Darin, had already committed conspiracy. We were all in on this together, and we all planned it with the intent of seeing it through to the end. I could've turned back at that point. I had no doubt Liv would work to get me fired, but my desire to pay off Rex and be done with all of this mess overshadowed that concern. In fact, if this went as I planned and I refused to give Liv and Darin any proceeds from the robbery, she would likely snitch to someone about our relationship, and that would be the end of my career—at Farrington anyway. But it would save me from the physical harm or possible death Rex had in store for me. Finding a new career was preferable to that.

I looked back at my watch—9:02. I exited the car, keeping my coat on and slipping on my gloves. Making my way through the pedestrian walkway, the scent of bread wafted through the air, from a bakery or perhaps a donut shop. Coming toward the big parking lot in front, I pulled my mask over my face, turned right, and entered the store.

I pulled my gun out of my coat pocket and pointed it at the woman behind the counter. She was stout, tall with a loose-fitting blouse and a myriad of bracelets that clanged together when she saw me. I turned, keeping my gun pointed at her, locked the door, and turned the "closed" sign outward to deter any potential customers.

She raised her hands, a look of horror splashed across her face. "You can relax. I'm not going to hurt you. Do you understand? That I'm not going to hurt you?"

"Yes," she muttered.

"Good. Do you have a safe?

"What?"

I raised my voice. "Do you have a safe?"

"Yes."

"Where?"

"It's in the back, in the office."

"Take me to it." She led me to the small office in back, her hands still raised. "Where's your husband?"

"He's sick. He's not here."

"You're the only one?"

"Yes."

She entered the office and approached a painting hanging on the wall encased in a thick frame. Placing her hands on each side, she lifted it, revealing the safe. She positioned the painting intending to prop it against the wall, but she let it go too soon and it crashed to the hard floor.

"Open it."

She sobbed, wiping her tears away as she began to work the combination. Her hands shook and I fought my impatience, waiting for her to reveal the contents, which seemed like an eternity. Noticing the phone on the desk, I ripped its cord from the wall, disconnected it from the phone, and threw it behind me in the hallway.

"Put the money in here," I commanded, opening the gym bag. "Fifty thousand."

"What?"

"Only fifty thousand, no more."

She took five large stacks of bills and placed them in the bag.

"You can close the safe," I said. She turned, her face to the floor, probably too scared to look me in the eye. I motioned toward the desk chair with my gun. "Have a seat. Now, from when I leave, I want you sit here for two minutes, OK?"

"OK."

"I've got someone watching you, so don't get up, don't use your phone, don't do anything until two minutes have passed. Do you understand?"

Yes."

"Good. After that, you can call anyone you want. Also, call your insurance company. You can get the money back, all right?" She nodded her head.

I put my gun away and exited the store, hoping she wouldn't take a chance and emerge from the chair before the two minutes expired. Walking briskly toward the car, I tucked the bag of money underneath an arm and removed the mask. I ran my gloved hand over my face, satisfying the itch the mask caused. Entering my car, I looked around to see if anyone might be watching. Seeing no one, I drove out of the lot.

Liv and Darin were expecting me, but I had no intention of returning to Liv's apartment. I needed to ditch anything that could tie me to the crime, so I ventured into the east side of Farrington, an industrial mix of new factories and long-abandoned ones. Finding an isolated street, I tossed the bag and ski mask into a gutter. I held onto the gun, however. It was registered to me, and if it ever went missing, questions would surely follow, such as when I noticed it was gone and why I hadn't reported it stolen. I put the money in the glove box underneath the owner's manual for the car which, for some reason, I still had.

I drove home after that, careful not to rouse any suspicion. I was calmer than I expected to be until I saw him in my rearview mirror, a mere minutes from home. A police car. Following me slowly on the main road before I entered my neighborhood, we came to a red light. I learned many years ago cops routinely run license plates through their system when they're stopped at a light. The chances were this officer was doing exactly that. If anyone saw my car at the jewelry store or worse, got my license plate, this was all over. The light stayed red for an interminably long time. I stared straight ahead, the cross traffic passing before my eyes, the vehicles nothing more than a blur in my tunnel vision.

Finally, the light turned green. I started slowly, aware I didn't know the speed limit on the road. *What was it? I had driven here thousands of times. Why couldn't I remember it?* A light beamed from behind me, illuminated in my rearview mirror. For a split second, sheer panic ran through my body—a lump in my throat followed by weakness and tingling in my hands. I felt relief—or something close to it—when I realized it was the car's turn signal. The cop changed lanes and passed me. I closed my eyes for a moment and said a "thank you"—to who or what I have no idea.

I parked in my driveway and gathered the money, stuffing what I could in the pockets of my coat and the rest in the back pocket of my jeans. Ms. Sorkelson, representative of old people everywhere who seem to live for early Saturday mornings, rambled toward my car. "I can't believe it," she blurted. I just can't believe it."

"What's   that?"

"You just missed Emily."

"What?"

"Yeah, she was here. She put something in your mailbox. I don't know what it is. Oh, I miss her. We talked for a few minutes. She seems happy. Anyway, I don't see you out and about much on a Saturday morning."

"Just running a few errands."

"How are things with your niece?" she cackled. I managed a smile, despite my stress level being through the roof.

"Not so great. I think we're finished."

"That's a shame. Well, more than one fish in the sea."

"I suppose so."

She walked away and I opened the mailbox to find an envelope with nothing on it except the phrase "OPEN IMMIDIATELY."

Chapter 20

LIV

Concocting my plan hadn't been difficult. The night after Darin was mugged, as I watched over him, tending to his battered and bloody face, I read a news story about a professor at a college in New York who had hooked up with a student. Deemed an "inappropriate relationship" in the statement from the school, sources said they had sex in his office and carried on a relationship for several months before she outed him. A woman scorned, perhaps because of his wandering eyes—he was also in a relationship with a coworker.

The college fired him and I guess the student went about her business as usual. While inappropriate for sure, it seemed harsh to fire him. They were consenting adults. But I didn't make the rules. And I didn't dwell on that story. I had my own to write.

It's amazing what you can find on the Internet, and more amazing is that you can get additional information for a little money. As I perused my class schedule for the upcoming semester, I noticed two of my professors were men. I would have Dr. Phillip Corter for accounting. His Facebook profile revealed a large, old man with silver hair, a wife of 35 years, and four kids. He seemed happy, but don't all people on social media? But his posts were filled with all sorts of messages about his enduring love for his wife. He was out.

I then turned to my Race and Politics course, taught by Dr. Matt Richardson. Handsome, for an older guy. Probably in his mid-forties. From the pictures, he seemed tall, with salt and pepper hair and a lean figure. A runner. Scrolling through his profile revealed a wife, or possibly ex-wife. There were many pictures of the two of them together until recently, and some messages on his page of statements such as "hang in there" and "let me know if you need anything." This could have been a death in the family or a divorce. I also saw no pictures of children or any references to any, which was good. Kids would only complicate things.

I paid to run a background search on him. He was squeaky clean except for some traffic tickets. He obtained a permit to carry a gun shortly after moving to Massachusetts. He was from Texas, after all. And, sure enough, a docket from a Probate and Family Court confirmed his wife filed for divorce the previous year. It seemed Dr. Matt Richardson was the perfect target. Men will do almost anything for pussy, and he was no different.

Saturday, February 18, 2017

"Something's wrong. He should have been here by now." I chewed my fingernails, a habit long ago broken because my mom excoriated me for it.

"Give him a few more minutes," Darin replied as he paced the floor of my apartment. We'd both been staring at the clock on the wall. It was almost ten o'clock. I couldn't see the front of the house from my apartment, so I kept opening the door hoping to see Matt coming down the hall, bag in hand. But each time, I was met with only the empty space of the hallway. And each time I didn't see him, my anxiety grew.

"Fuck this," I said, slamming the door. "I'm texting him."

"No. No texts."

"OK, then I'll call."

"No, don't do that either. Let's drive to his house."

We took my car and I felt it hard to control my speed. I was frantic that Matt hadn't come back and that he had either abandoned the plan or worse, had been caught. We entered his neighborhood and I slowed the car to a snail's pace. Driving by his house revealed no car in the driveway and the lights in the house appeared to be off. *Fuck*.

Darin convinced me to drive by the jewelry store. A stupid move, but I did it anyway, desperate to find out what happened. Maybe Matt would be there and we would at least have an explanation for his absence. Everything in the parking lot was normal except for a few police cars in front of the store. I couldn't be sure, but I thought I saw my grandmother out front talking to an officer.

"Oh my God, Darin." Tears found my eyes and a chill ran down my spine. "What the hell do we do?"

"Nothing for now. There's nothing we can do. We just lay low for a bit. You want to go to my house?"

"I think I'll go home."

"OK. I'll stay the night with you."

"No, I mean to my parents' house."

"What? Why?"

"I'm scared. I want to get out of here. This isn't right. He should have been back and he's not at his house. I bet you he went to the cops. That fucker."

"He wouldn't go to the cops."

"How do you know?"

"Because I know. He'd be stupid to do that, and he's not stupid."

"I don't care. I'm going to my parents' house."

"Whatever." That sounded ambivalent, and it hurt, but I didn't have the emotional capacity at the moment to put forth any objections. Worry eclipsed every feeling I had, and I couldn't get out of town fast enough.

I drove to my apartment and, after giving me a cursory hug, Darin sped off in his car. I threw some clothes and toiletries in a bag and started the two-hour trek to Weston. Texting my parents to let them know of my arrival, I soon received a call I knew was coming. My dad's face appeared on the screen, a goofy photo I took a few years prior that now served as his Facebook profile picture. I took a deep breath and told myself to act surprised.

"Hi, Dad."

"Hey, sweetheart. Are you on the road?"

"Yeah. Just left."

"I guess you haven't heard. Your grandpa called. The store was robbed this morning."

"What?"

"Yeah."

"Is he OK?"

"He wasn't there. It was only your grandma. She's fine. Obviously shaken, but she's all right."

"What did they take?"

"Money from the safe."

"The safe?"

"Yeah. They didn't take any jewelry, just money." My mouth fell open. My dad's words hung in the air and I didn't respond right away. "Liv? You there?"

"Yeah, sorry. Do they know who did it?"

"No. The police came and examined everything, but the guy was wearing gloves and a mask, so I'm not sure they'll find out."

"I didn't even know they had a safe."

"Yeah. That's where they kept a bunch of money. I told both of them they shouldn't keep so much cash there, but they obviously didn't listen.

"Well. I'm glad she's ok."

"Yeah, no kidding. I have to go, sweetie. We'll see you in a bit. Be careful."

"Will do."

I called Darin. My fingers couldn't scroll through my contact list quickly enough.

"Hey," he answered, the ambivalence still in his voice.

"You have to go find him now!"

"Who? Matt?"

"Yes."

"Why?"

"I talked to my dad. My grandparents have a safe at the store. I had no idea. Matt took the money and didn't take any jewelry. That's why he didn't come back. That piece of shit is stealing our money."

"I'm going over there now."

"Please be careful, baby. I don't think he would get violent, but you never know."

"He might not, but I will." Darin ended the call and I was torn on what to do. Because I already told my parents I'd be home, I decided to keep driving, the rest of my trip a self-induced hypnosis I couldn't recall later. On one hand, I was relieved Matt hadn't been caught. On the other, I worried for Darin. Money was ultimately the ticket to saving his life, and without the jewelry to pawn or the cash to pay Rex, Darin was as good as dead.

For lunch, my mom, uncharacteristically, planned a special meal when she knew I was coming—beef stroganoff with rice salad and steamed asparagus. It was my favorite dish when I was little, and the fact my mom still thought it was my favorite shows how disconnected our relationship was. It's like parents with grown kids who talk only occasionally. They have nothing to talk about, so they seize upon memories—how things were before the relationship deteriorated.

I didn't say anything, however. I played the good daughter and thanked her for making it. "This is nice, huh?" she remarked at the four of us sitting together for a meal since before anyone could remember. "It's so good to have everyone here."

"Why are you here anyway, Liv?" Sarah asked in her usual direct tone.

"I just couldn't stand being away from my baby sister any longer."

"Bullshit."

"Language," my father chimed.

"She's not such a baby anymore, you know?" my mom said. "Graduating in a few months and then off to college."

"Yeah, you know where you're going yet?" I asked.

"I've been accepted at Tufts and Northeastern. I just have to decide which one."

"No Harvard or MIT?"

"Please. But you couldn't get in there either. Changing the subject, how is Darin? The mysterious Darin." She widened her eyes upon uttering "mysterious" and strung Darin's name out.

"What's to tell?" *Other than Darin likely confronted my professor with whom we planned a robbery of Grandma and Grandpa's store.*

"I don't know. I'm just making conversation."

"He's great. He graduated last year from BC, still looking for something permanent in his field. Engineering."

"And he lives in Farrington?"

"Yeah, he moved there just for me," I said, batting my eyes.

"True love," Sarah replied, making a gagging motion with her finger.

I missed this banter. My mom and dad didn't say much, but the expressions on their faces showed they missed it, too. The carefreeness of the meal took away some of my worry. Maybe it was being away from Farrington or maybe being in our huge house made me feel insulated. Whatever it was, it was comfort. I couldn't help, however, checking my phone for any ding or buzz or ring I might have missed. I wanted to hear from Darin, but staring at my screen revealed only my wallpaper, a selfie taken a few weeks ago of Darin and I kissing during a snowfall, both of us smiling, his eyes cut toward the camera and mine closed.

"Liv, can you put your phone away?" my mom snapped. "At least while we eat?" I didn't respond, nor did I even acknowledge I heard her. It was exactly like her to ruin a good evening. I turned my phone face down and placed it next to my plate, staring at my half-eaten meal that now turned my stomach. I pushed my plate back and stood.

"Oh, don't do this," my mom complained.

"Do what?"

"Don't get all offended just because I told you to put your phone away."

"What makes you think I'm offended?"

"I know you, Liv."

"Yeah, well I know you too, Mom."

"What does that mean?"

"It means I know when you're trying to pick a fight. When you're trying to have everything your way. When you're still treating me like a kid."

"Well, you are still my kid, and this is our house. I think I have some say in how you act."

"All right. I'm going to my room and hey, look, I'm taking my phone." I waived it in the air. "You're free to do that too, Mom. Take your phone and go to your room. Or wait, maybe you already have a phone in there." I couldn't believe I said it the second the words left my lips. Her eyes narrowed and her mouth cinched. She didn't say anything. There was nothing to say, in fact. I turned to walk toward my room, and my dad ended the awkward silence with a plea for everyone to get along. I'm guessing my mom felt relief when he didn't address my phone comment.

I trounced to my room and shut the door like an angry teen. As I had done so many times in that room, I tried to block out the family squabbles by descending into my phone, jumping among the apps and hopping from one text to another. But it was too hard to concentrate. Darin hadn't contacted me and it had been almost five hours since I'd seen him.

I checked all his social media accounts. Nothing. I thought of calling Matt but wasn't ready to do that yet. He hated me and he had a right to, and I had no interest in facing that music. I would have been fine if I'd never spoken to him again. In fact, that was the plan. Get the jewelry from him, withdraw from his class, and he'd be out of my life.

I sat on my bed and let my mind drift. I stared at my closet door. It was inside that door that so many punishments had occurred, my mom banishing me for hours in the darkened space with no food or drink. It's one of my earliest memories—being locked in and crying, yelling, begging for someone to let me out. Early in my life, I had assumed my dad knew of her punishment tactics. After all, isn't that something that parents agree on—how to punish their children? As I aged, however, I suspected it was another secret of hers she kept from my dad. She never locked me in when my dad was home, so I doubt he ever knew. Reflecting on the cruelty and heartlessness of it, I resented my mom even more.

My mind continued to drift and I retreated under my covers. Sleep found me quickly, but it was restless and jarring, bringing an impending sense of doom I couldn't escape. I awoke and the room was dark and quiet, an eerie silence that heightened my worry. I checked my phone. Nothing.

Someone knocked on my door. "Liv?" my dad spoke from the hallway. "Can I come in?"

"Yeah."

"Hey," he smiled. "Can I have a seat?" He motioned toward my bed.

"Sure." He sat next to me, hunched over with his elbows on his knees. We hadn't spent a lot of time together lately, and I noticed his face had given way to age. A look of concern replaced the glee he exhibited at the dinner table. He seemed, for the first time I could remember, vulnerable.

"Liv, your mom is under a lot of stress. Please don't take that stuff personally."

"Dad, she treats me like a child."

"Well, to her you are a child. It'll always be that way. I know, you're grown and you have your freedom, but it's hard, especially with Sarah going off to school soon. I just think she's feeling lonely. And as a parent, I can tell you this: you'll never understand the love parents have for their children until you have a child of your own. She really misses you and she's concerned about what life will be like with both of you girls out of the house."

"Then why doesn't she show us that love? Why does she always seem distant? Why does she have to . . . be the way she is?"

"I don't have a good answer for you. And I know what you mean, and we've talked about it. We even went to therapy for a while."

"Did it do any good?"

"A little. Maybe. But we stopped going and things more or less returned to normal."

"Sorry, Dad."

"Thanks, sweetie." He kissed me on the forehead before exiting the room.

"Dad?" I was ready to reveal my mom's deep secret. He had a right to know. Her affair would explain so much of her behavior. It wasn't fair she kept him in the dark, especially after going to therapy and no doubt giving another reason for her distant behavior. I didn't doubt the deep love parents had for their kids, but that's something I never felt from my mom. And I didn't think she was sad about having both of her girls out of the house. She loved Andrew, and I had no idea whether she still loved my dad. But in the end, I couldn't do it. I couldn't break his heart. I couldn't stand to see the anguish on his face and to hear the confrontation that would inevitably follow.

"Yeah?" he answered, peeking his head around the door.

"What are you doing now?"

"The Bruins are on. The second period is about to start."

"Can I come watch with you?

"Do the Canadiens suck?"

"Yeah."

"There's your answer," he grinned, the light from the hall illuminating his face. He sauntered toward the living room with me in tow, my mom nowhere in sight. We dropped ourselves on the couch and placed our feet on the coffee table. I rested my head on his shoulder as our eyes fixed themselves on the screen, and that's exactly what I needed. In my own way, I had become detached, distant. Not in the same manner as my mom, but I was off in Farrington, living a double life, hooked up with my drug-dealing boyfriend, seducing a professor, and planning a robbery. I wanted to forget it all, to make it all go away. And in that moment, it did. I felt the love and protection only my dad could provide. I was home.

Chapter 21

MATT

Saturday, February 18, 2017

I took a chance the jewelry store would have a safe. I didn't know for sure, but it was a hunch—an educated guess that jewelry and money and a place for their safekeeping go hand in hand. I hid the money in the most cliché of all places—between my mattresses. It seemed obvious, but perhaps it was so obvious that someone, if they came searching, might not even think to look there. I was thinking of Darin, not the police. If the police came, they would find it and it would all be over anyway. The more likely scenario, at least at that point, was dealing with Darin. It was only a matter of time before he realized there was no jewelry and that I had taken money instead. I wanted to pay Rex off and deal with Darin later.

I sat at the kitchen table and opened the envelope, having no idea what to expect. *Why would*

Emily put something in my mailbox? Reaching in and grabbing the contents, I unfolded a piece of notebook paper, from which another piece of paper fell into my lap. I saw Emily's signature on it and, flipping it over, realized it was a check for fifty-thousand dollars. I stared at it in disbelief.

Spreading out the folds of the notebook paper, I began to read.

Matt,

I know you're probably surprised at this, but I was thinking about our conversation the other night and it seemed like you might be in some real danger. I honestly don't know if that's true. I don't trust you and you might be lying. If you are in danger, use this money to pay off whomever you owe money to. If you're lying, I can hope only that you feel guilty for taking it.

I asked my parents for the money. The good people they are, they didn't even ask me why I needed it. And they didn't ask me to pay it back, so you don't have to worry about that either. Growing up with privilege certainly has its perks. The check is made out to me, but I endorsed it.

I've decided to move back to Austin. The only reason we moved here was for your job and now that we're no longer together, there's no need for me to be here. I'll be moving back at the end of the school year and will find a teaching job back home.

Since I walked out of our house that day, we haven't really had any meaningful conversations. I'm not ready to start now and don't know if I ever will be, but this gives me a chance to say some things I've been feeling.

I don't know how you feel about what went wrong. I blame you for it all and I don't think you would deflect that blame. Don't get me wrong. I don't blame you for your addiction—your illness—I blame you for not trying to treat it. You chose it over me—it's that simple. Maybe you're happy, I don't know, but you hurt me. It's a hurt that will eventually go away (I think), but to think you chose gambling over me—after so many years together—is difficult to wrap my head around. I can't tell you how many nights I lay awake in bed asking myself why. I've stopped asking that question now. Which is a good sign, I guess. At least I'm moving in the right direction.

The way things deteriorated, I never took time to stop and ask myself hard questions, though, such as whether I still love you. Now that several months have passed (and many therapy sessions), I can confidently say now I don't. I stopped loving you at some point. I don't know when, though. Which is odd, right? I think it's easy to recall when you first realize you love someone, but falling out of love seems quite different in many respects. The feelings I had for you just slowly melted away like an ice cube evaporating in the heat of the sun. I do, however, care for you, and I don't want to see you harmed. I'm not sure how you feel, and it really doesn't matter, but I thought it was fair to tell you that.

Please don't contact me. Just accept this gift and please, for your sake (not mine), fix your life. Your addiction has held you in its grips for too long.

Take care,

Emily

After reading it twice, I stared into my living room, the setting of some brief but happy moments with Emily, and felt an odd mix of sensations— relief, regret, frustration, and guilt. It was a strange mélange of emotions simmering within. I wanted to talk to Emily, but I would honor her wish. Sitting at that table, however, and even though it had been months since our divorce, I missed her more than I ever had and perhaps more than I ever realized.

A knock at the door startled me. It was loud. Five quick raps followed by a ring of the doorbell, its sound lingering in my ears. Ann and Nancy had been asleep and began barking before they were fully awake. I climbed the stairs and peeked out my bedroom window. I saw a car I didn't recognize and the overhang obscured my view of the front porch, but I didn't need to see the person to know who it was.

Deciding to take the problem head on instead of avoiding it, I descended the stairs and silenced the dogs. Darin again rang the doorbell and was knocking on the door when I opened it. He said nothing but entered the house as if he owned it. I shut the door and he was already into his spiel. "Give me the money. I know you took money, so don't even try to bullshit me. My life depends on that money, and I'll kill you for it."

"Darin, slow down. Let's talk."

"Talk about what? There's nothing to talk about."

"You want a drink? Let me get you a drink." I was stalling, and I think he knew it. Noticing the check and Emily's letter on the table, I swiped them and placed them in a kitchen drawer. "I'm out of alcohol. How about some water?"

"Whatever." Surprisingly, he acquiesced and sat on the couch, his face rigid. His breathing seemed strained and I wondered if his injuries were to blame. Scabs covered the right side of his swollen face, and I could only imagine what his other wounds were. Handing him the water, I sat opposite him in the recliner. He gulped his drink, set the glass on the end table and stared at me, his steel, blue eyes doing their best to intimidate. "Well?"

"Well what?" I responded.

"You said you wanted to talk. So talk."

"Right. I'm just wondering who you owe money to."

"What's the difference?"

"Well, you roped me into this thing, so I think it's only fair that I know who's got you on the hook."

"Just a guy in Boston."

"Drugs?"

"Yeah."

"Don't get me wrong, and I don't want to assume, but I see your nice car out there, you seem to dress nicely. You don't seem like someone who needs money."

"So?"

"So why do it? Why get wrapped up in that?"

"Haven't you ever done something just because you wanted to? Something you didn't need a reason for?"

"I suppose. It just seems like a risky thing to get involved in, that's all." I realized my hypocrisy as the words left my lips. I had gambled and didn't need the money, and I owed a lot of money to someone who could do me great harm. But I wouldn't let Darin know we had so much in common. I couldn't show any weakness, and revealing my huge debt was the perfect way to do that.

"There's not much to say, man. I guess I like the thrill."

"So why not rob the jewelry store yourself?"

"Seriously? Aren't you a professor?"

"Of political science. Not of . . . whatever this is."

"The person who actually does the act takes all the risk. I like a thrill, but I'm not stupid. You apparently got away fine, but a lot could have gone wrong."

"And what about Liv?"

"What about her?"

"How much of this was her idea?"

He flashed a faint smile. "Try all of it."

"The whole thing?"

"Liv is not as innocent as you might have thought."

"No shit. Thanks for the overstatement of the year."

"I mean before all this. She's got some stuff in her past no one knows, except me."

"Like what?"

"Nope. I'm sworn to secrecy and anyway, you're probably the last person I'd tell."

"Fair enough."

"All right, man. Enough is enough. Give me the money."

"I don't have it."

"What the fuck do you mean you don't have it?"

"I gave it away. It turns out you aren't the only one who owes people money. I know you have the video and you can report me to the school, but I'm willing to deal with it."

"You remember what I said when I came in here? I said I'd kill you if I didn't get the money. Showing that video to someone is the least of your problems. So, either I get the money or you die." Reaching into his inside coat pocket, he pulled out a gun and stood. He walked over to me, the gun barrel looming larger as he approached. It resembled my gun—a small revolver but one I knew could kill me in an instant.

"Please!" I pleaded. "OK, I'll get you the money."

"That's a good answer. Now get up. Slowly." He kept the gun trained on me as I rose from the chair. My heart raced and I forced myself not to look at the gun. "Where is it?"

"It's in the kitchen."

"Go," he commanded, waiving his gun to my left. I walked, fearful with every step I would hear the blast of the gun—an accidental discharge or a trigger pulled with jilted rage. With purpose, I walked to the kitchen and opened the drawer containing the check. Upon seeing it, I knew I had to explain myself.

"OK, listen. This is a check for fifty-thousand dollars. All I have to do is endorse it and it's yours."

He crinkled his nose and furrowed his brow. "Why do you have a check? I want cash!"

"It's a long story, Darin. The point is, you get your money, and that's it."

"Liv said you took cash. Where the fuck is it?" He again pointed the gun directly at my face. I looked away.

"Listen to me! If you kill me, I can't sign that check and you won't get any money at all. And the way you and Liv were talking, I'm assuming you'll be dead in a few days if you don't produce the money, right?"

"Right," he responded, resigned to my reasoning.

"Then let me endorse this check. You can walk out of here, deposit this in a bank, and you can withdraw the money." He pursed his lips and I could hear the breathing through his nose. He swallowed hard and I knew I convinced him.

"Fine. Sign it. Hurry up."

I retrieved a pen nearby. Darin held the gun at my face as I put the pen to the paper. As I did so, I heard the click of him pulling back on the hammer. My throat closed and I tried in vain to swallow. I couldn't know for sure, but there was a good chance he'd kill me as soon as I signed the check.

A rush of adrenaline coursed through my veins. Fear took over. I swung my right arm around and, gripping the pen with all the force I could manage, I drove it into his neck and tackled him to the floor. He was silent, eyes wide with shock, and the loud bang of the gun echoed through the house. My ears rang as I tried to wrest it away from him, but he fought back, the pen still protruding from his neck, a grotesque sight made worse by the blood that poured from the wound. We rolled around on the floor, my mind preoccupied with getting the gun. The dogs began to bark, loud shrills of terror signifying something was terribly wrong. I held Darin down as best I could, but his body shook violently, convulsing this way and that. He managed to get on top of me as our hands tangled around the gun. In an instant, void of premonition or planning, the gun fired. The noise startled us—Darin's eyes exhibiting a mix of shock and terror.

I pushed him off me and he lay on his back, a deep hole now occupying his stomach. He screamed—a horrible shriek that seemed to last for several seconds. The metallic smell of the blood penetrated my nose and at once made me queasy. His hands found his wound and he managed to say nothing more than "Oh," no doubt surprised at the severity. A string of moans and groans followed another terrible scream.

I stared in shock at the gun in my hand and as Darin continued to yell, I slid it across the floor, out of reach. "Please," he begged. "Please. I don't want to die." He began to cry. Tears poured down the side of face, the final touch to the pitiful spectacle that was Darin Duclair—a massive gunshot wound to his abdomen and a pen extending from his neck.

"I'm sorry. I'm sorry." That was all I could muster. He continued to cry but the noise receded. His breathing became weaker and the deep blue eyes that were filled with rage only moments before, the same eyes that Liv fell in love with, were now empty, revealing nothing more than an unfocused, far-off gaze—the blank stare of death.

It's startling how quickly silence can come. Regardless of the cacophonous racket of one moment, the next can bring an overbearing quiet that, with its own power, pushes away the noise like the ebb of a tide. So it was in that moment. After Darin breathed his last, the only sound in the room was my breathing, rapid movements of my lungs gasping for air. I looked at him and smelled the blood. In a matter of seconds, I felt my stomach turn and my jaws tightened. I turned away from the corpse beside me and vomited, a sickening reminder of the breakfast I scarfed down that morning.

My decision to rob the jewelry store now had more serious ramifications than I could have imagined. A dead man lay on my living room floor, and turning myself in was not an option.

Chapter 22

LIV

Saturday, February 18, 1017

My dad and I both fell asleep watching the hockey game. I woke to the sounds of sports highlights and checked my phone. Only a couple of texts from friends. Nothing from Darin.

I imagined the worst. Rex had given him more time. Was it possible Rex had run out of patience? Did Matt have something to do with it? I stumbled to my room, bleary eyed and exhausted. I didn't want to call Matt. I was afraid to. What if he *was* the reason Darin wasn't responding? What might he do to me? What if Matt had set us up? What if he went to the police? Maybe Darin was in jail.

My heart ached. He wasn't with me and wasn't responding to me. I missed his voice and his silly texts filled with nonsensical emojis. I couldn't bear it anymore. I couldn't continue to be in the dark. I texted Matt and then called—a pattern I repeated all night and through the morning hours until I saw the sun began to lighten the sky. And each time, I received no response. I couldn't blame him after what I had done, but I wanted answers I wasn't getting. I lay back on the bed, trying to hold back tears, but it was pointless. I cried into my pillow like a scorned teenaged lover. Darin was my world. Without him, I had nothing.

I allowed my mind to drift to the night when I first met him, three years prior, trying desperately to cling to happy memories of the two of us together.

I had been to parties before, but I had never given a boy my number until I saw the handsome one across the room. He was unassuming, standing by himself, fiddling with his phone. He flashed a casual smile when he saw me, and went right back to his phone. I figured he was shy, so I approached him. Darin Duclair—it was such a cool name. Mine is boring. And he lived in the city. Sure, I lived right outside Boston, but he was from Beacon Hill—the heart of the city. He was sophisticated—a sophomore in college—and he talked about books and plays and music I only pretended to know about. I'm sure he saw right through my ignorance, but he was polite.

We ditched the party and drove around in his new Mercedes. His blue eyes captivated me and I was smitten. On our first date, a week later, he brought me flowers. That was a first for me. It was such a grown-up thing to do, nothing that would have even crossed the minds of any of the high school boys I knew. My dad invited him in before he took me out, and Darin made such a good impression even my mom remarked she was happy for me and wished me "good luck" out of earshot of Darin. We went to a fancy restaurant that served French food and he ordered for me, a relief because I couldn't pronounce anything on the menu. Afterward, we ate ice cream and strolled around Boston Common, ending the night by sitting on a bench and kissing. It was the perfect first date, and Darin was the perfect gentleman.

Chapter 23

MATT

Saturday, February 18, 2017

After adding my vomit to the floor that was now pooled with blood, I had only one thought: *I have to make Darin's body disappear.* I never considered going to the police. Robbing a jewelry store was bad enough, and making anyone believe I killed in self-defense was remote. I had the money to pay off Rex. I could dispose of Darin's body and leave the insanity of this past week behind. I wasn't proud of what I had done, but I wasn't willing to take the fall for it.

A thousand thoughts spun through my head. I had seen enough movies and read enough books to know it was usually the careless disposing of bodies that did killers in. In an effort to bury what they had done—literally—they got careless because they traded detail for speed.

I retrieved an old painting tarp, latex gloves, a shovel, and duct tape from the garage. The mirror hanging in the hallway adjacent to the kitchen revealed what a mess I was. Hair disheveled, shirt ripped, and three scratches ran the length of my neck on the left side. Blood stained my shirt and blood spatter dotted my face. My back and shoulder hurt. Our tussle lasted only seconds, but I felt as if I'd been in a car wreck.

I soaked a fingernail brush in soap and water and cleaned under Darin's fingernails. I then took his glass of water and washed it. After retrieving his keys, wallet, and phone from his pants, I removed his clothing. His phone kept lighting with texts and calls from Liv. Taking his thumb, I unlocked the phone and found the video of Liv and me in her apartment. I deleted it from his phone and from the cloud, erasing any hard evidence of my illicit relationship. Upon lifting him, I noticed he had an exit wound in his back, which meant I had to find two bullets, the first one that fired when I tackled him to the floor and the second one, which killed him. I spread the tarp across the floor and wrapped his body in it, securing it with duct tape.

I washed my face, the blood gelling with the water to creating a nauseating pink and sliding into the drain. I had to wait until the sun set to make my next move. The last thing I needed was someone to see me, even worse for Ms. Sorkelson to come for a chat. I buried my face in my hands as I sat on the edge of the bathtub, trying to come to grips with what I had done and what I was about to do. For all the lines one never envisions crossing, this had to be at the top of the list—taking another's life—the most forbidden of all sins. It went against every moral fiber I had yet here I was, in the process of hiding my evil deed.

I don't know how long I sat there, but the sun had set. My head and body ached and in some weird way, I welcomed the pain as a price for what I had done. I left my phone on the table and, walking through the kitchen, opened the back door and scanned my surroundings, ensuring there were no nosy neighbors clamoring about. With the sky dark, I walked around to the front and backed Darin's car up to the back of the house, hoping only that no one saw me driving the unfamiliar car.

I slid his body into the trunk along with the shovel, reentered his car, and exited my driveway. If a police officer happened to stop me, there was no rational explanation for me driving this vehicle. With that in mind, I drove the way of a boy scout—stopping completely at stop signs, signaling at every turn, and driving under the speed limit. Upon turning corners, the corpse shifted in the trunk with a thud, and the fear inside me grew.

When I set out on the road, I didn't know where I was going. I knew only that I needed to bury the body and to do it as fast as possible. As I tried to calm myself on what could've been the last drive of my life, I remembered reading about the mob, the aficionados of body disposal, and a common tactic was to bury a body in an already-occupied grave. That way, in case the police used cadaver dogs to search for the missing person, any alert that a dog gave to the police in and around a cemetery would be written off. I didn't know if any of that was true, but all I had was hope, which I hadn't had much of lately.

New Life Cemetery is a dark, ominous place even in the daylight. Giant oak trees cover its long, winding paths, surrounding headstones that go back to the eighteenth century. A remote area of the cemetery is a recent addition and a necessary one at that. Farrington is not a big city, but space was filling and land was at a premium, so the owners bought several more acres away from the main part, and it was here I brought Darin to his final resting place.

I parked his car behind a tree and walked around a few minutes until I felt soft dirt beneath my shoes. A new grave. I didn't bring a flashlight to avoid suspicion so I couldn't make out the name on the temporary marker. It was here I began to dig. Furiously. Mad with a purpose, knowing at any point, someone could stumble upon me in a situation, again, that offered no rational explanation. The cold wind whistled through the trees and betrayed my senses. Several times, I thought I heard cars or voices.

It felt like hours before I reached the casket at the bottom. Exhausted, I rolled Darin's body out of the trunk and dropped him in the grave. His body crashed into the casket, the walls of dirt muffling the thud.

As quickly as I had started, I began filling in the hole, cold dirt piling slowly on top of the corpse. Once satisfied the grave appeared as it should, I placed the marker on it and started Darin's car, driving toward the cemetery's exit. The two-lane road on which it was located was deserted, and I drove onto it with some sense of relief.

The police would find Darin's car. That much was sure, but I exerted some control over when they would find it. So, I went to the mall parking lot. The Farrington Mall is a relic from a bygone era and customers have dwindled through the years, but it still operated as a viable shopping option or a place for kids to hang out. It was well after midnight so the mall was closed, but I parked the car in an area I knew would be covered with hundreds of vehicles in a few hours.

Exiting the vehicle, I walked away from it as inconspicuously as I could. Darin's wallet, keys, and phone were in my pocket, a situation that made it even more imperative I get home as fast as possible without raising suspicion. It was a little over three miles home, so I had no time to rest. I started along the sidewalk, trying my best to duck the wind and stay warm.

I ventured past gas stations and fast-food joints, all closed for the night. A homeless person lay under thick blankets beneath a tree, a bottle of liquor within arm's reach. The streets were mostly free of vehicles, but I heard one approaching behind me. I kept walking, head up and staring straight ahead. *A cop. Shit.* He stopped along the curb, a sign for me to stop walking. He lowered the passenger-side window and spoke.

"Hey, how you doing?"

"Hey. I'm good."

"It's a bit cold to be walking, isn't it?"

"I kind of like the chill. Helps me to think."

He exited the car, walked around it, and stepped onto the sidewalk. I was frozen with fear and hoping my face didn't show it. "You have an ID on you?"

"Yeah." *Fuck.* I had my wallet in one back pocket and Darin's in the other, but I couldn't remember which pocket mine was in. If I pulled

Darin's out, this whole thing was over. *Which was it?* I typically carried my wallet in my left-back pocket but perhaps in my haste, I switched it. The cop eyed me, waiting for me to produce my ID, shining his flashlight on me. I reached back to my left, playing the odds, and produced a wallet. It felt familiar. Relief. I pulled my driver's license from it and handed it to the officer.

"So what are you doing out here? You're a few miles from home," he said as he studied my ID and handed it back to me.

"It's something I've been doing lately. Walking at night in the cold helps to clear my mind."

"Well, to each his own, but I don't like freezing my ass off."

"I find it invigorating."

He laughed and walked toward his car. "Be careful."

"Thanks." I resumed my walk. My hands tingled and my throat was dry. I tried in vain to get a deep breath. I had come so close to being arrested, and I would have been had the officer been more thorough. He would have noticed the dirt and mud on my right sleeve and the tiny specks of blood on my shoes. If he had gotten close to me, he would have seen the marks from Darin's fingernails on my neck that now burned with my sweat. Instead, I got a reprieve.

I made my way home and, waiting for me in the middle of the living room, was my next task. Fetching several trash bags, I began the unenviable chore of erasing the killing scene. Dawning rubber cleaning gloves and an allergy mask, I went to work, scrubbing feverishly and applying all sorts of cleaners to the floor. I filled the bags with paper towels and washcloths. My living room went from reeking of blood and vomit to the smell of a cold, sterile hospital room. Last, I vacuumed the floor and the couch where Darin had sat. I had seen way too many documentaries where juries convicted people based on fibers from clothing. I couldn't be too careful. After tossing my clothes and Darin's clothes into a trash bag, I searched for the two bullets. The first bullet lodged itself into a bookshelf across the room. I figured I could remove it with tweezers, but that would have to wait. The other bullet—the one that killed Darin--had nicked the ceiling and fallen under the couch. I grabbed it, tossed it in the bag, and took a shower, too tired to even think.

I stood still and let the warm water soothe my aching body. It flowed down my chest and back and I breathed repeated sighs, exhalations mixed with relief and worry. Repeatedly, I used the soap and shampoo to try to wash away the remnants of what I had done—to rid my body and soul of the stain that now occupied them. But that stain would be there forever. There was nothing I could do to erase it or escape the paralyzing thought that at some point in the future, a knock at the door could end my life as I knew it.

Liv kept reaching out, texting and calling both me and Darin, an incessant annoyance that led me to silence both phones. I removed the contents of Darin's wallet, burned them, and discarded the remains in one of the many trash bags I had piled next to the door. One by one, I hauled them out to the trunk of my car, again hoping I was free from the stares of any neighbors. Leaving once again, I dumped the bags in dumpsters around town, never putting two or more sacks into one receptacle. Next, I drove to the Chicopee Bridge that spans the Connecticut River and, satisfied no one was watching, threw Darin's phone and keys overboard, both making a faint splash before descending to the bottom.

As I drove home, drained, my hands shaking from terror, I couldn't shake the feeling I had forgotten something, that I hadn't completely covered my tracks. An unseen force, it nagged me and wouldn't relent. I entered the stillness of the house, only the clink of Ann and Nancy's claws on the floor and the jingle of their collars disturbing the calm after the storm. I lay on the bed and unlocked my phone to find fifty-two missed calls from Liv and twenty-seven texts. Like clockwork, the phone rang again. Liv. That would have to wait. For now, I needed sleep that wouldn't come. Instead, I lay in the darkness and tried to ease my troubled mind.

Chapter 24

LIV

Sunday, February 19, 2017

I couldn't go back to Farrington. I had no idea what awaited me there and the unknown was reason enough to stay at my parents' house. Rex was sure to track Darin down soon, so the farther I stayed away, the better. I slept for much of the day, worn out from the previous one. In needing an excuse not to attend my second week of classes, I faked an illness, vague complaints of a headache and stomach pain that, when I was young, would've elicited sympathy and round-the-clock pampering from my parents. Now, they met it mostly with indifference, the extent of my care being my dad offering to make chicken noodle soup and my mom bringing me an electric blanket. Only Sarah continued to check on me, an odd role for her and one I had never seen her play.

"You look like you've been crying," she said, delivering me a bowl of oatmeal. "Are you OK?"

"Yeah, I'm fine. I don't feel very good, but I'll make it."

"You think it's the flu?"

"Maybe. I don't think I have fever though."

"I'm not getting any closer to you, just in case." She made a cross with her forefingers, as if I were possessed with an evil spirit.

"Just the way I like it," I said, managing a soft smile. "So, we didn't really get a chance to talk last night because everything blew up. How are things around here?"

"Ugh. You know Mom. And Dad's always working."

"She's driving you crazy?"

"Definitely. I can't wait to get out of here."

"You only have a few more months."

"And it can't come soon enough."

"If I were you, Sarah, I'd move out of the city."

"Why?"

"If you don't, you'll find it way too easy to come back here and you won't exactly feel free, or at least not like you're expecting to. I'm two hours away. It's not far, but it's not like I can come home on some random weeknight. If you go to school in the city, you'll be too close."

"Yeah, true. I haven't thought about it like that. So, tell me," she said, her eyes lighting up. "What's it like?"

"What's what like?"

"Being independent. Free. Away from Mom and Dad."

"It's great. I can do what I want, see who I want, stay out as late as I want. I'm usually with Darin though." Saying his name caused a lump in my throat and a feeling that told me I needed to hide my expression. So I stared at my blanket, a holdover from decades ago that my parents got for their wedding, its silk edges fraying among the faded blue of the cotton.

"You're so lucky, Liv."

"Why do you say that?"

"You've got someone. I have no one."

"Stop. You'll find someone in college in a heartbeat. Guaranteed. College is crawling with men."

"Yeah, crawling is the right word. Horny snakes."

I chuckled. It felt good to laugh and for a second, I let my guard down. "They're not all like that. You just have to be careful. Choose wisely."

"Like you did."

I gave her a smile. She squinted at the invasion of the late sunlight that squeezed through the blinds, leaning down to hug me and turning her face away to ensure she didn't catch my nonexistent illness.

"I'll be in the living room," she said. "Text me if you need me."

"Will do. Thank you."

"I love you, Sis," she said, bounding off the bed and not looking back.

"I love you too." By the time I finished the sentence, my bedroom door was closed, and I was alone again. I fell asleep a short time later, but the sound of my dad's footsteps on the hardwood floor startled me awake.

"Sorry. I didn't know you were asleep," he whispered.

"It's OK."

"I'm turning in early. I have a long day tomorrow. Can I get you anything?"

"I'm good. Thanks, Dad." He smiled, turning the doorknob and closing the door without a sound, as if I were still asleep. The house was peaceful and quiet, only the heat kicking on occasionally and interrupting the tranquility. My brain was tired and I was exhausted emotionally, unable to devote any more mental energy to wondering about Darin or Matt or the police. I wanted to lie there, undisturbed, to put my cares in the back of my mind and just be. And for a while, I did. But the moment didn't last long.

Chapter 25

REX AND MIKE

Sunday, February 19, 2017

"You know where you're going?" Mike asked, the seat belt stretched across his flab.

"Yeah. Got it pulled up on my phone," Rex replied, checking the map. Estimated travel time: one hour, fifty-six minutes.

"I really don't want to be doing this," Mike replied, exasperated.

"Yeah, well, that makes two of us. But why? What else do you have going on?"

"Nothing, really. It's just that it's a fucking four-hour round trip packed into your little car."

"Stop complaining. You're getting paid. You want some food from the gas station? Will that help you out, little boy? Or should I say big boy?" Mike hated when Rex did that. He often made fun of his weight, jokes better fit for an adolescent male than a thirty-something. Yeah, he knew he was obese, and he had come to terms with it long ago, but the jabs still stung. He was too afraid to say anything, though. Rex intimidated him. He yelled when he didn't get his way and he once left him stranded on the side of the road when Mike angered him. Rex once left him in tears when he pointed his gun at him. But this was his life, and he was making more money being Rex's sidekick than he could ever make with nothing more than a high school diploma.

"Yeah, I want some food."

"Of course you do." Rex made an abrupt turn into a convenience store parking lot, his front bumper scraping the concrete. "My treat. What do you want?"

"Beef jerky. None of that spicy shit, though. And a Pepsi."

Rex slammed the door and walked inside. Mike waited, passing the time on his phone. A car pulled beside him, four giggling girls emerging. They were young, no more than twenty, all clad in tight jeans and sweaters. He stirred, longing for what he would never have. It had been so long since he'd been with one, and he was not boyfriend material. He didn't know how talk to them, much less make himself desirable. He justified his situation by telling himself he was content with the way things were. He was fine ogling from a distance, letting his imagination run wild.

"Here you go, numb nuts," Rex said, tossing the beef jerky onto Mike's lap. And diet was all they had." He placed the cold bottle in the cup holder next to his can of Mountain Dew. Mike hated diet drinks and worse than that, this one was generic, a store-brand guaranteed not to appease his taste buds. He observed the bag of beef jerky, "FLAMING HOT" written on the front. He had specifically said he didn't want anything spicy, but Rex didn't care or didn't listen, and nothing would change. Mike would remain silent and eat and drink what he didn't want.

"Before I forget," Rex said, pulling out onto the road, "you've got your gun, right?"

"Yeah."

"Just checking. This shouldn't be too hard of a job. That Darin is a pussy. A real pretty boy."

"You said he got mugged?"

"That's what he said, but that fucker's had enough time to get me the coke and he won't answer his phone."

"You think he ran off with it?"

"To do what? Sell it on his own?"

"Yeah."

"It's possible, but I doubt it. If he did, he's an idiot. I know where he lives. He'd be crazy to just ignore me and sell all that."

The rest of the trip was mostly devoid of conversation. Music that Rex liked and Mike hated filled the car. The GPS guided them off the freeway and into Farrington, past the college and the bars and restaurants that surrounded it.

"You ever been here?" Mike asked, ripping a piece of jerky with his teeth like a hyena picking at a corpse.

"Nope."

"It seems nice." Rex didn't respond. He agreed it was nice, but he disdained those who came from privilege. He grew up poor and tough on the streets of Boston, and Farrington had a reputation he loathed—rich, white kids who had everything given to them. They didn't know what it was like to have to work for their money. They were soft.

The two men meandered through residential streets, the occasional streetlight illuminating the otherwise-dark roads. The GPS alerted them of their arrival. Mike's head and face were sweaty from the beef jerky and snot ran from his nose. He wiped it on his sleeve as he exited the car. They both carried their guns on the inside pockets of their coats, each checking to make sure it was there before they got to the house. Making their way up the front walk, Rex studied his surroundings to ensure there were no prying eyes. He then knocked on the door, a loud disturbance in what seemed a quiet neighborhood.

"Darin!" Rex shouted, another knock met only with silence. "Fuck. Let's go to the back." The house was dark and there was no car out front. A neighbor dog barked from behind a wooden fence as both men entered the gate of the chain-link fence that surrounded Darin's house. Gazing through, they saw only darkness. "Do it," Rex commanded. Mike knew what he meant, and in one motion, his gun broke the glass of the back door, allowing him to reach his meaty arm through and unlock it.

The door opened into the kitchen and the air smelled of stale food. Rex used the light on his phone to navigate the way, Mike beside him with his gun drawn. If there was anyone here, they were deathly quiet. After searching behind every door and under the one bed that occupied the house, they knew they were alone.

"God damn it!" Rex took an empty beer bottle from the kitchen counter and slammed it on the tile.

"What do you want to do?" Mike asked.

"Search every drawer, look under the couch, in all the cabinets. If that coke is in here, we have to find it. After that, we trash this place."

They went about their business, pulling out drawers and spilling the contents on the floor. Darin's bedroom was soon a mess, underwear and tee shirts strewn about as if a tornado had come through. They emptied all the kitchen cabinets, silverware and glass and coffee mugs crashing to the floor. Rex, feeling all the rage and fear that came along with this dirty business, put his fist into the TV screen before knocking it to the floor. If he found Darin, he'd torture him until he confessed the whereabouts of the cocaine, and then he'd kill him, a bullet right between the eyes. He'd done it before. A recent transplant from California had, for some reason, assumed he could take money owed to Rex and abscond with it. But Mike tracked him down and Rex, with a smile on his face, pulled the trigger, the man crying and pleading for his life. It's not what he wanted to do—killing and disposing of bodies was messy—but it was business. And the moment word gets out you're soft, that you allow people to take advantage of you with no consequences, you're finished. They'll walk all over you like a cheap rug.

"Let's go," Rex said, opening the back door and motioning Mike out of the house. The air was cold and both men lowered their heads as they strode toward the car. They entered it and Mike finished off his drink while Rex fiddled with his phone.

"Where now?" Mike inquired. "Back home?"

"Nope. I need answers."

"How are you going to find him? That guy split, I'm telling you."

"353 Greenbriar Lane, Weston, Massachusetts," Rex spoke into his phone. He pitched it down in the center console once he had the directions. "Darin's got himself a girlfriend, and we need to pay her a visit."

Chapter 26

MATT'S DREAM

I'm in a car in a parking lot in some unknown location. I see a church in the distance, dark clouds surrounding its white steeple. It appears I'm lying in the front seat, but I can still see out of the car. And this car—whose is it? It's old and big and worn on the inside, the fabric of the seats giving way to the foam underneath.

There are three figures in the distance talking to one another. Their clothes are flapping in the heavy wind and the audible gusts shake the car. I look around the rest of the parking lot and it's empty. Desolate. As if no one has tread on it in years. Grass grows through the cracks in the pavement and it's dry, parched for rain. I don't like this place. I want out, but I'm having difficulty moving. My body feels as if it's made of lead, impossible to move. Even though I know I'm stuck, I continue to struggle, but it's fruitless.

Another gust shakes the car. The three figures are huddled together and in unison, they turn toward me and began walking. They aren't fast, but their walk is deliberate. I struggle again, tiring my body as I do so. There's a strange smell now. Metallic. Nauseating. I close my eyes in the hope the three figures are my imagination. I count to five. I turn my head and open my eyes to the empty lot. Nothing but low-hanging clouds and emptiness. I turn back, hoping I've erased the figures from my consciousness, but they're still there, inching toward the car.

I can make out their faces now. They all look the same—chalk-white with large, red eyes. They seem normal except for their demonic faces. They're all looking at me now. I'm struggling, fighting the heaviness but it won't relent. I need to escape. I need to get out of the car. There's a voice behind me. A girl's voice. I turn. Liv is in the back seat, smiling. Wearing a skirt, she spreads her legs. But as she does so, the smile fades away and she looks puzzled, confused at what's transpiring. She won't take her eyes off me, and now the confused look has transformed into worry. She opens her mouth as if to scream, but she is silent. Her eyes well with tears. I need her to help me but she seems paralyzed with panic.

The figures are closer. They surround me. One is in front of the car and the other two on each side of it. They move closer and I let out a yell from deep within me, my voice loud and echoing throughout the car. But then a hand—cold and damp—covers my mouth. It silences me and I can't fight back. I've used all the energy I have and now—in my final act—I surrender. My body goes limp. The red eyes peer down at me, satisfied with their work. A thousand images from my life flash through my mind as I begin to cry.

Chapter 27

REX AND MIKE

Sunday, February 19, 2017

"Jesus. This family is loaded," Mike said as he stared in awe at the large houses.

"Everybody here is loaded. How the other half lives." Rex parked the car on the street, eyeing his surroundings. Streetlights brightened the area and cameras dotted the large median in the center, evidence the neighborhood had spared no expense in warding off those who didn't belong. He parked his car on the street in front of a small park and killed the engine. The house loomed in the distance, two floodlights shining from the shrubbery. Snowbanks on each side of the long walk led to the front porch.

"All right," Rex instructed, "this has to be"—a tap on his window interrupted him, followed by a blinding flash of light.

"Shit, you scared me, man," Rex said, restarting the car so he could lower his window.

"Sorry about that," the man replied. "I'm just trying to see what you guys are doing." He wore a blue coat with a patch on it bearing his name—Rick. He had gray hair and a mustache that needed trimming. He held his mag light parallel to his right ear, illuminating the inside of Rex's car.

"Nothing. Just going to see a friend."

"Who are you visiting?"

"What does it matter?"

"I'm security for this street. It's my job."

"Yeah, well, it seems a little nosy."

"Look, these people pay me to watch the street at night and I know everybody who belongs here. And no offense, but you don't look like the Weston type."

"Oh yeah? Well you don't either," Rex shot back.

Although true, Rick didn't find the comment amusing.

"Tell me something I don't know." Rex turned his stare to the road in front of him, tired of the intrusive light. "Can I see some ID?" Rick asked.

"Are you a cop?"

"No."

"Then I don't have to show you shit."

"Then I guess I'll have to get the police here and you can show it to them."

"You're going to call the cops for someone parked on a public street? You guys must not have much going on around here." Rick reached for his cell phone and pulled it out of his pants pocket. Rex could feel the weight of his gun inside his coat. He could pull it out before Rick got a chance to dial the number and hit Rick in the chest. It wouldn't kill him right away. No, he needed time to think about how asinine it was to ask for his ID. If Rick would have gone about his business and left him alone, he would've gone home later to his wife or girlfriend or whoever was waiting for him in his shitty apartment somewhere in Boston. Rex could envision the hole in Rick's chest, blood pouring from it as he gasped for air.

But he thought better of it. A gunshot in this neighborhood would attract unwanted attention and defeat the whole purpose for the visit to Liv's house. "Don't worry about it . . . *Ricky*. We're heading out." He sped off, squealing the tires on the pavement.

"Shit!"

"What now?" Mike asked. Rex ignored him, his narrow eyes focused ahead, trying to determine another way to get to the house. Mike knew not to ask again. He knew Rex heard him and chose not to answer. There were certain things he learned the hard way not to do, and asking Rex a question twice was one of them.

Rex circled the park and pulled onto a main road, mostly deserted at that late hour. He parked the car in front of a meter, half expecting another Rick to intrude on his personal space. But no one came.

"All right. Here's what we're doing. We have to go in the back. The house is right over there," he said, pointing in the general direction of the massive structure. "Keep your ski mask on. Don't take it off for anything. There are tons of cameras around here. And another thing. Take your gun, but don't use it unless you absolutely have to. We don't need a lot of noise."

"What if we have to, you know, get rid of somebody?"

"Then we'll mess with that when the time comes. All I want to do is find Darin."

They walked through the edge of the park. A swing blew in the wind. The slight squeak of the chains rubbing against the hooks accentuated the eerie setting. The woods behind the house were thick, populated by tall evergreens amidst the patches of snow on the ground. The air was crisp but both men were too nervous to be cold. They approached the wooden fence that surrounded the backyard. It was sprawling, eight feet high with rounded slats at the top. Rex pulled himself up, his shoes doing a small walk up the fence until he was able to hook his left leg over the top, which he used to propel himself into the yard. He fell with a thud and lay still, ensuring he didn't disturb anyone or anything. He was so intent on getting into the house he hadn't considered a dog might be waiting for him, but one never appeared.

He crept toward the patio, squatting as he approached a chair at a large picnic table. The chair was heavier than he expected, and it took him two tries to hurl it over the fence. Mike placed his large shoe on the seat of the chair, the fabric straining underneath. With a grunt, he pulled himself up as best he could, the top of the slats digging into the fat of his gut. He winced at the pain and slowly, after rocking back and forth a few times, spilled over the side, crashing to the ground. The impact knocked the wind out of him. Rex stared at him waiting for him to move. He did, eventually, gasping and moaning. He rose awkwardly, using the wet ground to propel himself upward.

"Fuck, that hurt."

"Shhh," Rex exhaled, as if he needed to stress the importance of being as quiet as possible. They stared into the house. It was dark except for the living room. On the couch lay a girl watching a large

TV. They crouched behind the table. Rex, in his typical lack of forethought, had not once considered how to get into the house through the back door, so the two men stood there, hunkered like soldiers determining how to advance on a battlefield. Mike still reeled from his entrance to the yard, and now he fixated on the girl. Her dark hair was in a ponytail and a sweatshirt swallowed her petite frame. She cozied under a blanket and it appeared to Mike she was asleep, but then she stirred and rose from the couch.

The two men ducked as the girl moved toward the back door, grabbing a trash bag. Rex had to think fast. He pulled his gun out as the girl opened the door. She turned to her right to place the bag in the large bin when Rex approached her from behind.

"Don't move," he said has he grabbed her, pointing his gun in her face. He wrapped his gloved hand around her mouth as she screamed. "Shut up. I'm going to take my hand off your mouth. If you make any noise at all, I'll kill you. You got it?"

Her eyes were wide with panic. She feared for her life and didn't dare make a sound. She could get out of this. She just had to comply, and so she did. Rex moved his hand away from her mouth. "Good," he announced. "Now I'm going to ask you some questions, OK?" She nodded. "Answer calmly, and don't do anything stupid."

"OK," she muttered.

"Who's in the house with you?"

"My parents and sister."

"Where are your parents?"

"They're in bed. Upstairs."

"Is your sister Olivia?"

"Yes."

"And where is she?"

"In her room." The girl pointed toward the long hall that led to Liv's bedroom.

"Good. All right. Let's go inside." The three walked into the living room. Mike shut the door behind them. "Mike, you take this girl . . . I'm sorry, what was your name?"

"Sarah."

"Sarah. Lovely name. Mike, why don't you take Sarah, and I'll go have a talk with Olivia." Rex shoved Sarah toward the big hands of Mike, who grabbed the back of her neck and pushed her down the hallway. There were two doors at the end of that hallway, one to the left and one to the right. The one on the left was completely closed. The other was slightly ajar, and Mike directed Sarah through the doorway. It was her bedroom, where she had spent so many hours, and none as unpleasant as what was to come.

Chapter 28

LIV

When I was nine, my aunt took a trip to Spain. I didn't know where that was at the time, but I knew it was far away and, from what my parents said, it sounded like a lovely place, an almost magical destination. When she visited our house after returning, she walked in with several bags filled with delicious food and souvenirs. She gave my parents their gifts first and then she gave Sarah hers. I can't remember what they got, probably because I was so enthralled with my own.

The box was blue, emblazoned with "Capitán" on the top. I opened it, and it was the most beautiful figurine I had ever seen. Made of matte-white porcelain, the bust of a girl hugged a white horse's head. The girl's eyes were closed and a pink flower adorned her flowing, blonde hair. The top of a yellow dress covered only one shoulder, leaving the other one bare. It was heavy—over two feet tall and almost two feet wide.

I loved that figurine. I would regularly dust it and carry it around the house, despite my parents' fears I would drop it. Eventually, as with most anything a child receives, it became just another part of my room. As my attention turned to other things—makeup and movies and music and boys— the figurine sat on my dresser, neglected but always beautiful.

Sunday, February 19, 2017

My dad left the bedroom and I was alone again, in the dark with treacherous thoughts I didn't want. I had not yet fallen asleep and was still conscious of my surroundings, but I was in that state of limbo where image after image flashed through my weary brain. I heard a thud, as if something hit the ground outside. I turned on my back to hear for another noise and eventually did. The back door opened and I walked to my window to peer out. It was there I saw them—two men with masks and guns and Sarah, her face distorted with terror. My instinct was to reach for my phone, tucked away in my sweatshirt pocket, but the three came inside, and I worried about the sound of my voice carrying outside my bedroom door.

So, I walked over to my dresser and lifted my figurine, cold and heavy in my right hand, and I waited, holding my breath. I stood behind my door. My heart raced. *Please let this work.* My doorknob turned and the light from the distant living room showed the faint image of the man, his back to me, looking toward my bed with his gun pointed in that direction. With all the strength I had, I hurled the figurine at the side of his head. It broke as it knocked his head against the wall and he crumpled to the floor. I jumped over him and ran. I didn't see Sarah, but every fiber of my being told me to escape the house. The front door was too far away, so I exited the back, clad only in a sweatshirt, sweatpants, and socks. I didn't dare look back and I managed to scale the fence, falling to the cold ground on the other side. I screamed as I ran. My feet hurt as I trampled the sticks and small rocks that peppered the ground. Slipping on a patch of snow, I fell, gaining speed as I descended down a hill and hitting my head on a fallen tree. I heard the terrible sound, a crunch, like someone taking a hammer to a watermelon, before everything went dark.

Chapter 29

REX AND MIKE

Sunday, February 19, 2017

Rex lay on the floor, stunned, his head pounding from the blow. He took his right glove off and reached underneath his ski mask to check for blood. He felt it, warm and wet on his fingers. Gathering his wits, he stood but had to steady himself against the doorframe. He heard a commotion in the living room and, rushing down the hall, saw a man descending the long staircase.

"Stop," Rex screamed. "Right there." The man raised his hands and reversed his stride, an awkward exercise in climbing the stairs backwards. Rex held his gun out, coming closer to the man.

"Please," the man begged. "Take whatever you want."

"Oh, I will. Don't worry. Turn around." The man complied as Rex jammed the gun into his back. They entered the master bedroom. The man's wife sat on the bed and, as Rex flipped on the light, he saw her terror-stricken face, mouth agape and eyes filled with fear. Rex shoved the man onto the bed and stood in front of it, continuing to point his gun in their direction.

"Now listen. I don't want any lies. I don't have time for that shit, so I'm going to ask you a question. If you lie to me—and I'll know you're lying—this is going to get a lot worse."

"Just, please, take whatever you want," the woman begged.

"Shut up!"

The couple couldn't look at the figure with the black ski mask. The instrument that could kill them was only feet away and they lowered their gaze in terror. They prayed silently, begging God to spare their life and their girls' lives. Their material wealth now meant nothing, endeavors through the years to obtain it now seemed pointless.

"OK, question number one. Do you know Darin Duclair?"

"Yes," the man responded. "He's our daughter's boyfriend."

"Good answer. Next question. Do you know where he is?"

"No. I swear."

"Has he been here in the past week?"

"No. He hasn't been here in a while."

"Do you have money in the house?"

"Yes."

"Where?"

"In my closet." The man pointed to his left.

"All right. You're doing good so far. How much?"

"I think it's ten thousand."

"How the other half lives, indeed."

"OK, you," Rex commanded the man. "Get up. Go to the closet. Slowly. One stupid move and I'll blow you away." The man strode toward a safe, tucked away upon a shelf among his clothes. Rex continued to point the gun at the man's wife who refused, still, to look at it. Mascara-laden tears streamed down her face. She failed to remove her makeup when going to bed, a habit she vowed to discontinue but one her depression perpetuated. The man fumbled with the combination and opened the safe with a click. It occurred to Rex there might be a gun in the safe and, in a wave of panic, turned the gun toward the closet. But the man was broken. He reached inside and pulled out several stacks of bills.

Rex located a leather bag on a chair. Or was it a big purse? It was brown and shiny and still had a price tag hanging off the strap. "Put the money in that bag. Is there anything else in the safe?"

"No," the man answered as he dropped the money in it, the stacks causing a low thump as they fell.

"Can you tell us where our daughters are?" the woman cried.

"Well, you don't need to worry about that, but since you asked, one of them is safe. She's downstairs. The other? She was naughty. She took off. Ran out of the house after hitting me." Both parents knew right away he referred to Liv. She was a fighter. They thanked God that at least she was OK. But they both wanted this nightmare to end. They wanted to hug their kids, nothing more. As the man put the money in the bag, he conjured up the nerve to look at the man in the ski mask. Blood descended his neck. He was wounded. Maybe this was his chance. He could lunge at the man before he had time to react. He could take the gun away from him and hold it on him until the police arrived. But what if he failed? What if the man saw him coming? If that were the case, the man would kill him. No, it was better to comply. Do what the man said and live to tell the tale. He was obviously after Darin anyway.

"Back on the bed," Rex said. The man slid toward the headboard and huddled next to his wife. "All right. When we started this, you two were supposed to answer truthfully. And you've done well so far, right? Go on, say it," he commanded. "Say 'I've done well.'" The couple complied, muttering the words through their anguish.

"Very good," Rex replied. "Now, let's have some fun."

*   *   *

Mike led the girl into the bedroom, shutting the door. He was twenty-eight years old and, not once in his meager existence had he been alone with a girl or woman in a bedroom until then. He never had any confidence to approach one, much less ask one on a date. He was too fat, and nothing in his personality—so jaded now to the point of cynicism—could overcome that trait.

But here he was, alone with a girl, eighteen, who told him her name was Sarah. Her long, dark hair reached the middle of her back and her smell was divine. "You don't have to cry," he told her. "Just sit on the bed." She obeyed, wiping the tears from her cheeks with her shirtsleeves. Mike held the gun to his side. He was erect and wanted her, but he didn't want it to be like this. He wanted to talk with her first and get to know her.

"I'm guessing you're in high school." It wasn't a question, but she assumed he meant it as one.

"Yeah. I'm a senior."

"That's cool. I remember my senior year."

"I'm going to college next year," Sarah said, figuring she could engage Mike and diffuse the situation. But it had the opposite effect on him. That a pretty girl such as her was talking to him in such close proximity was more than he could bear. They were all alone, for now undisturbed, and his imagination ran wild.

"Something to look forward to, right?"

"Definitely."

"OK, I need you to do something," he said, rushing his words.

"What is it?"

"Take off your clothes."

"Please. Why? I won't tell anyone about this, I swear."

"Do it. I don't want to hurt you." He was happy she stopped crying. That made things better. Crying ruined the mood. Ashamed and scared, Sarah stood and removed her sweatshirt and pants. Mike stared at the lithe figure before him. His desire grew and his heart raced. He clinched his teeth, his lust overcoming any remorse he would have for what he was about to do. He had done this once before, and the power he was able to exert over a woman was as much of a turn on as his sexual desire. "Take them off."

Sarah slid her bra and underwear off, trying her best to shield herself from the leer of the repulsive man behind the ski mask. He held the gun in his left hand and, putting his right hand between his left side and left arm, removed his right glove. He touched her, running his sweaty paws across her breasts and down her back. The gun was inches from her head. She was powerless and her anticipation of fear for what was about to happen was more than she could bear. She began to cry again.

"Turn around," Mike commanded. Unwilling to wait for her compliance, he spun her around and bent her over the side of the bed. The gun pressed the back of her head, he unzipped his pants, and he entered her. She cried harder, her arms barely able to support herself as the revolting heap of filth behind her continued his attack. She reached within her to think of something, anything, that would take her mind away from the moment, but she couldn't. The moment was too much. She winced in pain and closed her eyes, squeezing more tears out. They descended her cheeks before falling to her bedspread. She heard an awful noise from behind her, Mike grunting as he finished his disgusting deed. He backed away from her, ordering her not to turn around. Tossing the gun on the bed out of Sarah's reach, he zipped his pants and once again admired her figure. He moved his hand along her back and buttocks before lifting the gun. He knew what he had to do. It wasn't what he *wanted* to do, but he knew Rex would require it. In fact, Rex would be livid when he found out how careless he had been.

He grabbed the gun and backed away from Sarah. He had done this enough to know if he were too close, blood would stain his clothing. He heard Sarah whimper and sniff and, for a brief moment, he paused and managed an "I'm sorry" before pulling the trigger. The sound echoed in the room, causing his ears to ring. Blood spattered the wall and Sarah's limp body slid off the bed and onto the floor, blood gushing from her head and mouth. Her eyes remained open in a horrid stare of death. Mike thought of a second shot but saw no rhythmic movement of her body indicative of breathing, so he refrained. She was dead, and now he would wait for the inevitable tongue lashing from Rex.

* * *

"So, when's the last time you two had sex?" Rex inquired, staring at the frightened couple. No one spoke. "Am I speaking English? When's the last time you fucked?"

"Um. Like two weeks ago," the man replied. "Three weeks, maybe."

"Oh, my. Has the flame of passion died? Such a shame. You know. I never got your names." He trained his gun on the man.

"I'm Todd. She's Pam."

"Todd and Pam. I bet you two were the all-American couple back in the day. Am I right? Of course I am. Good looking, probably grew up rich. Everything going for you. What a life. You two are certainly better looking than I am, although you'll have to trust me on that because, well, I'm not taking off this mask. And at the risk of being rude, I can't tell you my name either. I hope that's ok, Todd." Todd nodded. "And Pam?"

"Yes," she replied.

"All right. I feel like we know each other now. We're getting somewhere. Now, let's get back to that no-sex thing. I'm not one to pry, but an attractive couple like you should be fucking on a regular basis. I mean, Todd. Come on. Look at Pam. That body. Sure, she doesn't look like she did in college, but still. She's worthy of a fuck, right? Right?"

"Yes."

"Exactly. So let's fix that. I need you two to undress. And hurry." Rex knew Liv might call the police, but his sadistic desires outweighed his worry. The couple complied, discarding their clothes amidst the messy covers on the bed. Both feeling embarrassed, they brought their knees to their chest, fearing the further instructions that were to come. "Wow. Pam. You are a beauty. And no fake tits. You know, a lot of women get implants, and for what? To impress someone? A husband? A boyfriend? Her girlfriends? It's so stupid. Let them be, I say. As a red-blooded, American male, I can tell you we prefer them natural. And Pam, darling, can you lower your legs and spread them a bit?" He struggled to breathe as the intoxication of power overtook him. "Very good," he said as she obeyed. "I'm starting to like you more and more, Pam. And Todd. You might be a little short in the meat department, but I've seen worse. And hey, it's not the size of the dog in the fight, correct? So tell me, Todd, what do you like to eat?"

"What?" Todd responded, puzzled by the question.

"It's a simple question."

"I—"

"Me? I like a steak. Sure, I can do Italian or seafood. But a nice, juicy steak, medium rare, that's hard to beat. But you know what's even better than a steak? You know what will have your mouth watering at just the thought of your tongue touching it? I think you know. Say it."

"What?"

"Say it. What am I talking about?"

"Vagina," he mumbled.

The answer amused Rex. "Vagina. You're so polite. Technically, you're correct, but the term I was looking for is 'pussy.' So yeah, there is nothing sweeter in this whole world than sticking your tongue between those two folds of flesh. And I can tell from your wife's that she gives quite the dining experience. I have to say, I'm a bit jealous. Well, perhaps if we had more time I could enjoy the feast as well. But for now, Todd, I want you to eat her out. But hold on, one thing first. You know, my view is a little obscured in this mask and I'm assuming this will be quite a show, so I changed my mind. I'm going to remove it."

He lifted the ski mask from his face, revealing his cruel eyes. Neither Todd nor Pam looked at him, but they began to cry, loud moans at the realization of what Rex removing his mask meant. "Much better," he smiled. Pam screamed as the shot from downstairs rang out. It was sudden and unexpected, like a jolt of bad news that, in its surrealness, hangs in the air and takes a second to process. Rex turned toward the bedroom entrance, his eyes wide. Todd, acting on instinct, lunged toward Rex, but it was no use. Rex, upon hearing the commotion, turned and fired his gun four times. Todd's body lay limp on the floor and Pam continued to scream. Rex turned toward her and the two exchanged looks. His evil eyes were the last thing she saw. He raised the gun and fired twice, hitting her in the face each time.

He turned and, with his heart racing from the rush of the kills, bolted down the stairs and into the hallway toward Sarah's room. Opening the door, he saw the girl's nude body slumped on the floor and Mike, as if contemplating what he had done, sat on the edge of the bed, off in the distance. But Mike was not contemplating what he had done—he was worried about Rex's reaction to it.

"I've got a bag of money upstairs. Let's get the fuck out of here."

"Hold on," Mike replied.

"What is it?"

"It was stupid, I know, but I couldn't help it."

"What—what did you do?"

"I came in her."

"What? You stupid fat fuck! Couldn't help it, my ass. Now your DNA is all in that girl. Fuck!"

"Sorry, man."

"Shut up. Don't talk." Rex thought for a few seconds. "All right, go to the garage and find a gas can or lighter fluid." Without speaking—as Rex instructed him—Mike wandered toward the garage, sifting around the belongings next to the expensive cars that he could never dream of owning. After turning on a light, he found a gas can, large and heavy, next to a lawn mower untainted by dirt or grass, as if it hadn't been used in years. He brought the container inside the house, carelessly banging it against the doorframe.

"Start pouring," Rex commanded. Mike opened the can and began pouring the pungent liquid over Sarah's body and onto the floor and bed. Following Rex upstairs, he did the same to Todd's and Pam's bodies, soaking the bed and the floor around it. Rex retrieved a candle lighter from the hearth and touched it to the carpet. Everywhere Mike had poured the gas erupted in flames, the heat instantaneous. He grabbed the bag of money and the two walked downstairs, repeating the process in Sarah's room.

In a matter of seconds, smoke alarms sounded throughout the house, and Mike and Rex exited through the back yard, scaling the fence as they had earlier. They rushed through the woods toward Rex's car, stumbling and slipping on the slick terrain.

If they had taken more time, if they had been more cognizant of their surroundings, they would have noticed Liv lying limp on the forest floor only a few feet away, fresh blood covering one side of her face. She remained unconscious but when she awoke, her world would never be the same. All she cared about in her young life was gone, forever to remain a memory in the recesses of her dark, depraved mind.

Chapter 30

MATT

Sunday, February 19, 2017

I couldn't sleep for hours after my disturbing dream—the three figures haunted me after I forced myself to wake. What little sleep I did get was fretful, full of tossing and turning and the fear wrapped its tentacles around me, crushing my chest in the process. I didn't believe in premonitions or omens in dreams. That was nonsense. But I couldn't shake the idea that the dream was significant, that it served as a warning of some sort. Or maybe it was nothing more than my active brain—disturbing thoughts and images greased with alcohol and paranoia. I found it hard to breathe. I expected a knock at the door, an invitation from the police to answer a few questions at the station. Or worse, an officer ordering me to turn around as he slapped the handcuffs on me, my freedom gone in an instant.

But no knock came. The house was silent and remained so. Even Ann and Nancy seemed to have felt the weight of my deed from the previous night, and they slept undisturbed by any vehicles that dared linger too long in front of their property, which usually brought their wrath. That entire Sunday was a haze. I moved from my bed only occasionally and as night fell, I immersed myself in the comfort the bed brought and soon, a deep slumber followed.

A few minutes before midnight, my phone rang and jolted me awake. The blaring sound in the darkness disoriented me and I had to catch my bearings. It was Liv again. I couldn't keep avoiding her calls. The more I did, the more suspicious I seemed.

"Hey," I answered.

"Matt! Matt, please! You have to come get me!"

"What? Where are you?"

"I'm near my house—my parents' house. I had to run. Two guys broke in and now the house is on fire. Please, I'm begging you" She was frantic. The panic in her voice was genuine, too real for even someone who had played me for a fool a few days ago. While I had no interest in helping her after what she did, I wanted to keep her and myself as far away from the police as possible, so I relented.

"Send me your location."

"OK. There's a parking lot on the far side of the park. Pull into a spot and I'll come to you." I ended the call. I didn't know what happened at her house, but I had my suspicions. Darin owed someone money and, considering he hadn't paid, they had sought revenge. But why Liv's house? Yes, she had an obvious connection to Darin, but it seemed implausible she would be involved in anything like drugs or gambling. Or maybe it wasn't. Less than a week ago, I had taken her for a smart, well-adjusted young woman who, in a minor error of judgment, had chosen to sleep with her professor. I had since learned there was much more to Liv Powell than I realized. I'd give her the smarts, but she was far from well adjusted. At the very least, she was troubled and at the most, a depraved soul who thought nothing of ruining another's life.

The GPS on the phone guided me closer to her parents' neighborhood. She sent me the address to the house and knowing I wouldn't meet her there, I wanted to drive by it out of curiosity. But I got no farther than the end of the street. Police cars and firetrucks consumed the entire block, their flashing lights an ominous sign amongst neighbors whom I was sure weren't used to seeing them. They gathered outside their houses, many clad in pajamas and heavy coats, their desire to rubberneck superseding their need for warmth.

I circled back to the far side of the park and pulled into a parking space, as Liv instructed. It was dimly lit and the woods nearby gave it a gloomy setting. I turned the engine off and the headlights followed soon after. Then, illuminated only by what little moonlight there was, Liv emerged from the trees that surrounded the park. She jogged toward the car and swung the door open, triggering the inside lights, which revealed her wound. Blood matted her hair and had run onto her cheek and neck. It was dry and her face appeared swollen and scratched. Her eye was partially shut.

"Go!" she said. I put the car in reverse, speeding away and eyeing my rearview mirror in the process. Whatever occurred at Liv's house—in a neighborhood such as hers—was sure to have the police on high alert for any suspicious activity. Hanging around a park at two o'clock in the morning was the type of commotion that would draw unwanted attention.

We drove in silence until the lights of the city faded behind us. "Liv, what happened?" Her head was against the headrest and I thought for a moment she was asleep. But she spoke. Her voice was faint and broken and the sound of the tires on the freeway almost drowned it out.

"Two guys broke in. They had guns. I was in my bedroom but I was able to get out."

"How?"

"I hit one of them."

"Do you know who these guys were?"

"I'm not for sure because they had masks on, but I'm almost certain it's the guys who Darin owed money to."

"What about your parents and sister?"

She began to cry. "I don't know. Oh, my God. I don't know, but I'm afraid they're dead."

"You have to go to the police."

"I can't. Darin will get in trouble. I can't do that to him. Do you know where he is?"

"No," I lied.

"I talked to him on the phone Saturday morning and he said he was going to your house."

"My house? Why?"

"He knew about the money. He knew you didn't take any jewelry. Just the money. Why? Why did you do that?"

"Because I didn't need to take any jewelry."

"Yes you did. That jewelry was worth a lot more than whatever you got out of the safe."

"Well, let's just say I made an executive decision, OK?"

"Executive decision? Whatever." If she had not recently endured what I'm sure was the scariest moment of her life and if she wasn't injured, she would have pressed me enough to confess why I took that money from the safe. But she didn't pursue it, and I didn't offer more information. She sat, silent again, broken. She felt her cheek and then her head, exploring the severity of her wound. Wincing in pain, she began sobbing.

"I think you need to go to a hospital."

"No. I'm not going to a hospital."

"Liv, you're hurt, and head injuries are serious."

"I can't."

"You know the police are looking for you, right? They're probably at your apartment right now."

"Then take me to your house."

"What?"

"Please, I don't have anywhere to go."

I sat in silence, staring at the stripes on the road. I was drowsy and the past two days—the past week—had me exhausted. I felt Liv staring in my direction, waiting for an answer. I knew I couldn't say no. She had nowhere to go and, if she did go to the police, there was a good chance I could be implicated in Darin's disappearance, the robbery, or both.

"Fine."

"Thank you," she whispered.

Neither of us initiated any conversation in the car after that. An odd thing, considering less than a week ago we were in a relationship. What that relationship was, I had no idea, and I never bothered to analyze it. In hindsight, of course, it was a farce, built on lies my desire wouldn't allow me to detect.

We entered the back door of my house and walked through the kitchen. I couldn't help but look at the spot where I had killed Darin. It was now pristine, but I wondered what Liv's reaction would be if she found out. I vowed I would never tell her but at a minimum, I had to prepare for her suspicion of me, which I suspected she already had. She was wobbly as she entered the living room and fell onto the couch. As I turned on the light, I saw her head wound was worse than I'd imagined. The blood on her swollen face combined into a grotesque image and her eye—the one not swollen shut—was red from crying. She shuttered at the sudden light that illuminated the living room.

"Sorry," I said, turning it off. "I need to doctor your head, Liv. At least clean it up a bit. I have some pain meds too."

"OK." I offered my hand and she took it, rising from the couch in a deliberate manner, like a drunk trying to hide her inebriation. I led her to the bathroom where she sat on the counter. Scrounging up rubbing alcohol and gauze and bandages—things I rarely used and was surprised I even had—I went to work. She grimaced as the alcohol contacted the gash. I soaked the blood as best I could and, upon smelling it, had to fight my nausea. It was a stark reminder of what I had done almost forty-eight hours earlier. I stood close, her legs on either side of me. Her smell was familiar and it took me back to the moment we first kissed, a passionate, rushed embrace that kept me longing for more. Despite what she did to me—lying, preying on my vulnerabilities, and blackmailing me—I had compassion for her. The rest of her family was likely dead, and I couldn't grasp the pain that would bring if true.

"Do you want some Vicodin?"

"Yes. Please."

"I also have an Ambien." She nodded her head. I handed her a cup of water and she swallowed the pills simultaneously, looking pained in the process. For the first time since she entered my car near the woods, she looked me in the eye. It was a look of brokenness and remorse, nowhere near indicative of the confident woman she was a few days ago. I bandaged her head as best I could. I had no idea what I was doing and upon completion, the bandages around her head and on her face were a haphazard mess of white, akin to what a child would produce when playing doctor.

"I have a spare bedroom. You can sleep in there." I helped lower her from the counter and led her upstairs. She slipped under the covers and turned away from me, lying on the uninjured side of her body. I sat in the chair next to the bed, one I'm not sure I had ever sat in since Emily bought it at a flea market so many years ago. I wanted to observe Liv. For what, I didn't know, but she likely had a concussion, and her slipping into a coma—or worse—would spell trouble. Then, in the pitch black of the room, she spoke.

"Matt. I'm not a good person."

"Liv, now's not the time for self-loathing. You need to rest."

"It's true. I'm not. She slurred her words as the Vicodin and Ambien tugged at her conscience. I wondered how much she knew she was saying and how much was the work of the drugs. "I've done some things I'm ashamed of. Things I never should've done." She paused and, thinking she was done speaking, I began to rise from the chair. She made a moaning sound, however, and I realized she was crying. She started talking again. "I wonder what he's doing now, what he thinks of me."

"Darin?"

"No. Eric."

"Who's Eric?"

"He was my cheer coach. I accused him of rape." She garbled her words and there were inordinate pauses after each few.

"Did he rape you?"

"No."

"Why did you accuse him?" I waited for a response that never came. Listening in the deathly silence of the room, I heard only her breathing, deep and rhythmic as her slumber overtook her.

I stumbled across the hall to my bedroom desperate for sleep but also curious about what Liv had confessed. Her guard was down after taking the pills, and I had little doubt what she said was true. A simple web search confirmed it. From the *Weston Daily*, dated January 6, 2012.

A former cheerleading coach pleaded guilty yesterday to statutory rape and was sentenced to no more than 15 years in prison. Eric Brandt, 34, was the coach of the Pyramid Spirit Cheer Squad in Boston. The allegations surfaced last year after one of the cheerleaders, aged 15, accused him of raping her in his office. Although he initially denied the accusation, his attorney, Paul Calnor, said this was the best outcome under the circumstances. "These are difficult cases for a lot of different reasons, and my client wants to begin to put all of this behind him. A long, drawn-out trial is not the way to do that," the defense attorney said. "Pleading guilty was an agonizing choice, but this is how we can start the healing process."

On the other side, District Attorney Haley Olman said she was pleased with the sentence. "Mr. Brandt is a sexual predator, and he is going away for a long time. We're happy with the sentence and knowing he is away for such a long time will give peace of mind to the young girl he violated."

Because the victim is a minor, her name is not being released.

My blood ran cold as I read the article. Did Liv falsely accuse this man? I had to find out. Given what I had learned about her over the past few days, it wouldn't surprise me. Staring at the screen trying to process the information, I clicked on a headline that caused my heart to race: *House Fire Kills Three*. It confirmed my worst suspicions.

A house fire on a quiet street in Weston revealed a grizzly scene. Investigators confirmed three people have died at 353 Greenbriar Lane. Although authorities haven't released the identities of the bodies, a source revealed two of the deceased are Todd and Pamela Powell. The other is one of the couple's daughters, although the source could not confirm which one. Neighbors confirmed the couple had two daughters, Sarah, aged eighteen, and Olivia, aged twenty.

Authorities suspect arson. They have not revealed a motive yet, but investigators confirmed a safe inside the house was open. "This does not appear to be an accidental fire," Detective John Dimati said. "It seems deliberate, and we're still investigating whether it was the fire that actually killed the victims."

Asked why someone would set a fire after killing the victims, Detective Dimati responded doing so is almost always because the perpetrators are trying to cover up a crime. He also stressed this is an ongoing investigation. "*Right now, there's a lot more that we don't know than we do know.*"

I sunk back into my bed, too tired to undress. I checked my watch—almost 5 A.M. Sleep was futile at that point. The realization I had to teach a class in a few hours turned my stomach, but I knew I had to do it. Not arriving, along with Liv's absence, could raise suspicions. The police would be looking for her and I had to pretend, somehow, among all of this chaos, everything was normal. More importantly, I needed to learn who Olivia Powell really was.

Chapter 31

MATT

Monday, February 20, 2017

The alarm on my phone startled me awake. I resisted the temptation to hit the snooze button and rolled out of bed, my left knee creaking as I pushed myself upward, stretching and reaching for the ceiling. I peeked in on Liv. She was sound asleep. I couldn't get out of my head what I knew and she didn't—her family was dead. I decided against waking her. She needed rest and not knowing the horrific news for a little longer would make no difference. I showered and dressed in a hurry and, upon seeing she was still asleep, texted her.

> Headed to work. Help yourself to anything in the kitchen. Feel free to shower, etc. I'll be home later.

I went through the motions while teaching. I heard some students talking about the fire. Liv didn't seem close to any of my other students, but news travels fast, and now even casual acquaintances knew of the tragedy. The vacant desk that was hers distracted me. A week ago, she had enticed me, playing with her hair, smiling at me, spreading her legs after a night of sex. Now, the desk was empty, a metaphor for her life, upended after a senseless act of violence. As I muddled through my lecture, I wondered if she knew yet.

I canceled my second class, chalked up to being under the weather. It was a luxury I had being able to leave early, a trade-off any professor will tell you is the welcome byproduct of years of schooling and a mountain of student loan debt. Students milled about in the halls and on the lawns of the campus, braving the chilly weather as if hoping against hope it was winter's last gasp.

I pulled into the driveway and made my way to the front door, uneasy about what was to come. Either Liv knew her family was dead or I would have to break it to her. I walked in. Ann and Nancy greeted me as always and, in a matter of seconds, the welcome turned into the anticipation of a treat. I gave them each one and they hurried off, content to chew out of my presence.

I ascended the stairs as light on my feet as possible in case Liv was asleep. As I walked down the hall, a sound emanated from the bedroom. A familiar sound. The same I had heard the previous night. Liv sat on the bed, her back against the headboard, sobbing. I had no words, nothing of comfort. Not because I didn't want to offer her any, but because there is no blueprint for such a situation. "I'm sorry, Liv."

"When did you find out?" she asked.

"Early this morning."

"I saw the news and a bunch of people are calling and texting."

"Have you answered anyone?"

"No."

"Don't feel like you have to yet. Do that only when you feel ready." She nodded as she dabbed her eyes with Kleenex, her knees against her chest. It was odd, but I wanted to comfort her, to hold her and give her some reassurance. But doing so was a futile gesture. If she sought that, she would offer it. I didn't know what our relationship was at that point. To describe it as dysfunctional is an understatement.

"Can I get you anything?" I offered.

"No, thanks."

"Liv, I know you don't want to talk about it, but the police are looking for you. They want to talk to you."

"I know. It's all over the news. Evidently, I'm missing."

"Do you want me to drive you to the police station?" She blew her nose, dabbed her eyes, and discarded the Kleenex among the dozens of used ones on the floor near the bed. She sighed and shook her head. "I don't want to pressure you, but what's your plan?" I asked.

"My plan? Are you kidding me? What kind of plan could I possibly have? My parents and sister are dead, my house burned down, and now the police are looking for me. I'm open to any suggestions."

"I think it's a good idea if"—the doorbell rang and interrupted me. A loud knock followed. The dogs sprang into action, their barks filling the house. I rushed down the stairs, quieted them, opened the door, and saw a short man in an overcoat who offered a handshake. He was balding with a pockmarked face, likely older than I was.

"Dr. Richardson?"

"Yes," I replied, shaking his gloved hand.

"I'm Detective Monroe with the Farrington Police Department. How are you?" *Shit.*

"I'm OK. What can I do for you?" I was alarmed and did my best not to show it. I knew, however, detectives had almost a sixth sense, keen at spotting when someone was the slightest bit uneasy when answering questions.

"We're looking for Olivia Powell. We understand she's one of your students at the college."

"Is she in trouble?"

"We're not sure. Right now, we're just trying to make sure she's OK. There was a situation at her parents' house and as far as we're concerned, she's a missing person. We'd like to talk to her." I stepped out on the porch and closed the door. He seemed puzzled but backed away to give enough room between the two of us.

"I mean is she in any kind of trouble with the law."

"No, we don't think so. We know she was in the house but escaped. She's not a suspect if that's what you're asking."

"OK, thanks." I paused, unsure of what to do. I couldn't keep Liv hidden in my house. She would have to talk to the police eventually. "She's here. Upstairs."

"She's here? In your house?"

"Yeah."

"Why is she here?"

"She called me to come get her. I know all about the break-in and the fire. She has a head injury."

"How did that happen?"

"She said she hit a tree."

"A tree, huh?" His reaction told me he didn't believe me.

"Yeah, when she escaped."

"Dr. Richardson, I know you said she called you, but why you? Her grandparents live here in town. And I'm sure she has friends. Why call her professor?"

"I guess that's something you'll have to ask her."

"Yeah, I think so. Do you mind getting her? I need her to come to the station so I can talk to her. Or if you prefer, I can talk to her here inside the house." *I can't have him walking through my house. What if I neglected to clean something or left something out? A spec of blood. One bullet was still lodged in the bookcase.*

"I'll go get her. Hang on." Liv must have heard who was at the door because she was descending the stairs as I walked in the living room. She looked at me, the edges of her mouth drifting outward. Not quite a smile but a look of resolution, as if to say, "Ok, here we go."

"Please be careful with what you say," I whispered. She hugged me. It caught me off guard, but I returned it.

"Thank you," she said. "For coming to get me," clarifying her gratitude. She moved toward the door, shoeless, only socks covering her feet, and mud caked the back of her sweatshirt. I followed her out and stood on the porch, trying my best to look casual and not have my face reflect the anxiety that swelled within me.

"Thanks, Dr. Richardson," the detective said from the front walk. He opened the passenger door for Liv and, as he rounded the car, gave me a wave. I returned it and gave a half-hearted smile, almost frozen with unease. Liv wasn't a suspect, but they would pry her for all kinds of information. The robbery of her grandparents' store would be addressed. Would Liv protect me? Sure, she was in on it, but what did she have to lose? And what about Darin? Liv knew he was coming to my house to confront me. Would she divulge that information? That thought terrified me to my core and as Detective Monroe pulled away from the curb, I knew it wasn't the last time I'd see him.

Chapter 32

LIV

Monday, February 20, 2017

The inside of the detective's car, some kind of Ford, stank. A lemon-scented air freshener tried to mask the stench to no avail. It was probably the remnants of old fast food. At least that's what I figured, judging from what detectives did in movies. They sat on stakeouts, ate, and got fat. Detective Monroe seemed no different. The thin hair that lingered atop his head was unkempt and his belly protruded beneath his overcoat.

He didn't say anything to me after we got in the car, which was awkward. I was in the front seat and was torn between not wanting to talk and the uncomfortable silence. He pulled into the police station, a large, brick building with several windows. Untarnished cement surrounded it and saplings dotted what little grass there was near the entrance. The faint smell of fresh paint and new carpet wafted through the air as we traversed a long hallway. It reminded me of the first day of school.

"Let's have a seat in here, Olivia," Monroe said. He motioned me into a small room with a folding table and chairs. Already in the room, sitting at the table, was a handsome man whose impressive height I noticed when he stood and extended his hand. He had a rugged look about him and lines of age on his face and a few days growth surrounded a warm smile.

"Olivia, I'm Detective Dimati from Weston. Detective Monroe and I are going to ask you some questions." He diverted his eyes and studied his laptop screen.

"OK."

"You understand you're not under arrest, right?" Dimati asked.

"Yes."

"You're free to go at any point. Sound good?"

"Yeah."

"All right. You live in Farrington, correct? You go to school here?

"Right."

"Why did you go home to your parents' house in Weston?"

"No reason, really. I would visit them sometimes."

"Did anything seem unusual to you that weekend? Anyone behaving strangely? Any odd phone calls?"

I shook my head. "No."

"Do you know of anyone your parents owed money to?"

"No."

"Can you describe for me what happened? If you miss any details, don't worry. You can always come back and fill those in."

I told them about everything I saw, how the men had forced my sister into the house at gunpoint, and how I had hit one of them over the head with the figurine.

"That wound on your head. How did that happen?"

"I slipped and hit a tree when I was running." The detectives eyed me, a scrutinized look that resulted in an uncomfortable pause in the rhythm of questions, which forced me to drop my gaze toward the table.

"Olivia, you can tell us if someone hit you," Monroe chimed in as he lowered himself in the chair next to Dimati. "You're not in trouble, but we need to know the truth."

"No, it was a tree. I swear."

"Did it knock you out?" Dimati asked, resuming his questions.

"Yes."

"And what happened when you woke up?"

"Um, I called Matt to come get me."

"Matt. That's your professor?"

"Yes."

"And why did you call him?"

"I was scared and I figured he'd come and get me."

"Why did you figure that?"

"Because we're friends."

"Don't you have any other friends? People closer to your age?"

"Yeah, but I didn't want to call them."

"So, you just figured Matt, out of the kindness of his heart, would drive the two hours and pick you up in the woods?"

I didn't say anything. I might not have been under arrest, but they suspected me of knowing more than I was letting on.

"How long have you known Matt?"

"Not long."

"Are you two in a relationship?" I lowered my eyes again as both men scribbled notes on their legal pads.

"Olivia?"

"We were," I answered.

"Were what?"

"In a relationship."

"What kind of relationship? Sexual?" Dimati could tell I was reticent. "Don't worry. It's not a crime to have sex with your professor. The school might not like it, but I don't care. We need to know because it's relevant to our investigation."

"Yeah. Sexual."

Detective Monroe opened his laptop and turned it on. A loud hum emanated from it, and he spoke. "Olivia, we've been asking around. It appears you're also in a relationship with Darin Duclair. Is that right?"

"Yeah."

"So, I guess you're aware he's missing."

"Yes."

"Do you have any idea where he is?"

"No. I've tried calling and texting him, but he won't answer."

"Which phone did you call him from?"

"My cell phone."

"Do you have it with you?"

"Yeah." I flashed it after removing it from the pocket of my sweatshirt and he asked to see it, no doubt to verify I had called and texted Darin as I claimed. After several minutes of perusing my texts and call log, he handed it back to me.

"Do you have any other injuries, Olivia?" Dimati asked.

"No."

"OK, I want you to watch this," Dimati said as he opened his laptop and turned the screen toward me. "This is surveillance footage from the break-in. The equipment was torched, but all of that video is uploaded to the server maintained by the private security company that patrols the neighborhood. It's a good thing. Otherwise, we'd have nothing." He hit play on the video, the black-and-white image springing to life. I saw the two figures in the backyard. Sarah came into view—*oh, God, my sweet sister*—before the two men overtook her and forced her into the house. I knew, looking at the two men, it was Rex and Mike, the two drug dealers from Boston. Identifying Mike was easy because of his girth, and it was reasonable to conclude his partner was Rex. Monroe continued the video until I could be seen, running out of the house toward the fence.

"You're quick," he said as he paused it. "And lucky." He resumed the video, fast forwarded it to when Rex and Mike scaled the fence, and paused it again. "Olivia, do you have any idea who those guys are?"

"No," I lied.

"No idea at all?"

"No."

"I'm guessing you know your grandparents' jewelry store was robbed on Saturday, right?

Monroe   asked.

"Yes."

"Have you spoken to either one of them?"

"No."

"Do you know if Darin has a gun?"

"He does."

"You happen to know what kind?"

"I'm sorry. I don't know much about guns."

"Is it a revolver? Can you see the cylinder, the part where you load the bullets? The thing that spins around?"

"Yes."

Without introduction, Monroe turned his laptop toward me and hit play, showing me footage of Matt robbing the store. I tried my best to remain expressionless. "We obviously can't identify the man because of the mask, but do you have any idea who that is?"

"No," I lied again. "You think it's one of the guys who broke into my parents' house?"

"We're not sure. I don't think so, though. This guy," he pointed at the screen, "is taller. That doesn't mean they're not connected though."

He sat back and folded his hands over his belly, seemingly frustrated over the lack of any leads. Dimati sat in silence, twirling his pen in his fingers and staring at his notes.

"All right," Monroe said. "I think that's it for now, unless you have anything," he remarked, turning to Dimati, who shook his head. "Olivia, do you have somewhere you can go? Maybe your grandparents' house?"

"Yeah, I can go there."

"For various reasons, I don't think it's a good idea if you go back to Dr. Richardson's house, for you or him. I'll give you a ride."

It was another awkward ride that silence dominated. I gathered from Monroe's attitude he wasn't talkative or his job had beat him into submission. Either way, he was a man of few words. I guided him toward my grandparents' house, whom I had called warning of my arrival. He parked at the curb and handed me his card. "If you think of anything, call me, OK? Anytime, day or night."

"OK."

"I'm really sorry about what happened, Olivia. I know it's not easy. If you're having trouble processing this, we have a counselor who can help you sort through it. And believe me when I tell you this. I've seen countless cases where people have lost friends and family members. The grief will catch up to you. It will find you, sooner or later. And when it does, you have to deal with it."

It was a surprisingly touching display from him, a side I hadn't seen and one I figured he didn't possess. I thanked him and exited the car. My grandmother stood on the porch, tears in her eyes. I didn't know if they were tears over the tragedy or tears of joy I was alive. It was probably both. She eyed my head wound for a split second before embracing me. We hugged for several seconds, and I began to cry. My parents and sister were gone, and the guilt I felt was a massive weight upon my shoulders from which I was sure I would never find relief. My grandfather was waiting inside. The redness of his eyes was blatant but he tried to hide it. His generation still carried the stigma of a crying man being a weak one. He hugged me without a word and sauntered off to the kitchen, going to devour whatever sweet treat my grandmother had prepared. Its aroma filled the house and somewhere, deep within me, I felt a sense of calm. My mind drifted back to my younger years when my family would visit this house. The alluring smells from the kitchen were constant, my grandmother ensuring we never went hungry.

The guilt, however, soon took over again. My grandparents had always loved me without condition. And how did I repay them? By conspiring to rob them of their hard-earned money and terrorizing them in the process. Then I thought about my past. The stealing, the blackmailing, the lies, the false rape allegation. My desire for revenge had sent an innocent man to prison. And now, my blind love for Darin had caused a series of events over which I now had no control. In that moment, as I reclined on the couch, despondent, I wasn't sure I could go on with my life. I wondered why I should even want to live.

Chapter 33

MATT

Monday, February 20, 2017

The Massachusetts Correctional Institution—Holfield is located 100 miles due north of Farrington. It opened in the early 1900s and, since that time, the state continued to add buildings, so today it houses almost 1,000 inmates. I drove to the parking lot, finding a spot about a hundred yards from the facility. Guards poised in towers above the concrete wall with razor wire kept watch and eyed me as I walked through the pedestrian entrance.

A small, old man with glasses sat behind a clear plastic divider. "How can I help you?" he asked, peering over his frames.

"I'm here to see someone."

"An inmate?"

"Yeah."

"Do you have an appointment?"

"No."

"What's the inmate's name?"

"Eric Brandt." He typed on his computer keyboard and jotted some information on a sheet of paper. After doing so, he handed me a clipboard with a piece of paper attached.

"Fill this out, front and back, and sign it. Hand it back to me when you're done." I got the feeling this old man, probably close to retirement, was a former prison guard or possibly a former cop. Whatever the case, he gave me orders in the style of someone not used to being questioned. I put in the necessary information on the sheet and handed it back to him. "Walk down this hallway," he pointed. "At the end, you'll see a metal detector. Go through that and take an immediate left. You'll see the visiting area there. Pick a spot with a vacant phone. You have thirty minutes once the inmate appears."

"Thanks."

"Yep," he replied, without looking away from his computer screen. He pressed a button and a loud buzz sounded, unlocking the outside door.

I had never been in a prison and my paranoia grabbed hold of me as I traversed the walkway. *I could end up here.* After passing through the metal detectors, I sat by one of the phones and waited, nervous about my encounter. There was only one other visitor there, a woman who, if I had to guess, was talking to her son. I waited a few more minutes, staring at the cinderblock walls and metal fixtures that surrounded me. The lighting was bad and I felt sympathy for the people who had to work in the depressing environment. With a clang, a guard opened a metal door and through it walked Eric Brandt. He appeared different than the picture in the news story. A large beard and mustache covered his face and he had a belly which, considering he was a cheer coach, probably didn't exist before he landed in prison. He gave me a perplexed look and sat on the metal bench across from me, behind the clear divider. We each lifted a receiver.

"Hi, Eric. My name is Matt Richardson. I live in Farrington and teach at the college. One of my students is Olivia Powell." His eyes narrowed at the mention of the name, as if he were skeptical of my reason for being there. I could also tell, however, he was intrigued.

"OK?"

"If you wouldn't mind, I'd like to ask you about your case, about her accusations against you."

"Well, what do you want to know?"

"Did she make it up?"

"Wow, you like to get right to the point, huh?"

"Sorry. She said something that makes me think what she accused you of isn't true."

"Why would she tell you this?"

"We were just talking."

"This is the kind of stuff you talk about in class?"

"No, we were . . . at my house." *Shit.*

"Oh, I get it. You two have a thing going on. Nice. I can understand it. She was always cute. I bet she looks great now, huh?"

"Yeah," I answered, knowing he was fishing for more information. Understandable, considering his entire world was devoid of female interaction.

"Well, watch out for her."

"What do you mean?"

"She's a psychopath."

"Why do you say that?"

"Seriously? You have to ask? What kind of person besides a psychopath could make up a rape accusation and send someone to prison?"

"So, it's not true?"

"Of course it's not. She made the whole thing up."

"Is there any truth to it at all?"

"None at all."

"Why would she do it?"

"I'm sure she was upset because I was a little hands-on with the girls, if you know what I mean."

"Like inappropriate touching?"

"You could say that."

"But that's sexual assault."

"Please," he said, indignant. "Touching a girl's leg is one thing, rape is quite another."

"So you were framed?"

"Yeah. She set the whole thing up. That bitch put her panties in my office along with a box of condoms. It was a total lie. I never raped her. Hell, I couldn't rape anyone."

"Why did you plead guilty?"

"I wish to God I hadn't now. I figured it was the best thing at the time. For me, for my family. I also didn't think there was much of a chance of getting a not-guilty verdict. There was so much evidence. None of it was true, of course, but try getting a jury to believe that. And with a guilty verdict? They would have thrown the book at me." He shifted his weight and observed his surroundings. "So, tell me, what exactly did she say?"

"She said she accused you of rape and that it wasn't true. I'm not sure she was aware she was saying it, though. She had taken a sleeping pill and some pain medicine."

"You have to help me," he pleaded, inching toward the divider.

"How?"

"You have to tell someone."

"Who?"

"My attorney. Paul Calnor. C-A-L-N-O-R. Look him up. Back when all this happened, his office was near downtown on the west side. Please. Just tell him what you told me."

I was reluctant. Relaying this message to an attorney meant the nature of my relationship with Liv might see the light of day. It also meant if she found out I talked to Eric's attorney, she could reveal the robbery out of nothing more than revenge. I didn't think she would, but Eric's words—"she's a psychopath"—hung in the air, and they made me uneasy. On the other hand, this was most likely an innocent man I was talking to, incarcerated for several more years for something he didn't do.

"OK. I'll talk to him."

"Thank you."

I thanked him for meeting with me and exited the prison, eager to leave it. Finding the attorney's information on my phone, I input directions into my map and headed toward Boston. As I was doing so, Liv texted me.

The cops know about our relationship. Just telling you in case it comes up. I responded with a thumbs-up emoji and, against my better judgment, replied.

Where are you now?

At my grandparents' house. I'll text you later.

I didn't know why she would text me later. I wanted nothing more to do with her and, considering what had transpired, I doubted she would want anything to do with me either. I didn't reply and instead focused on racing toward Boston.

Calnor & Associates was in a small, nondescript building near the Charles River. I stepped inside and a stunning woman—presumably an assistant—greeted me from behind a semicircle desk. Had I seen her in another setting, I would have presumed she was a model. Her dark red hair that encompassed her face made her fair skin stand out.

"Hi, can I help you?" she asked, giving a cursory smile.

"Yeah, I'd like to talk to Mr. Calnor."

"We're just about to close. Would you like to make an appointment?"

"Well, not really. I live about two hours away, and I don't need legal services. I need to talk to him about a case he worked on several years ago. It won't take much time." A man emerged from an office from across the room. His suit jacket brushed the Ficus plant near the doorway.

"Janine, you have to move that damn thing. I hit it every single time I walk out of here." I assumed he was talking to the woman in a playful way, but when I turned my head back toward her, she rolled her eyes. "What can I do for you?" he asked.

"Can we talk in your office?"

"Yeah, it has to be quick though. My son has a hockey game in an hour and if I don't make the faceoff, my ex won't let me hear the end of it."

"OK, it won't take long." I followed him into his office, a small room with a cluttered mess of folders that covered his desk and the immediate floor space around it. His tired eyes and drooping face—indicative of too many hours in the office and not enough rest—gave him a weathered look. He stood just inside the door and shut it as I walked in. He stared at me, as if waiting for me to begin. I told him about Liv's statement and that I had talked to Eric.

"Eric Brandt and Olivia Powell. I remember that case well. Poor bastard. He flat-out told me he was innocent. But then again, almost all my clients say that."

"Did you believe him?"

"It's hard to say. I always found it difficult to believe that a cheer coach would close his office door, rape a girl right after practice was over, keep her underwear and condoms in his desk, and expect nothing would come of it. It never made sense. If he did, it's one of the most brazen, idiotic things a person could do."

"So you think he set her up?"

"I'm inclined to think so."

"So why did he plead guilty?"

"I talked with him a long time about that, of course. He decided it was better than rolling the dice and going to trial."

"Did you ever interview Liv?"

"Olivia?"

"Yeah, sorry. That's what she goes by."

"No. Never got to depose her. If the case had gone much further, I would have. And I was looking forward to cross examining her at trial."

"So what can be done?"

"About what?"

"Eric Brandt is innocent."

"Mr. . . . I just realized I don't know your name."

"Matt Richardson."

"There's nothing to be done. That case is over. Eric pled guilty of his own volition, and that's that."

"Yeah, but what about Liv's statement?"

"What about it? She made that under the influence of drugs. There's not a judge in the world who would do anything with that. And if she denies making the statement—which she most likely would—all that leaves us with is you claiming what another person said and, as any first-year law student will tell you, that's hearsay." He was right, and it troubled me. The look on my face must have shown it.

"Look, I can tell that upsets you, but there's really nothing to be done. If you can convince her to testify to that in open court or at least sign an affidavit, then we might have something. But good luck. People who make false accusations don't typically turn around and come clean. When it comes down to it, criminal law is all about saving your own ass, or as much of it as you can. If she did make the whole thing up, she's not going to risk her own ass now. And between you and me, Eric was a bit of a scumbag. Every single cheerleader who the police interviewed said the same thing. He liked to touch the girls. Depending on how all that went down, that might be a crime in and of itself, and there are plenty of people who would want him locked up just for that. Look, you've done your good deed. You're a good citizen. If she says anything else, let me know. And one more thing. Here's your free legal advice for the day, stop seeing her. I've seen pussy get more men in trouble than anything else. And she's one of your students. If she did make the whole rape thing up, you're playing with fire. You seem like a nice guy. Be careful."

"Duly noted," I replied. I didn't need his advice, but I was thankful for the meeting. I left the building and walked to my car, parked on the street.

Vehicles zipped by as rush hour was in full swing. Entering the car, I reached in the glove box and retrieved the money I owed Rex. I was ready to rid myself of it. It had become a symbol of the disease that had derailed my life. Two figures passed on the sidewalk next to my window. A man and woman, arm-in arm. Paul Calnor and his beautiful assistant. The man who had just told me about the dangers of "pussy" was a divorcee in a relationship with his assistant who was probably twenty years his junior. I shook my head at the obvious irony. I wondered if he had also "ruined" his life, but fully aware I had also fallen prey to the same thing.

The sun had set before I arrived at Rex's. Parking on the street in front of his building made me sick to my stomach. It made me think of things I didn't want to—addiction and money owed. I hadn't made any kind of a conscious choice to quit gambling, but the situation I had put myself in necessitated it, and staring at the small food store below his apartment felt like something out of a former life, a cloud of memories I couldn't quite grasp yet couldn't shake from my psyche.

I knocked on the door and, as always, Mike answered. He raised his eyebrows and jerked his head up—a quick, wordless greeting. I walked down the hallway and into the bedroom as I had done so many times. Rex was lounging on the bed and staring at his phone. The room smelled of gasoline and I guess I made a face that showed my repulsion.

"Matt," Rex said, stringing my name out longer than necessary. "Yeah, I know. It smells like a goddamn gas station in here. Numb nuts Mikey here had a little incident. So, you'd be pretty stupid to show up here without money. What do you got?" I reached inside my coat pocket and pulled out what I owed him.

"Impressive," he said, taking the money. "I figured Mikey would have to pay you another visit. He reached under the bed to put the money away and, as he did so, I caught a glimpse of the right side of his head. A wound with dried blood appeared on his temple, a bruise surrounding it. I was curious about it but didn't dare address it. I always had the attitude that the less time I spent in that apartment, the better. Plus, Rex always struck me as a loose cannon. I could see him flying off the handle at someone for saying the wrong thing.

"So you ready to make another bet?" he asked.

I shook my head and pursed my lips. "No, I'm out."

"What?"

"Yeah, I'm done. I can't do that anymore."

"Why not?"

"Well, the last one didn't exactly go well, and I'm not a big fan of baseball bats."

He laughed. "Understandable. Well, if you ever get the urge again, you know where to find me. And you know, I do other stuff too, so if you ever feel the need, let me know."

I figured he meant his drug business but I didn't want to pry. "All right," I nodded. I walked out of the apartment and down the stairs, wanting never to set sight on it or Rex and Mike again. It wasn't until after I sat in my car that it became clear. The smell of gas. The head wound. I knew Darin was involved with people from Boston. Rex and Mike could have been those individuals. The hair on the back of my neck stood. I was likely just in the presence of murderers, the cold-hearted killers of Liv's family.

Chapter 34

LIV

Tuesday, February 21, 2017

I woke to the smell of bacon and stumbled into my grandparents' kitchen. My grandfather had the newspaper spread out on the table, sipping his coffee. "Hey, Liv. Let me get you some breakfast."

"No, I can do it. Thank you." I went to the stove, scooped some eggs, and snatched a few pieces of bacon before sitting at the table.

"I'm sorry," he said, realizing the newspaper was in my way. He shook it and folded it twice before setting it down again. "I've been in touch with the funeral home. The funeral will be on Friday." A funeral. The last thing I wanted to think about. I dreaded them, and the thought of going to see my parents and sister buried was crushing.

"Sweetheart," he said, his eyes looking above his reading glasses, "do you have anything to wear to it?"

"Yeah, at my apartment." I owned a black dress my mom had given me. I didn't like it but for a funeral, it was perfect, if there was such a thing. "I just need a ride."

"I can take you."

"Where's Grandma?"

"At the jewelry store."

"And you didn't go?"

"She wanted to go alone. She's taking this hard. And you know how she is. She'll bury herself in something to avoid dealing with it. She was out of the door before I got up. How are you?"

I didn't know how to answer that question. I was numb, bathed in grief and guilt. I felt trapped. I could confide in my grandparents only so much. There was only one other person who knew the truth, and that was Matt, who likely never wanted to see me again. I shrugged my shoulders in response and stared at my plate.

"You know you can talk to me. And you know you're welcome to stay here as long as you need."

"Thanks, Grandpa." It was a nice offer, but I wanted to be home—a place that no longer existed. I felt the sting in my nose that precedes a cry, but I held back.

"Your mom . . ." tears filled his eyes, "she was going through a lot."

"What do you mean?"

"I only know this because she confided in your grandma, but your mom had been fighting depression for years. She never told anyone and I don't think she ever sought help."

"She definitely never told me, but thinking back on it, the way she acted, her demeanor, it makes sense."

"And your dad. He knew and he tried his best to talk her out of it, to make her happy. But that's not how it works. She needed professional help."

"Why didn't she get it?"

"She got pills, but she needed counseling, too. And she never got that. I also wonder if she was bipolar. She was very proud, your mom. I guess it was the way we raised her. She wasn't much for touchy-feely type stuff."

"Tell me about it."

"Yeah, I know she could be hard on you girls, and I'm sure that got worse as her depression progressed."

"Did Grandma try to get her to see someone?"

"Yeah. She begged her, to the point where there were many times I heard your grandma crying on the phone with your mom. I was afraid your mom would kill herself."

"Do you know if she ever tried?"

"I'm not sure. It wouldn't surprise me."

"I had no idea. I knew she was withdrawn but I never thought she might be depressed or bipolar."

"I don't want you to get the wrong idea, Liv. This didn't have anything to do with you or your sister or your dad. It was nothing you did that caused her depression."

I appreciated his statement, but I couldn't help thinking I at least exacerbated it. My attitude and personality must have sent her to a darker place. It's no wonder we rarely talked in the year leading to my departure for college. Another wave of guilt washed over me. I felt tears welling in my eyes.

"Grandpa, I hate to bring this up, but what condition were their bodies in?"

"I talked to the detective yesterday. The bodies were burned pretty badly, but there was enough there they could identify. They were all shot. The detective said the doctor who performed the autopsy thinks the gunshots killed all of them, not the fire which, in an odd way, is a relief. At least they didn't suffer by being burned alive. And Liv, I don't want to tell you this, but you're going to find out sooner or later." He took off his glasses and rubbed his face before sighing and looking at the ceiling.

"What is it?"

"They're pretty sure your mom and Sarah were sexually assaulted.

"What? Why do they think that?"

"They were nude." I rested my elbow on the table and placed my forehead in my palm. Just when I thought the news couldn't get worse, the unwanted images of Rex and Mike subjecting my mom and Sarah to their revolting desires made me sick. I shot up from the table, my chair screeching across the floor as I pushed it back.

"What is it?" my grandpa asked, looking stunned. My chest felt tight.

"I'm sorry, Grandpa. I can't be here anymore. Can you take me to my apartment?" He paused and gave me the only answer he could.

"Yeah, sure." Still without shoes, I walked to the car. I thought about what my grandpa had said, how my grandma liked to avoid dealing with anything heavy, and maybe I was the same way. I felt trapped in the house and I needed out, like a diver who needs to come up for air. He didn't say much on the drive over. He was never one for many words, but I knew he was hurting, and I imagined he would show his grief soon. It was like a soda can that had been shaken, and only the slightest opening would cause it to spew forth. I also needed to process what had happened. I didn't know how to do that, but I knew I wanted to be alone. The past week had been a whirlwind, and I wasn't sure my brain had fully processed everything that had occurred.

I thanked my grandpa and waved as he drove off to accompany my grandma at the store. Walking in, I realized I didn't have my keys. They were in my room at my parents' house, burned and melted, likely under a pile of soot. I walked to the end of the hallway and knocked on the landlord's door. He opened it after I knocked a second time. He was intimidating to look at with his old, chiseled face and perpetual frown.

"Hi," I opened. "I don't have my keys and I was wondering if you could let me in." He saw my head, bloody and bandaged, and surveyed my ragged clothes.

"Why don't you have your keys?"

"It's a long story. I just need you to let me in, please."

"You should keep your keys on you all the time."

"Look," I replied, growing more exasperated by the second, "I don't need a lecture."

"Well, it sounds like you do. Now I'll have to get another key made if you've lost yours. Did you lose it?"

"Yeah."

"Figures."

I wanted to hit him. I wanted to pound his face with my fist and shove his shriveled body into the wall. "God damn it, will you just fucking let me in?

Please!" His eyes widened. He fumbled with his keys and stormed past me.

"Which one?" he inquired.

"Number 4." He opened it and slammed it back into the doorstop, after which I slammed it shut in his face. He yelled something I couldn't decipher and I told him to fuck off, amidst the tears that were now streaming down my cheeks. I walked to the bedroom and fell into my bed, bawling into my pillow. I thought about what Detective Monroe had said: *The grief will find you.* The grief had found me, and the weight of the world was on my shoulders.

Chapter 35

MATT

Tuesday, February 21, 2017

Killing Darin haunted me and I couldn't erase the tragedy of Liv's family from my mind. I had no sexual or romantic feelings for her any longer, but I empathized with what she must have been going through. The sudden loss of an entire immediate family was unfathomable to me.

That was my mindset as I dragged myself to work, which was meaningless to me at that point. I went through the motions in my lectures and didn't stick around my office for more than a few minutes, only long enough to satisfy any students who needed to speak to me. None showed, so I left, eager to escape to my home. I stopped at the liquor store for a bottle of wine, the solution to numbing my feelings, albeit a temporary one.

As I approached my house, a familiar car sat along the curb. I pulled into the driveway as a man emerged from the car. Detective Monroe. *Shit.* I smiled and waved as if happy to see him.

"Dr. Richardson," he greeted me as I exited my car.

"Hey."

"I really like this house. I meant to tell you that the other day, but it slipped my mind. These old colonials have real charm."

"Thanks. I'm actually thinking of selling it."

"Is that right? I'm interested, but there's that minor detail of a cop's salary." He gave me an odd smile, which I felt compelled to return.

"What can I do for you?"

"I was wondering if you'd mind coming to the station with me. We talked to Ms. Powell yesterday and we're trying to get as much information as we can. We think the disappearance of Darin Duclair and what happened to her family might be related. And I know you and Ms. Powell were in a relationship, so I'm hoping you can shed some light on all of this."

"Yeah, I can come with you. I'm not really sure what I have to offer though."

"I appreciate that. You never know. Sometimes talking through this stuff can yield some new clues." He opened the passenger door to his car and stared at me. I knew I could refuse to go with him. I had the right to do so, but rejecting his invitation would make me more of a suspect than I might have already been. *Stay calm. Breathe.* I sat in the car. An 80s song played on the radio. Odd, I thought. I never considered detectives would listen to music on the job. He turned it off when he got in and pulled away from the curb.

"I have to say this. I know you know it, but it's protocol. You know you're not under arrest, right?

"Yeah, I know."

"This is completely voluntary."

"Right."

"It's such a strange thing," he said.

"What's that?"

"That Darin, Olivia's boyfriend, goes missing the same week her parents and sister are murdered." He turned his head toward me. Our eyes met. It was a look I didn't like. He turned back and focused on the road before speaking again. "It doesn't seem coincidental. What do you think?"

The question surprised me. I wasn't prepared to give any kind of a theory, and I stammered before I could put a coherent response together. "It does seem strange it would all happen in the span of a few days. They could definitely be connected, but I'm sure you've seen stranger things." He turned his mouth downward, as if he were considering that possibility.

"Definitely. I've seen some strange stuff for sure. But more often than not, things like this are connected. What I can't figure out is why they would target Olivia's house in Weston. It's a mystery, no doubt about it. But really, that's Weston PD's case. We're working on only the disappearance of Darin." I didn't respond, mostly because I didn't think what he said warranted one. I also knew, however, he was fishing for information, so I figured the less I talked, the better.

"Oh, you know what?" He snapped his fingers as if he just remembered something. "We need to take a short detour. Is that OK? It involves another case I'm working on and it's on the way to the station anyway."

"Yeah, that's fine." *A detour? Where?*

"You probably know how it is, given your profession. Trying to juggle ten things at once."

"Yeah, I know what you mean." He turned on Sycamore Street. I had a sinking feeling in my stomach, and the longer we spent on that road, the worse it got. The surroundings were familiar. The strip mall with the grocery store and next to it, our destination. Holland Jewelers. I swallowed hard and tried my best to mask my need for a deep breath.

"You know about this robbery, right?"

"Yeah. Liv told me."

307

"Liv. I didn't know she went by that. I need to talk to the grandmother for just a second and give her an update." He drove into a space in front of the store and slammed the car into park. "You know what? If it were up to me, I'd let you stay in the car, but it's against department policy to have anyone besides an officer alone in a cop car."

"Oh . . . OK." *Shit.* He led me into the store. It all came back to me. The layout. Liv's grandmother behind the counter. The office door at the end of the hall, wide open. My heart raced and I tried to remain calm. I felt my face become flush.

"Mrs. Powell? Detective Monroe."

"Oh, yes. Hi." She came out from behind the counter and shook his hand before turning toward me.

"Oh, this is Dr. Richardson," Monroe said. "He teaches at the university." I smiled and gave a small wave. "What is it you teach again?" Monroe asked, furrowing his brow.

"Political Science." I knew what the detective was doing. He was trying to get me to talk in the hopes that Liv's grandmother might recognize my voice. *That meant I was a suspect in the robbery, but how?*

"That's right. I couldn't remember. It turns out, Mrs. Powell, that your granddaughter is in Dr. Richardson's class."

"Is that right?" she responded. "So you know Liv?"

"I do."

"Poor girl. We're all going through so much, but I just can't imagine how she feels." An old man emerged from the office. He appeared to have a limp and pulled his glasses off his face, grabbing the temple with one hand.

"Hey, Detective."

"Mr. Powell, how are you?"

"What's the latest?"

"Well, that's what I came to tell you. We really don't have anything, unfortunately. We've studied the surveillance footage and put information about the robbery on our website but so far, we don't have any leads." The grandfather glanced at me but seemed uninterested in who I was, and I wasn't about to offer an introduction. "Now that I think of it, Dr. Richardson, had Olivia, sorry—Liv—been acting strange at all that you could tell, either before or after the robbery."

I shook my head. "No."

"Can you describe her demeanor, just from what you observed?" *This guy is relentless.*

"She's attentive. A good student. She speaks up occasionally. She seems—*seemed*—happy." The grandmother was looking into the display case but when I uttered the sentence, her head jerked up and she stared at me. I caught her glare but averted my eyes. Everything was silent. My words hung in the air, and I dreaded what was coming next.

"Hmmm, OK," the detective replied. "Sorry, guys. We don't have anything at this point, but I'll keep you updated."

"Why did you ask about Liv?" the grandfather asked. "You don't think she was involved." Although it was a question, he turned it into a statement, almost accusatory in its tone.

"No. We're just pursuing everything at this point. As I said, I'll keep you updated."

We exited the store and as I sank into the passenger seat of the detective's car, he leaned in his opened door and looked at me. "You know what? Stay put. I have to tell them one more thing." He trotted back inside, the door shutting behind him. I was on to him, but what I didn't know is whether he knew it. Did he underestimate me and think I was so naive that I wouldn't see what was going on, or was he so brazen that he knew I knew and didn't care? Either way, I had to be careful. Outside of Liv, there was nothing—that I knew of—that could tie me to the robbery, but I never planned to come close to that jewelry store again.

"Sorry about that," Monroe said as he slammed his car door. "Darin's case is frustrating, but so is this one. A robbery, which is not all that unusual, but the guy didn't take any jewelry and asked for only fifty-thousand dollars. Don't you find that weird?"

"Yeah, it is."

"I guess Liv told you all about it." His look oscillated between the road and me.

"Yeah, she told me the basics."

"What a week for that family."

He pulled into the station parking lot amidst a row of marked police cars. I exited and breathed in the cold air and, walking in, it occurred to me I had never been in a police station. That was good, I suppose, but walking in among the bustle of people coming and going unnerved me. The detective led me back to a small room, perfectly square and filled with a folding table and folding chairs. I sat in one as he walked across the hall and grabbed two bottles of water. Handing one to me, I uncapped it and drank, saturating my dry throat and mouth. I continued to grip it as I set it on the table and tried to remember everything I had read and watched about police interrogations. I knew there were things suspects did that caused cops to believe or disbelieve them, and I probed the recesses of my mind to recall that information. But I couldn't recall anything. My nerves warred with my rationality.

"OK, Dr. Richardson, again, you know this is completely voluntary, right?"

"Yeah."

"You can end the interview at any time and we can have someone drive you home." He had his phone on the table beside him and he seemed distracted, as if he were reading a message. He uncapped his pen and flipped a page on his yellow legal pad, and went to work.

"I think a good starting point is to talk about your relationship with Liv."

"OK."

"When did you meet her?"

"Last week, in my class."

"And you developed a relationship with her, correct? Beyond just the normal student-teacher relationship, I mean."

"Yeah."

"Did it turn sexual?"

"It did."

"Did you ever meet Darin Duclair?"

"Yeah."

"And where did you meet him?

"I saw him at Liv's apartment."

"And what was the occasion?"

"What do you mean?"

"Why were you both there at the same time. I'm guessing Liv didn't tell her boyfriend she was in a relationship with her professor, so I'm wondering why you two were at her apartment."

"I showed up, unannounced." And with that statement, the lies began. "I didn't know she had a boyfriend until then."

"And what was that interaction like?"

"Awkward."

"How did Liv react when she saw you?"

"She was surprised. And I was surprised to see another man in the apartment."

"Did you speak to Darin?"

"Yeah, briefly."

"Did he know of the nature of your relationship with Liv?"

"No. Or at least I don't think he did."

"So how did Liv explain your presence to Darin?"

"She made up a flimsy excuse about me being there to help her with an assignment."

"Did he buy that?"

"I'm not sure."

"Did you ever get into any kind of a physical altercation with Darin?"

"No."

"Ever get into an argument?"

"No." He paused his rapid-fire questions and retrieved his phone. My face was hot. I had my coat on and I wanted to take it off, to relieve me of the heat I was feeling, but doing so might give the impression I was flustered or wanted to stay, that I wanted this probing detective to ask me anything he pleased. After what seemed like a full minute of silence, he resumed.

"Had you ever met Liv's grandparents before today?"

"No."

"Have you ever been to Liv's house in Weston?"

"No."

"So let me ask you this. What do *you* think happened to Darin?"

"Well, I heard he was involved in drugs with people back in Boston."

"Who did you hear that from?"

"Liv."

"But I thought you said you didn't know about Darin before you showed up at Liv's apartment unannounced."

Shit. Think. "I didn't. She told me after he went missing and after the fire."

"So you think some people back in Boston are responsible?"

"Yes."

"For his disappearance and for the fire?"

"It makes sense, I think."

"See, I just don't understand why they would do what they did to Liv's family. Do you think Liv was involved with these guys as well?"

"No. No way."

"What makes you say that?"

"Because I know her."

"You've known her for a week."

"What's your point, Detective?"

"My point is even if we think we know someone, they could still be hiding something. Kind of like a professor having sex with one of his students. I bet people around here would never suspect you of that." I didn't respond but stared at him and he back at me. It was a low blow, but not unwarranted. "You see what I mean?" he asked, a smile creeping onto his face. "People have all sorts of secrets. But usually those secrets don't result in a missing person, a triple homicide, and arson."

"Right."

"And you know, as a detective, I have to come up with theories. It's kind of a starting point when we start gathering evidence. And so I'm working on a theory with this case." He put his pen on the legal pad, on which he had written nothing, sat back in his chair, and folded his arms. He stared at me for several seconds, and I did my best to maintain eye contact. "And here's mine. I think you know what happened to Darin."

"Why would *I* know what happened to him?"

"Because you're the common denominator here. Your connection to Liv. Your interaction with

315

Darin at her apartment. And I don't want to jump to conclusions here, but you had an incentive to kill Darin."

"Kill him? What makes you think he's dead?"

"It's a pretty safe bet, wouldn't you say?"

"No, I wouldn't. He's an adult and he's been missing for a little over two days, right?"

"Correct."

"Who knows what kind of shit he's in to. I already told you about the people from Boston."

"But you would agree you had an incentive to kill him, right?"

"No, I wouldn't agree to that at all."

"You had this relationship with Liv, and then you find out she has a boyfriend. You want him out of the picture. It makes sense."

"Detective, you can call it what you want—incentive, motive, whatever—but the idea I could kill someone out of jealousy over a relationship is ludicrous. I had been in that relationship with Liv for only a few days. That's hardly any time to develop any kind of jealousy."

He smiled. "You should be on my end of things. I've seen people kill for a lot less."

"And I said kill someone out of jealousy. Hell, I couldn't bring myself to kill anybody over anything."

"So you think Darin just skipped town, huh? A guy with a house here, a pretty girlfriend? You think he'd leave without telling her anything?"

"I don't know. As I've said, I don't really know him."

"Look, Dr. Richardson, all I'm trying to do at this point is eliminate you from having any connection to this case. As soon as I can do that, I won't need to talk to you anymore. So please, just give me something. Something I can hold on to so I can say, 'OK, he's not involved.'"

"You're asking me to prove a negative."

"Where were you on Saturday?"

"I went to Liv's apartment early in the morning. That's when Darin was there. I left there after about a few minutes and then I came home."

"Was Darin still there when you left?"

"Yes."

"What did you do when you went home?"

"I don't remember exactly what I did, but I stayed there."

"All day?"

"Yes."

"You didn't go anywhere?"

"No."

"Did anyone visit you at home? Any neighbors or friends or family?"

"No."

"Do you have a doorbell camera by chance?"

"No."

"Any security cameras around your house?"

"No." He sat up and rested his elbows on the table. His demeanor and age told me he was a veteran at this, but his face began to show signs of frustration. It gave me hope as the panic inside my head raged.

"Would you mind if we came and had a look around your house? Maybe stepped inside and looked around for a bit?" I knew the police didn't just "look around." If I gave him permission to come in, they would conduct a thorough search.

"Why do you want to look in my house?"

"Again, we're just trying to eliminate you as having any connection to Darin's disappearance."

"I'd rather you not."

"You'd rather us not?"

"It's a no, Detective."

"If we were to come in your house, say we got a warrant to do so, we wouldn't find any evidence Darin was in your house? No fingerprints or DNA? Anything like that?"

"No."

"So Darin never set foot in your house?"

"No." He dropped his head and rubbed the back of his neck with one hand while he lifted the pen with the other. He took a big gulp of water and sighed after swallowing.

"Would you be willing to take a lie-detector test?"

Fuck. "No." I paused. "Detective, I appreciate you're trying to solve a case. I know you're looking for information, but I don't have any more information other than what I've told you."

"You do realize taking the test and passing it will eliminate you from being a suspect, right?"

"The only thing I realize is that you're zeroing in on me because you have no leads at all. If you did, you wouldn't be wasting your time with a college professor whose only error in judgment was having sex with one of his students."

He glared at me as I uncapped my water bottle and took a sip. It was only after I set it down that he replied. "All right, Dr. Richardson, that's all I have for you now. I'll get an officer to drive you home. And I almost forgot. We found Darin's car in a parking lot at the mall. We had it towed in this morning and forensics has it right now." He stared at me as he stood, fixing his gaze on my eyes. That wasn't information he almost forgot. It was information he was holding back, trying to make me squirm, and it worked. "I'll let you know if we find anything." I stood and turned to walk out of the door, feeling my pulse in my neck. As jumbled as my thoughts were at that point, I had the clarity of thought to remember to take my water bottle. It had my DNA on it, and leaving it with Detective Monroe was not a risk I could afford. I stuffed it into my outside coat pocket as I exited the station, following my officer-escort to his car. As much as I didn't want to believe it, I was in trouble. As soon as I entered my house and the officer drove out of sight, I called Liv, desperate for her to answer. We had to get our stories straight. If not, I'd be the lone suspect in the disappearance of Darin Duclair, and there would be nothing I could do to make the police think otherwise.

Chapter 36

MATT

Monday, February 20, 2017

I called three times with no answer, after which I texted her "URGENT." She called me back and we agreed to meet at her apartment. When I first drove there to meet her the previous week, excitement and anticipation enveloped me, and the butterflies in my stomach wouldn't settle. Now, as I parked outside the gate and walked toward the entrance, none of that was present. I was panicked, knowing the slightest discrepancy in either one of our stories could spell the end of my world as I knew it.

She opened the door and, as expected, appeared haggard. My poor bandage job was gone, the wound exposed.

"Hey," she said before making her way to the couch. I sat beside her and laid everything out, all I could remember that I had told Detective Monroe.

I repeated it again for emphasis and to make sure she understood.

"I've got it. Jesus." She rolled her eyes.

"I just want to make sure. The slightest difference in our stories could raise a red flag."

"I know, Matt, I know."

"And Liv, I think I know who killed your family."

"Yeah, so do I."

"You do?"

"I knew it the night it happened. It's those guys from Boston."

"What guys?"

"There were these guys Darin was delivering drugs to."

"You know their names?"

"Yeah. Rex and Mike."

My blood ran cold. "Oh my God."

"What is it?"

"It's true."

"What's true?"

"I know them."

"How?'

"I placed some bets with Rex in the past."

"Bets?"

"Yeah. On games."

"How much money?"

"Quite a bit."

"Tell me."

I knew this was it. I couldn't keep it from her any longer considering what happened to her family, and I figured I owed her an explanation. "My last bet was fifty thousand."

Our eyes met and I watched with dread as the realization swept over her face. "I knew it! You son of a bitch!" She took a pillow from the couch and hurled it at me. She screamed, an ear-piercing wail that echoed throughout the room. I expected someone—probably her landlord—to knock on the door or call the police.

"Liv, please. I didn't know Darin owed them money. I didn't even know he was involved with them. And I never dreamed whoever he was involved with would do that to your family. You have to believe me. Had I known that was a possibility, I would have just taken the jewelry like we planned."

"Yeah, well, you didn't did you? You decided to go it alone, and now my family is dead."

Is this all my fault? Don't you bear some responsibility? This was your harebrained scheme to begin with. You're the one who tricked me. This was a dangerous game and you got in over your head. That's what I wanted to say to her but as she lowered her head and it shook with sobs, and as her shoulders slumped farther, I couldn't. I didn't need to beat her up any more than she already was.

"Liv. Listen. You have to go to the police. You have to tell them you know who did it."

"I can't," she replied.

"Why not?"

"For starters, I already told them I had no idea who could have done it. If they know I lied about that, they'll become more suspicious. Also, I'm terrified. Rex and Mike can track me down and they would have killed me that night. I'm sure they'll come after me."

"I'll put you up in a hotel. That way, there's no way they can find you." She nodded her head.

"Let me pack." I sat there in silence, an awkward passage of time as she stirred around in her bedroom and the bathroom, filling a suitcase. She retrieved a black dress and shoes I assumed were for the funeral.

We walked in silence to my car. I placed her suitcase in the backseat and she sat in the passenger seat, staring out the window, a clear sign she didn't want any conversation, least of all from me.

I drove to University Inn, a sprawling, old-style motel half a mile from campus. I asked for a weekly rate, which I was given, though I guessed Liv would be there longer. If she refused to tell the police what she knew, Rex and Mike could still come after her.

She wasn't safe in her apartment and, while I considered having her stay with me, that could only cause problems for me in the future. I had played with that fire once, and I didn't intend to get burned twice.

I drove her around to her room and handed her the key. "Thanks," she said, not quite meeting my eyes. "I didn't tell you this before, but the police said my mom and sister were probably raped."

"Oh my God, Liv. I had no idea." She turned away to open the door and I thought I saw her roll her eyes, as if expressing the idea I didn't care what happened to her family. The truth is I did care. And a deeper truth, which I didn't want to admit, was I felt guilty. If I had done as she and Darin instructed, Liv's family would still be alive. That thought haunted me, and I couldn't erase it from my mind. She opened the back door to retrieve her suitcase.

"Liv," I said, turning to face her, "I'm going to make this right." I didn't know what I meant at the time I said it, but it would become clear later. She eyed me for a few seconds, told me she would talk to me later, and shut her door.

She wheeled her suitcase behind her and I waited until she opened the door to her room before I left. She turned and gave me a wave, an empty gesture, perhaps her trying to give me the impression she would be OK. But I knew different. She would never be the same.

Chapter 37

LIV

When I was ten years old, a girl I knew who lived on our street got sick. I wouldn't call us friends. She was a couple of years older than I was, but we played together occasionally. One day, my mom told me the girl was in the hospital. The doctors said she had a virus and they were working their best to treat it. The next day, my parents went to the hospital to visit the girl and her family while Sarah and I stayed with a neighbor. My parents came back sooner than I expected and they were quiet, both of them with somber looks about them. When I asked how the girl was, my mom told me she was dead. It was so sudden, so shocking, so final.

That was the only funeral I had ever attended until the day they lowered my family into the ground. I remember the wails from the girl's mother, asking "why" to no one in particular. She collapsed in someone's arms and her husband tried to lift her. It was a heart-rending scene, the gravity of which was reinforced throughout that day by adults repeating a phrase that shouldn't have to be uttered in the first place: no parents should have to bury their child.

The worst part for me was the open casket. I never knew such a thing existed, but one-by-one, we filed past the deceased girl. She was so still and peaceful, as if she were only asleep. She had a red bow in her blonde hair and a red and white dress that I overheard her mother say was her favorite. I didn't know what to do as I walked past her, so I got my cue from the adults. I wished later I had told her goodbye.

It was that experience that led me to dread funerals. As I got older, there were a couple of funerals I could have gone to, but I concocted an excuse to stay away. The thought of death and the impermanence of life unnerved me, and I avoided dwelling on the subject because it forced me to think about my own mortality.

Friday, February 24, 2017

On that cold Friday morning, my grandparents picked me up from the motel. I lied and told them I was staying there because my apartment was being remodeled, a story they seemed to buy. We traveled in silence to the chapel at the cemetery. I was thankful they were there, both for support and the fact that they made the funeral arrangements. The chapel on site was small, which forced many of the mourners to stand along the wall on each side. We walked into the complete, shattering silence and sat near the front. Relatives were there whom I hadn't seen in years. Vague faces from years past gave me sympathetic eyes as I studied my surroundings. The worst site, a site seared into my brain forever, was the three caskets at the front. My grandparents spared no expense in them and, in a sign the chapel architect had never considered more than one casket would occupy the transept at a time, the one on the left was perpendicular to the others. I found it odd there was no distinction of who was in which casket.

A preacher found his way through the crowd and stood behind a lectern. My attention drifted to and from his words. Much of what he said was loosely connected stories from each of my family members' lives, I'm sure supplied by my grandparents. Some were heartwarming, others funny to lighten the mood. I was numb, however. I was physically exhausted from crying and emotionally drained, so much so that I needed a different emotion to overtake the ones that had been present for the week. I willed myself to use what little energy I had on something else, and what I felt surprised me. As I viewed the three caskets, I felt anger. Why didn't any of my family members put up a fight? Did they just comply in the hopes they would live? Why was I angry with them? Then, in a rush of emotions, I felt guilt for feeling anger. After the guilt, though, came rage—a deep, palpable fury from within. I thought of my mom's and dad's last moments. Did they think of me before Rex or Mike pulled the trigger? And what about Sarah? What was she thinking in her last moments, when one of those disgusting animals had their way with her? My heart raced and my hands were sweaty. I wiped them on a Kleenex from a box next to me on the pew. I realized my tears had stopped. My heart still ached, but my anger had taken over. I was seething as I sat listening to the preacher wrap up the eulogy.

As the pall bearers carried the caskets to the hearses, which would drive them to their final destination, hugs from family members and strangers inundated me. Some of my family had words of comfort, and some had no idea what to say. Which was fine. I didn't know what to say either. Really, what *was* there to say? No words uttered in that moment would make any difference in my life or take away any of what I was feeling because of the unspeakable tragedy. My family was gone, I was alone, and nothing could bring me out of the dark depths of sadness and ire.

My grandfather purchased three plots in a new part of the cemetery, away from most of the other gravestones. We drove along the gravel road and parked near a large tree, still devoid of leaves in the dead of winter, allowing the sun to shine through. As I stood on the uneven terrain, trying to balance in my heels, the sun warmed the back of my neck and my mind drifted far away from the terribleness before me. The crowd at the gravesite was many times smaller than the one that had gathered in the chapel, and as they bowed their heads and cried or paid their last respects, I gazed off into the distance. I wondered what my future held, and I longed for a certainty that wasn't there. I knew only one thing in that moment: I wanted revenge, and there was nothing in this world that would stop me.

After the graveside service, my grandparents drove me to the charred remains of my childhood home. My car sat in the driveway as it had on that fateful night. It was undamaged, but the rubble around it was a miserable site. Piles of bricks and blackened wood made parts of the house unrecognizable. I could have walked around, but doing so would have served no purpose. The disaster of the previous Sunday had eclipsed any fond memories I had of growing up in that house or playing in the back yard or riding my bike on the street. All that remained was horror.

As I drove toward Farrington, relieved to leave Weston behind, I called Matt. He answered right away, as if expecting a call. "Can you meet me at Maxwell's tomorrow morning?" He hesitated to answer before finally agreeing. I didn't know if he would help me—I wasn't even sure what I needed help with, but he was the only person I could count on to keep a plan secret. Payback was vital and if he wouldn't help me, I would go it alone. It was a risk either way, but the level of risk is always diminished when you're blinded by hatred.

Chapter 38

LIV

Saturday, February 25, 2017

Despite it being almost noon, a crowd engulfed Maxwell's, which served only breakfast food. Families getting a late start on a Saturday and others trying to erase hangovers dominated the scene. I thought of the night, almost two weeks prior, Matt and I had met here. It seemed like forever had passed since I weaved my web and ensnared him, concocting my plan I now wished had never entered my demented mind.

He arrived before I did, sitting in a booth with his back to me as I approached. A green hoodie masked part of his appearance, but I knew it was him. I recognized the hands that gripped his coffee cup as the same ones that traversed my body several days prior. I scooted into the side opposite him. He gave me a "hey," his face expressionless. He took the liberty of ordering me coffee, which I appreciated. I let the warmth of the cup soothe my hands before I started speaking.

"Matt, I don't really know what to say or even how to say it."

"Liv, I didn't come here—"

"Please, just let me finish. "I know this will ring hollow, but I have to say it. I never meant for any of this to happen. I didn't want anyone to get hurt. I was thinking of only getting Darin out of his situation, nothing more. I don't know why I didn't tell Darin to just . . . rob the store himself." I whispered those last four words, suddenly concerned my voice was carrying. "It was a stupid decision and it started something I'll never get over. I realize it's my fault—my fault for getting you involved in this and it's my fault Darin is missing or dead. I blamed you at first, but I know you don't deserve that blame. You didn't want any of this and I forced you into it. So, for what it's worth, I'm sorry." I teared up, unfurled my napkin containing my silverware, and dabbed by eyes. A waitress came to our table but retreated when she saw me.

"Well, thank you for your apology. Considering what's happened to you, I'm not sure it's necessary, but thank you." I doctored my coffee and avoided making eye contact with him as I stirred it. "How are you holding up?" he asked.

"I'm kind of numb at this point. The funeral was yesterday and I really just don't want to think about any of it."

He looked out of the window next to us. "I see you got your car."

"Yeah. Thankfully I had an extra key in my apartment." When we first met here, our conversation had flowed smoothly. In the ensuing meetings, we had exchanged words without much effort at all. There was an ease to our conversations that resembled a solid couple. Now, in the aftermath of the chaos I wrought, there was a deep chasm of silence between us. Everything uttered seemed contrived, planned out like a boy and a girl on a first date. The waitress came to our table again and we declined to order anything else. After several seconds of silence, he spoke.

"So, is that why you called me, to apologize? I mean, no offense, but that seems like something you could've done with a phone call.

"That's only part of it."

"What is it?" he asked.

"Let's go talk in my car," I said, turning my head and scanning the crowd. I didn't feel comfortable talking in the diner any longer, especially as people hovered about waiting for a table.

"OK." He slid out and stood, pulling a five-dollar bill from his wallet and dropping it on the table. We sat in the front seat of my car and I could still feel the warmth of the heated air. He pulled his hood off of his head and I gazed upon his full appearance for the first time that morning. The front of his messy hair dropped toward his sad eyes. A few days growth gave his mostly gray beard a prickly appearance. I wondered what he really thought of me. I wondered if my family's death bothered him, or if it was something he could put out of his mind at a moment's notice.

"What is it, Liv?" He sounded put out.

"Rex and Mike are still going to come after me. They know I'm a witness to the crime, and they know I can identify them both. I can't keep living in that motel forever. I appreciate you footing the bill for it, but I have to move out. I need something else. Maybe I'll leave Farrington, I don't know." I was rambling, avoiding the topic. He sat and listened, however, patient with my stammer. "I'll just put this out here. Wait. Are you wearing a wire?"

"A wire? Are you kidding me? You honestly think I'd go to the cops?"

"I . . . I'm sorry. I don't know."

"Liv, I have no interest in seeing you get arrested. You've suffered enough. What do you want? Why did you call me out here?"

"I want Rex and Mike gone." I stared straight ahead, again avoiding eye contact.

"Gone how?"

"You know."

"Dead?" I turned and glared at him and he got the message. His lips parted slightly and his eyes widened.

"Liv, I can't get involved in anything like that."

"Matt, I'm begging you. Please. They'll kill me. They won't even think twice about it. You saw what they did to my family. They're probably looking for me now. I can't let my death be the end of this."

"Liv, please go to the police."

"I can't. I told you. Rex and Mike will kill me for sure or send someone else to do it. And I don't want to talk to that detective anymore. Trying to keep our stories straight and avoid slipping up—it's too much. It's easier if Rex and Mike are out of the picture."

"Easier? Easier how? Exactly what do you want me to do?" I realized I hadn't thought it through. I knew what end I wanted, but I didn't know the means.

"I don't know," I replied, shaking my head. "I just can't keep living in fear. What they did, what they did to my family, it will haunt me for the rest of my life, and the thought of them out there, living their lives as they please, makes me angry."

"I understand your desire for revenge."

"No, you don't. Sorry, but you don't. You can never understand what it's like unless it happened to you."

"Fair enough, but think about this for a second. Suppose you did . . . kill them, or I did. What then? How many people get away with something like that? Hardly anyone."

"OK, professor, but that's some flawed logic. There's no way to know how many people get away with murder because no one volunteers they murdered someone and didn't get caught. If there's no body, that is."

"Fair enough again," he said.

"Will you at least think about it?"

"About helping you kill Rex and Mike? No, I won't. I won't even entertain the thought. I don't want anything to do with this. You've got your whole life ahead of you. Don't make a tragic mistake and ruin it. There's no guarantee Rex and Mike will come after you. They probably already killed Darin, so they have no use for you."

"Maybe, but there's no guarantee they *won't* come after me either."

"What are your plans, Liv?" he asked, trying to change the subject. As much as I hated it, I knew he was right. I couldn't kill and get away with it. I didn't know how I would go about it and even if I did attempt it, there's a chance I wouldn't be successful. That would be a sure death sentence for me.

"I don't know," I answered. "I'm going to withdraw from the college. I don't know if I'll reenroll. Maybe I'll move somewhere else. I don't want to go back to Weston."

"Not to sound like a parent, but do you have money?"

"I've got enough for now. My parents' attorney called me and talked about their wills. I'm getting their bank accounts and most of their stuff. What wasn't burned, anyway."

"I'll keep paying for the motel room if you need me too."

"Thanks, but I'm checking out today. I guess I'll go to my apartment. Before that, I'm going to Darin's house. I want to look around, see if I can find anything that might give me a clue as to what happened to him." I stared at him for a brief moment before averting my gaze, willing myself not to cry. He moved his arm toward me, as if he might make some type of gesture, a touch of the hand perhaps or even a hug. In the end, however, he opened the car door and stepped outside.

"Please be careful, Liv," he said, bending down to make his face visible.

"I will." With that, he shut the door and walked away. I cried, another loud sob that had become commonplace in the past week. I couldn't escape my emotions, all bubbling beneath the surface of my broken soul. I pulled out of the parking lot and headed toward Darin's, struggling to see through the cloud of tears.

I pulled into the small driveway, adjacent to a neighbor's yard. Clouds had taken over the sky and the wind accelerated, causing a loose shutter on a front window to bang against the house. I figured the police had been here, but the front door was locked. I walked around the side of the house and entered the backyard, slipping through the gate of the chain-link fence. Wet leaves covered the tiny porch, as if taking refuge under the awning from the snowfalls of the season. I turned the doorknob and pushed the door open, my shoes crunching the broken glass from a pane in the door window.

I flipped a light switch in the kitchen and nothing happened. I flipped the one I assumed controlled the garbage disposal and still, nothing. Walking into the kitchen, I noticed broken dishes and what appeared to be a broken beer bottle. The living room revealed the TV face down on the floor. I walked into Darin's bedroom, the soft soles of my sneakers making scant noise on the hardwood floor. I was conscious about being quiet, but I wasn't sure why. There was no one here. The house was desolate. Abandoned, as if Darin had left in a hurry and never returned. I lay on his bed and could still smell him, that familiarity for which I longed. I hugged his pillow and did my best to relax, drifting off only to jerk myself awake several times. Finally, I let myself go and fell into a deep slumber, wrung out from the exhaustion that was my life. When I awoke, the house was pitch black inside, a sign I had been out for several hours. I turned my head to the left and jumped. The faint outline of a figure loomed over me, and I felt the cold, hard steel against my neck.

Chapter 39

MATT

Saturday, February 25, 2017

Mrs. Sorkelson knocked on my door, ready to shoot the breeze. I opened it, only to get a phone call a few seconds later. "I'm sorry. I have to take this," I said, before looking to see who it was.

"No problem, honey. We can talk later."

I shut the door and viewed the call screen. It was Liv. I answered and heard nothing but sobs. "Liv?"

"Matt, you have to come here please."

"Where?"

"Darin's house. I'll send you the location."

"Are you OK?"

"No."

"What's wrong?"

"Please. Just get over here."

"I'm leaving now." I couldn't imagine what it could be. I thought for a split second she might be on to me—that she might have found out I killed Darin. But there was nothing in his house that could connect me to him or any evidence I was the one who ended his life. I drove in a hurry, still aware that one failure to signal or run of a red light could mean another run-in with the police.

I parked on the street and saw Liv's car. It appeared no one else was there. There were no lights on outside the house nor inside. The front door was ajar, open only a few inches. I eased it back, the hinges squeaking louder the farther I pushed it.

"Liv?"

"I'm in here."

"Where?"

"The bedroom." I pulled my phone out and used the flashlight on it. Even so, it was difficult to navigate my way toward her voice. My shoes knocked into clutter on the floor and I asked her to speak again.

"Here." I walked down a short hallway, following her voice and trying in vain to adjust my eyes to the dark. As I neared the bedroom, I heard her whimpers. Entering after pushing the door open, my light revealed a grisly sight. Liv was tied to a chair, nude. Her hair, parted in the middle, revealed a face streaked with blood. Blood also covered her abdomen and she moaned.

"Oh, my God,"

"Please untie me." I reached behind the chair. Rope bound her hands together and her ankles were tied to the legs of the chair. I struggled to untie the rope and use my phone light at the same time, dropping my phone twice in the process. Finally, I freed her arms and then concentrated on the rope that bound her to the chair. With her assistance, we freed her. I helped her stand and felt her full weight in my arms. She put her head into my chest and cried. I held her, both for her comfort and support. After what seemed like minutes, I led her to the bed, where she sat, shivering. I scanned the floor for her clothes and handed them to her. She dressed, gingerly moving her limbs.

"Let's get you out of here," I said. "Can you walk?"

"Yes." She took my hand and I led her to my car. Thankfully, there were no passersby or neighbors to witness the curious scene. "You shouldn't drive," I said, opening the passenger door. We'll come back for your car later." She didn't object and, with frail and gentle movements, sat in the car.

"Liv, you have to tell me what happened."

"It was Rex. Only him."

"What did he do?" It sounded like I was prying, but I needed to know if her injuries required a hospital visit.

"He cut me. My face and stomach. They're not deep."

"Jesus Christ. What did he say to you?"

"He threatened me. He said he still needs the money for the drugs Darin never delivered and if I can't get it, he'll kill me. He also made a point of telling me not to go to the police."

"So what did you say? Did you tell him you'd get the money?"

"I told him the truth. Once the judge signs off on all that stuff, I can pay him. I told him my lawyer said four or five months."

"Is that true?"

"No. I have no idea how long it will take. I was just buying time."

"Are you hurt anywhere else?"

"He slapped me and shoved me to the floor. He also . . . raped me."

"Oh, God, Liv. Do you want to go to the hospital?"

"No. They have to report sexual assaults to the police."

"You could say you don't know who did it."

"Yeah, but they'll ask for a description.

"So make one up."

"No! Please, just take me to your house."

"I'm sorry. I'm not trying to hound you. I just want to make sure you're thinking clearly." She said nothing in response. After a few minutes of silence, we arrived.

I let her in before me and she made a beeline to the bathroom, where I had doctored her injuries less than a week ago. She washed her face and, fulfilling what I thought was my responsibility, I treated her new injuries. "You should take a shower. There are towels in the linen closet," I said, pointing behind her.

"Thanks." I shut the door and wandered to my bedroom. I wanted to be alone with my thoughts, but a clear mind escaped me. For the second time in a matter of days, Liv was in my house injured at the hands of Rex. He was a menace, terrorizing everyone he encountered. He made me uneasy from the moment I met him, but I could never have envisioned he was capable of murder or rape. I knew different now. He was a nightmare, an unchecked keg of explosives that could maim or kill in an instant. I knew even after Liv paid him the money—if she was indeed able to do it—Rex's terror would never stop. He had no reason to. He knew Liv's family was dead and that she had a lot of money coming. He could continue to wreak his havoc on her life, a turmoil from which she would never recover.

I lay back on the bed and stared at the ceiling, unsure of what to do. Fitting, because at that point in my life, there wasn't much I was sure of at all.

Chapter 40

MATT

Four Months Later

"You sure you don't mind doing this?" I asked, speaking into my phone.

"Not at all. I mean, I don't know what it's for and I'm not one to ask too many questions, but yeah, I'll do it."

"I appreciate it, Doug."

"What are friends for, right?"

"True. Expect a call soon. I don't know if it'll be from my phone or Rex's, but it's coming. And of course, I'll give you a heads-up if this falls through."

"You're not in any kind of trouble are you?"

"I thought you said you weren't prone to questions."

"Good point. Just checking on you though."

"Yeah, I'm fine. I appreciate it. So you need me to go over any more details?"

"No, I'm good. I got it."

"All right. Let me know if you need a refresher."

"Will do."

"Hey, how's the weather down there?"

"June in Texas. You know how it is. It's already hot and the worst is yet to come."

"I don't miss it at all."

"I don't blame you."

"Thanks again, Doug."

"Don't mention it."

Since that previous February, I tried my best to concentrate on my work at the college. On some days, I could. Other days, however, were more difficult. Darin's last gasps for breath plagued me, and knowing the investigation into his disappearance was still open and that I was probably still a suspect nagged me, like a gnat buzzing around me I couldn't get rid of. Always there, lurking, following my movements. I considered resigning from the college with the hope that being far way would help, but to do what? To go where?

I also couldn't stop thinking about Liv. The image of her tied to the chair with blood pouring down her face appeared in my dreams several times. I talked to her three times since that horrific night. The first time was when I took her to retrieve her car from Darin's. The second was by pure coincidence when we saw each other at a coffee shop near campus. Her smile was back, but I knew her well enough that it was only on the surface. The pain behind her eyes was obvious and I could only imagine what her nights alone had been like. I almost invited her to dinner but I refrained. I didn't trust myself and, despite her apparent mea culpa, I didn't fully trust her either. I figured the more distance we had between us, the safer I was.

Yet I couldn't escape the fact that on some level, I cared for her. What troubled me is I didn't know why. Why should I care for her at all? She had done nothing for me except lead me on and give me false hope for a few days, preying on my pathetic, hedonistic desires. But there she was, occupying my thoughts. Perhaps I wanted her to be who I thought she was when we first met. And maybe deep down, she was. But it also pained me to think of what her future held. Whatever time she bought from Rex was running out, which brings me to the third time Liv and I talked and, as it turned out, would be the catalyst to set the events in motion that would forever transform who I was. She texted me in March that her grandparents, for some unknown reason, were contesting her parents' wills. The reason, at least from Liv's perspective, was immaterial. She was supposed to have enough money from her parents' estate to pay off Rex.

Now, none of that money was coming anytime soon. Her text was simple yet jarring:

> My grandparents are contesting the wills. I won't get the money for a long time, if at all, which means I can't pay off Rex. I knew it would end like this. Anyway, I just thought you'd want to know.

She had resigned herself to accepting her fate—the same fate that resulted in her family's death. I texted her back, something pathetic along the lines of everything working itself out. I knew, however, the situation was dire.

I'm going to make this right. Those were the words I said to her as we parted ways in the motel parking lot, and the same words I repeated to myself after her text. I was, by nature, a problem solver, and I couldn't let Liv's predicament go untouched. I already felt guilty for my role in the whole mess: if I had taken the jewelry as Darin and Liv wanted me to, Darin and Liv's family would still be alive. I'd still be a robber, but I wouldn't be a killer. That ship had sailed, however. The guilt ate away bits and pieces of me every day, and I couldn't bear the thought of not intervening in Liv's Rex problem knowing if she didn't pay him, she would likely die a horrible death.

Well, if you ever get the urge again, you know where to find me. And you know, I do other stuff too, so if you ever feel the need, let me know.

Those were Rex's words before I left his apartment for what I thought then was the last time. He used them as an enticement, a way of seizing upon my weakness. I used them as well, but as an opportunity. Over the remaining March and all the way into June, I placed small bets with Rex. He had agreed to forego his usual policy of not accepting bets less than a thousand dollars. So, these were not big bets, but they were just enough to keep me coming around and currying favor with him as someone who always kept his word and paid what he owed. He was his despicable self as usual, talking down to me, laughing at his unfunny jokes, smiling his disgusting grin. Walking in that apartment and conversing with him and Mike—murderers, likely rapists, and otherwise unhinged psychopaths—unnerved me, but I kept my resolve.

The last time I visited, I laid the trap. "You hinted a few months ago if I was interested in anything else to let you know," I said, causing him to look up from his phone.

"So what are you looking for? I can get you almost anything you want."

"We're talking drugs, right?"

He crinkled his nose and laughed. "You're such a square. Yeah, we're talking drugs. I never took you for a drug man though. But maybe the pressures of teaching have gotten to you, huh?" He smiled, staring at his phone again.

"Not to use. To sell."

"To sell?" He looked up from his phone again. "What are you talking about?"

"Cocaine."

"I've already got people delivering that to me."

"OK, but I doubt it's as much as I'm talking about."

"How much are you talking?"

"At least two kilos a month."

"Get the fuck out of here. Two kilos?"

"Yes."

"You know how much money that is? Where are you getting that kind of blow?"

"I have a contact in Texas. He gets his supply from a guy in Mexico. They make a delivery on a private plane twice a month. That guy in Mexico said he can supply more if the demand is there. I talked to my contact and told him there's demand up here. Think about it. The whole Boston area. Rich suburban kids who have money to spend. College kids. The demand is almost endless."

"You don't think there are already people dumping coke around here?" he asked, not distracted by his phone any longer.

"There are. But I guarantee you there's demand that's not being met. Who are you distributing to?"

"Mostly people in the neighborhood."

"Right. And in small quantities, I'm sure. We're talking two kilos. You sell that on an agreed-upon price. The guy in Mexico and my Texas contact take their share, I take my cut, and you keep the rest."

"How much?"

"Mexico takes fifty percent, Texas takes ten, and I take ten. Everything after that is yours." Rex stared at me, as if waiting for me to say something else. An inordinate amount of time passed before he spoke.

"Not going to lie, professor. This sounds pretty good. You got a number for the Texas guy?"

"I do." I relayed the number to him and, to my surprise, he dialed it. I figured—or was hoping—he would wait to make the call so I could warn Doug, but Rex was impatient. He put the phone on speaker.

"Hello?" Doug answered.

"Yeah, this is Rex from Boston."

"Who?" *Shit.*

"Rex. From Boston. We both know Matt." He turned toward me, fishing for my last name.

"Richardson," I said.

"Richardson," Rex repeated.

"Oh yeah, yeah. Hey, I'm glad you called."

"So, tell me about this deal."

"Well, I'm assuming Matt filled you in at least a little, but I can tell you what you need to know."

"Tell me about this guy in Mexico."

Doug began his story. "I don't know his actual name. He goes by El Cuchillo. It means The Knife."

"I'm not really looking or a Spanish lesson, man."

"Yeah, sorry. He's former cartel. Now usually former cartel members are six feet under or chopped up in little pieces, but this guy is a distant relative of El Oso, a major cartel player.

"I've heard of him."

"Yeah, I figured. Anyway, El Cuchillo wanted out for whatever reason, and El Oso ordered his guys to stay away from El Cuchillo, not to touch him. El Cuchillo promised not to infringe on the cartel's territory and in exchange, El Oso promised not to kill El Cuchillo."

"I feel like there's more to this story," Rex said, almost sounding disinterested.

"There is, Doug continued. "So when El Oso got arrested a few years ago, El Cuchillo got concerned that maybe El Oso's guys would come after him or maybe cut a deal with the Mexican or

American authorities. So, after that, El Cuchillo kind of went into hiding, and he's mostly into small shipments now. I know two kilos is a lot to us, but down there, that's a drop in the bucket."

"So how did you meet this El Cuchillo?" Rex asked. I was even more nervous than I had been earlier. Doug was giving a great performance, but all it took was one slip, one discrepancy, and Rex would bail out and, in a terrifying thought, take out his frustration on me. My heart raced faster and swallowing became difficult. Listening to Doug recite the story we concocted made it sound ludicrous, so farfetched that no one in his right might would believe it.

"Tijuana. Last year, I was down there with some friends and—if you've ever been there, you know this—but it's really easy to score drugs. I bought some coke and I was in this bar and this guy started telling me he used to be in the cartel, like bragging about it. I thought he was full of shit. But then he tells me to come out to his car. That made me nervous, but he opened his trunk and there was a shit-ton of coke in there. I guess he sensed I had money and for whatever reason he trusted me, because he asked if I'd be willing to sell it if he got it to the States. My first thought was no way, too much risk. But when I heard he could get it there by plane, and all I'd have to do is take it, cut it up, and sell it, I told him I was in."

"Didn't it worry you the guy could have been a cop?"

"Funny enough, it never occurred to me at the time. Maybe it was the tequila that clouded my judgment. But I'm glad it did because I'm making tons of money. And if we open this thing up there where you are, you and I will both be making more than I'm making now."

"So how do you know Matt?"

"Matt and I go way back. We went to college and law school together." Rex turned to Mike, sitting on the bed and hanging on every word in the conversation.

"Mikey, what do you think?"

Mike shrugged his shoulders and raised his eyebrows.

"Honestly, it sounds pretty good." Rex turned to face me. I felt compelled to say something. Doug had given the performance of a lifetime, but I was afraid of continuing the conversation any longer. The more words were exchanged, the greater the risk was that Rex would detect the lies.

"Hey," I chimed in. "Why don't we continue this later?"

"Is that Matt?" Doug asked.

"Hey . . . Ryan." I almost said his real name before remembering his alias. Does that sound good to everyone?" I asked, glancing at Rex. "I tell you what. Why don't you and Mike come to my house, we'll get some dinner, and hash out the details?" This was it. This had to happen if my plan was going to work. Rex stared at me before fixing his gaze upon Mike. He turned to me again, furrowing his brow and crooking his mouth in apparent consideration of the invitation.

"Yeah, that sounds good."

"All right. You guys free tomorrow night?"

"Yeah, we can do that."

"How about seven o'clock, my house? You've got my address, or at least Mike does," I said, trying to inject some humor in referring to when Mike paid me a visit with his baseball bat.

"OK. We'll be there."

"Hey, we'll be in touch, Ryan," I said, raising my voice to ensure Doug could hear me and letting him know the conversation needed to end.

"Yeah, I'll talk to y'all later. Rex, good to speak with you. Looking forward to our new relationship."

"Yeah, same. Talk to you later." I bid Rex and Mike goodbye and descended the stairwell for what I hoped was the last time. I couldn't believe I was going through with it, but I was energized, ready for revenge.

Chapter 41

THE DINNER

Breathe, Matt. I had to keep telling myself that as my heart raced. I was a nervous ball of energy, pacing around the house and peering out the front window. A few minutes after seven o'clock, just after delivery of the food, they arrived. Rex was dressed nicer than usual, wearing a collared shirt and jeans. Mike was in tow, wearing a baggy shirt and pants as usual. I opened the door holding a bottle of wine as they approached the house.

"I hope you guys like Italian."

"Who doesn't?" Rex answered.

"OK, good. I got a few different dishes from Rocini's. It's the best Italian food in Farrington. I know you guys have better options in Boston, but this stuff is damn good." I shook each of their hands and ushered them inside."

"Matt," Rex started, "nice place you got here. You must be doing all right."

"Yeah, I like it, but I'm probably selling it soon. You want to buy it?"

"No offense, but Farrington is too small for me. I'm Boston, born and bred."

"What about you Mike?" I turned to him and smiled.

"No way. I have to maintain this guy's little nest in Southie," he replied, sticking his thumb out toward Rex.

"Understandable. Well, hey, let me give you guys the tour before we dig in to the food."

"Such a host. I'm already impressed," Rex said. I showed them my office and the kitchen. I pointed to the back yard where Ann and Nancy lay, chewing on scraps from a rawhide bone. I made the conscious choice of locking the pet door so I wouldn't have to deal with them. I needed to rid myself of all the distractions I could. I led my two visitors upstairs, stopping in the hall and pointing to my bedroom and the spare bedroom across from it. Rex stood close, making me uncomfortable. For some reason, it occurred to me only then they could steal something or worse maybe attack me and leave me for dead. These were two bona fide murderers I let into my house. I steered them back down the stairs toward the kitchen.

"So, you're not married?" Rex asked.

"No. I was, but I'm recently divorced."

"Oh, that sucks."

"Yeah, but it was amicable."

"So, no lady friend then?"

"No, I wouldn't say I'm doing too great in that department."

"Well, we need to fix that."

I waived him off. "I think I can manage, but thank you."

"You sound like Mikey here. No prospects at all. I mean, you'd think that some girl out there wouldn't mind him, right? Although they're not always willing when they're with you, are they Mikey?"

"Shut up," Mike retorted. I had a feeling this was a reference to the rape of Liv's mother or sister, or maybe both. I couldn't be sure, but it renewed my quest for revenge and my purpose for inviting them.

"Let's eat, gentlemen," I said, extending my hand toward the square dining table. "You two can sit there." I pointed to the chairs facing away from the kitchen. I began unpacking the food. "All right, three huge containers here. Spaghetti with meat sauce, fettuccini Alfredo, and the third here is lasagna."

"What a treat," Rex replied, dishing the food onto his plate. "I think I might like you, Matt. And not only because you give me a lot of money." As usual, he laughed at his joke. I returned a snicker to placate him. "You better get yours quick, though, or Mikey will eat the whole damn thing."

"I forgot," I said, rising and hurrying toward the kitchen. "I have garlic bread warming in the oven." I took the bread out, taking time to consider the absurdity of this whole scene. I invited these two psychopaths into my home, of all things gave them a tour, and now I was feeding them. If I hadn't been so nervous, if I hadn't grasped the gravity of the situation, I would have laughed. But it was all too real, and the moment of truth was approaching, like a freight train barreling along the track, unable to stop and sealing the fate of everything in its path.

"Here you go," I said, placing the bread in the center of the table.

"Matt, you're going to have to invite us here more often," Rex said, snatching a piece of bread.

"Well, maybe I will since we'll be in business together."

"Yeah, about that, so who's making the run up here from Texas?"

"It'll either be Ryan or he has someone else who can do it."

"I have to tell you, Matt, I'm in. It sounds like a good deal. Doesn't sound too risky on our part. Nothing riskier than what I'm doing now, anyway. But I got a question." He set his fork down, clanging it on the plate and staring at me. Those cold, dark eyes I had seen too many times and never wanted to see again pierced my gaze. "Why cut Mikey and me in on this. Why not have your buddy run the coke straight to you?"

"I don't have the connections you do, Rex. I don't even know anyone who's into this other than you. And if we didn't do this deal, El Cuchillo will just find someone else and it'll be them making money instead of us."

"Fair enough. Yeah, let's do it."

"Excellent. Let's finish eating and I'll call Ryan and we'll get the whole thing set up." I twirled some spaghetti with my fork, trying to hide the quiver in my hand. "Oh, shit. I'm a terrible host. We don't have anything to drink. I was opening a bottle of wine earlier and got distracted. Red is all I have. That's all right, I hope?"

"It's perfect," Rex replied. "I'm more of a beer guy, but we're celebrating, right?"

"Exactly. I'll get some glasses." I returned to the kitchen, eyeing the two bottles of pinot noir sitting side by side on the counter. Both from Napa, I had grown to love the reds from the Saul Ganniff Winery. The bottle on the left, from 2014, the one on the right, from 2015. Only one year's difference, but a crucial one. I aligned the three large glasses and began pouring, the deep red swirling around as it settled in. The aroma, strong and sweet, made my mouth water. Finishing the pours, I made my way to the table, steadying the three glasses in my hands.

"Here we go, guys. Rex, Matt," I said, placing their glasses in front of their plates. "How about a toast?" I offered, raising my glass. "Here's to money, money, and more money." We all laughed. Theirs was genuine, mine contrived, as an actor would do setting the tone for a scene. "Cheers." We clanked our glasses and drank.

I took the glass from my lips, savored the taste, and sighed. "That's so good. There is nothing like a good pinot."

"That's really sweet," remarked Mike.

"You know," Rex said after guzzling over half of the pour "it's like you're broadening our horizons, Matt. Like I said, I'm not much of a wine guy, but I could drink this all night."

"Then by all means, drink up." I smiled as we continued to drink, relishing in the moment and eyeing my supposed business partners across the table. A bead of sweat formed above Mike's upper lip. His glass was almost empty. He took a deep breath in and sighed, reclining in his chair. Rex tugged at his collar.

"Gentleman, let me read you something," I said, pulling a folded piece of paper from my back pants pocket. Setting my glass on the table, I unfurled the paper and stared at Rex and Mike, looking more uncomfortable by the second. "I got this information from the Internet and, while I tell my students to be careful not to believe everything you read on there, this seems pretty accurate." I began to read: "'Meet *Atropa belladonna*, the beautiful lady, commonly known as deadly nightshade. There's a reason it's called deadly. Yes, it can kill you. The sweet berries from the plant are toxic to humans. As few as ten berries can kill an adult male.'" I paused my reading and revealed my secret. "I poured out some of the of the wine from your bottle and replaced it with some berries from my backyard. Fifty berries in all, squeezed to perfection to give you guys the perfect amount of deadly sweetness. And I've been waiting for this moment, four months to be exact—the perfect moment when the belladonna are in full bloom, the berries young and ripe. Shall I continue?" It seemed an odd reaction, but instead of looking at me as those words parted my lips, both men stared at the glasses that contained the poison they had just ingested. I stared down at the paper and resumed reading. "'The immediate onset of symptoms includes blurred vision, rapid heartbeat, and loss of balance. Soon after, delirium, hallucinations, and convulsions result. Often the plant of choice for assassins throughout history, ancient Romans were known to dip their arrows in the poison to guarantee the death of all those they pierced. One of the deadly ingredients in the sweet berries of the plant is atropine, the name of which stems from Atropos, one of the three fates of ancient Greece. She had two sisters. One spun the thread of a person's life, the other measured it, and it was up to Atropos to cut it, causing death.' Gentleman, Atropos has just cut your thread."

"You son of a bitch!" Rex said, bursting out of his chair and trying in vain to reach me. He collapsed and his writhed on the floor in a sickening motion, his limbs twisting as his body convulsed. His face contorted and he grasped for a breath. Mike fell to the side and landed on his hands and knees. His eyes were wide with terror before he fell on his face. A violent jerk of his torso followed. He lay still before his legs twitched.

I sat, finished my glass of wine, and stared at my two victims. Rex's chest and Mike's back rose and fell, and the pace of their breaths became slower and slower until the poison sucked the life out of them and they breathed their last.

The silence was deafening. I don't know how long I sat there, but the sunlight of early summer that had illuminated the living room faded away, and darkness took over, perhaps a metaphor for my heart. The self-analysis would come later, however. For now, I had a double murder to conceal.

Chapter 42

THE DEAL

I made the now-familiar drive to the remote part of New Life Cemetery. Loading Mike into the trunk tested my strength and Rex's body in the backseat, mere inches away, frightened me. A part of me expected him to rise and attack me, wrapping his hands around my throat as I struggled to steer the car and stay alive. I kept looking in the rearview mirror, a useless act because it was dark, but each time hoping I didn't see his eyes glaring back at me.

As far as I could tell, the cemetery was deserted. I found the same spot from four months earlier— the grave without a permanent marker. I removed the temporary one, stuck the shovel in the dirt, and began to dig. When burying Darin, although it was exhausting, the cold February air had allowed me to barely break a sweat. Now, a warm, breezeless, June night meant I was drenched within minutes. I worked hard and fast, knowing even in this remote area I was not immune from prying eyes or some wanderer scuttling about. I was wary of cemeteries anyway, and I had no desire to meet anyone hanging out at one at night.

As I neared the bottom of the grave, the dirt piled high to one side, the stench of rotting flesh slapped me in the face. I knew it was coming, but nothing prepared me for the strength of it. I turned toward my car to try to get a breath of fresh air when I saw her. I gasped and dropped the shovel. My instinct was to run but I fought it. There was no way out.

"I knew it," Liv said. "I knew it all along. You killed Darin."

"Liv, it's not what you think. He was going to kill me. I had no choice."

"Bullshit. If that's true, why didn't you tell me? Why was I forced to follow you around, waiting for you to slip up?"

"I didn't want to tell you. I was scared. And after what happened to your family—"

"What—you thought I couldn't handle it?"

"No, it just didn't seem to matter as much."

"Didn't matter? How could you say that? I loved him!" She inched closer. I retreated a step toward the grave, afraid of what she might do. "After my family died, he was all I cared about." Her voice broke and her attempts to inhale sputtered.

She grabbed the shovel and lifted it, pointing the tip in my direction. "I should kill you. I should kill you right now and throw you down there with him."

"Liv, hold on. Aren't you wondering what I'm doing here? Darin's been dead for months. This has nothing to do with him."

"So, what is it then? Why are you here?"

"Open the back door of my car." She didn't move at first, as if distrustful of what I was planning. After a few seconds, though, she walked toward the car, still holding the shovel and not taking her eyes off of me.

"Oh my God," she said as the door swung open.

"That's right. And Mike's in the trunk. They were going to kill you, Liv. You knew that. They were a menace, and it was either them or you." She said nothing but backed away from the car. To my relief, she dropped the shovel.

"Why? Why did you do it?"

"I told you. It was either them or you."

"That doesn't answer my question. Why did you care if they killed me?"

"I . . . I don't know. Maybe I felt guilty Darin was dead. Or maybe, for some inexplicable reason, I still cared for you."

"I could go to the police."

"You won't. You know I'm right. Plus, I know about Eric."

"What?"

"I know about Eric and your made-up story."

"What do you mean?"

"Stop. You know exactly what I mean. That night you were at my house after you hit your head. I gave you Vicodin and Ambien. They made you talk. I know you made up the rape allegation against him." The silence lasted for seconds. Although it was hard to see because of the dark, I think she had her mouth open, stunned at the news.

"I was young. It was a dumb thing to do."

"Yeah, it was. But are you willing to turn me in knowing you'd be punching your ticket to prison? I told you, I didn't intend to kill Darin or even hurt him. He had a gun pointed at me. It was an accident. And if it wasn't for you and your scheme, none of this would have ever happened. I didn't ask to get involved in any of this shit."

"I know," she replied, resigned to the fact I was right.

"So, do we have a deal? No one talks."

"Yes."

"Say it."

"No one talks." She seemed to look me in the eye for only a second, turned, and walked away. I didn't know if her car was parked nearby or if she walked to the cemetery. Regardless, I could do nothing but hope no one saw her.

I finished covering up—literally—my crime. The dirt fell into place, I replaced the marker, and drove home, weary. Afterward, I drove Rex's car to the mall and parked it near where I parked Darin's. Eventually, someone would find the car and report Rex and Mike missing, but I doubted anyone could tie their disappearance to me. I discarded their phones in the Connecticut River, as I had done with Darin's, and made the trek home. After a meticulous cleaning of my house, I relaxed as best I could, but sleep proved elusive. And I wasn't sure it would ever come easy again.

The events of the past four months had so warped my sense of justice that I could rationalize killing two people to atone for killing one. Or maybe I did still care for Liv and I was worried for her safety. Regardless, a nagging truth kept haunting me and never stopped: killing Rex and Mike had been easy. It was so easy it worried me. Who had I become? What was this role I was now playing? Had meeting Liv transformed me into a criminal, or had those inclinations always been with me, ever present, ready to surface at any moment? In the end, it didn't matter. They were there, and they weren't going away.

Epilogue

The blue latex gloves made my hands sweaty. I placed the stacks of money in the brown envelope, sealed it with tape, and checked the address one more time to make sure I had it correct. Lowering my car window, I dropped the envelope in the mailbox and drove away. The Hollands would soon get their money back. In what is surely my distorted sense of right and wrong, I felt more guilty about taking their money than I did killing Rex and Mike. I couldn't undo that, but I could undo at least some of the harm I had caused by participating in the robbery.

As I drove across the parking lot, I spotted a car exactly like Darin's. I did a double take and stared at the driver, an old man with a scowl. I looked away only when he raised his middle finger. Seeing the car took me back to the interview with Detective Monroe. He tried to make me sweat when he told me the police had found Darin's car, but the detective hadn't contacted me again. I'm sure the forensic team thoroughly searched the car inside and out, but evidently I was careful enough not to leave any clues about my connection with it. But Darin's disappearance was an open investigation, and that thought disturbed me. I knew cold cases could be reopened at any moment. All it would take is a curious detective, a persistent family member of Darin's or, my biggest fear, the police finding his body. My most treacherous thought—a place I willed my mind not to go—was that something at the bottom of that grave could link me to the death of Darin, Rex, Mike, or all three of them. If that happened, if my grand scheme ultimately backfired, my life as I knew it was over. I would die in prison.

Pulling onto the road from the nondescript shopping center, I saw Liv filling her car with gas. She used a squeegee to clean her windshield and her back seat was filled with what appeared to be clothing. I assumed she was going on a trip, maybe even moving away from Farrington. I turned right and made a quick U-turn. Driving slowly past the gas station, I caught her glance. She gave me a hollow smile and waved. I returned it and drove home.

I wondered how much of Olivia Powell I really knew. Was she, as Eric described, a psychopath? Or was she merely a troubled person, confused, warped by something in her past that caused her deviant behavior? I didn't figure I would ever get the answer to that question. She would forever remain a mystery to me—a seductive Siren who lured me into a trap and, almost as quickly as she came into my life, vanished from it, likely never to return.

I pulled into my driveway. For the first time in years, I felt some sense of calm. It was probably fleeting, but I enjoyed the moment. I appreciated the surroundings, the fullness of the trees and the flowers in bloom accentuated the beauty of the house, a place I would soon leave. In the backyard behind the small, fenced-off area, the belladonna thrived—the beautiful lady, so innocent looking on the outside but deadly on the inside, a perfect metaphor for my former student, Ms. Olivia Powell of Weston, Massachusetts. The plant's purple, bell-shaped flowers reached for the sun and the large leaves provided shade to the dark berries that hung below, tempting, deadly, waiting patiently for their next moment to shine.

THE END

ABOUT THE AUTHOR

Gavin Beck is from Dallas. He practiced law before he realized teaching is a lot more rewarding. He is an avid reader and a lover of music, traveling, and sports. Several authors have influenced his writing, including Patricia Cornwell, John Grisham, and James Patterson. *No One Talks* is his debut novel. Gavin lives with his wife and kids in Texas, along with two dogs, a cat, and two guinea pigs.

Connect with Gavin:
Website: gavinbeckauthor.com
Twitter: @gavinbeckauthor

AUTHOR'S NOTE

Dear reader,

I hope you enjoyed this book and that it fulfilled for you whatever you typically look for in a novel. I would appreciate it tremendously if you could take a few moments out of your busy day to leave me a review. I value your time, and the review can be as short or as long as you want. I also read and respond to every email at gavinbeckauthor@gmail.com

www.ingramcontent.com/pod-product-compliance
Lightning Source LLC
Chambersburg PA
CBHW032131190626
46814CB00005BA/1645